DESIDRA'S AWAKENING

A fever had ravaged her all through the night, and she'd heard her mother crying and a minister chanting. Candles sputtered at the ends of her four-poster bed.

"Let her go in peace," the minister had said. One by one everyone had slipped from the room, leaving her alone.

She'd wanted to scream after them, "I'm not dead yet! Hear me! I want to stay with you!" But she was unable to make a sound or exhale a breath.

While she lay there frozen with fear, a giant void had opened and invited her in, but before she could step across its threshold, a dark creature had suspended itself over her bed. Slowly it lowered itself onto her body and softly kissed her. What was this thing? An angel come to take her to heaven?

She clung to its comforting presence, but pleaded to stay. "Don't take me yet."

The entity held her, growled, and sank two sharp fangs into her neck. She was in agony for a while, but then a feeling of sensual intrusion and ecstasy overcame her. Slowly and voluptuously the vampire drank her blood and made her drink some of its own.

On that night Prince Romano had redeemed her and doomed her forever.

D1085885

THE WORLD OF DARKNESS

VAMPIRE
Dark Prince
Netherworld
Blood Relations
Blood on the Sun

WEREWOLF
Wyrm Wolf
Conspicuous Consumption
Hell-Storm

MAGE
Such Pain

WRAITH
Sins of the Fathers

Strange City (an anthology)

Published by HarperPrism

Blood on the Sun

Based on
Vampire: The Masquerade

Brian Herbert and Marie Landis

HarperPrism
An Imprint of HarperPaperbacks

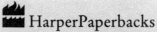 **HarperPaperbacks**
A Division of HarperCollinsPublishers
10 East 53rd Street, New York, N.Y. 10022-5299

This is a work of fiction. All the characters and events in this
book, although based upon World War II, are fictitious, and any
resemblance to real people or events is purely coincidental.

ISBN 0-06-105670-7

HarperPrism is an imprint of HarperPaperbacks.

HarperCollins®, ®, HarperPaperbacks™, and
HarperPrism® are trademarks of HarperCollinsPublishers, Inc.

Cover illustration by Joshua Gabriel Timbrook

First printing: October 1996

Printed in the United States of America

Visit HarperPaperbacks on the World Wide Web at
http://www.harpercollins.com/paperbacks

❖ 10 9 8 7 6 5 4 3 2 1

Dedicated to our mutual relatives, Cooper Landis and
Beverly Herbert, who shared our love of books.

MEMORANDUM

TO: General Abel Baker
c/o War Department
APO 7-88834 AL

DATE: January 3, 1945

Regarding the information you recently furnished our office concerning AWOL soldiers you have been unable to locate and their supposed proclivities, I advise you to be extremely discreet. Your insistence that "vampires" have infiltrated the United States Army is a disturbing statement, and one I must question.

I'm certain you realize the effect your theory would have on the American public. The average citizen would no doubt equate your words with some sort of Satanic operation being promoted by the United States government.

Our President commands you to drop your investigation immediately and to see the post psychiatrist as soon as possible.

Respectfully,

C. Whitefox
Director of Special Investigations
U.S. War Department

1942

1

On a cold morning in the spring of 1942 a flock of bird-like creatures descended and lit on the peak of the tallest office building in Seattle. They chattered momentarily, then pitched off the roof down into shadows. Below them steam rose from a metal grating that concealed an underground city lying beneath the streets. One by one the brownish-gray creatures slipped through the grating and transmuted into pale human shapes.

The Kindred had returned from their Blood-hunt.

Their Elder, Prince Romano, spoke to them, his snow-white ponytail tossing. His tone was harsh and the words threatening. A falcon sat on his shoulder, its hooked beak bloodied by its evening prey.

Romano's black eyes glittered with anger. "Have I mis-interpreted your words, Desidra? Do I hear you correctly? You say we owe mortals something? What favors do you plan to bestow upon them? What insanity are you proposing?" He looked around. "Do the rest of you give credence to this rot?"

In audience stood fifteen figures, wavering shadows fluttering in dim light, advancing and retreating with each word their Elder uttered. Desiccated, drained of their juices, their bodies crackled like dry leaves blown along a dusty roadway. The Kindred were hungry. The results of the night's Blood-hunt had been poor.

Prince Romano paced slowly back and forth. His lean body towered over the shadowy figures. "Answer me!" he cried. "Have you forgotten your allegiance to your sire? I made you! All of you! If it hadn't been for me you'd have rotted in your graves long ago, eaten by worms until only your disassembled skeletons remained. Instead, I've given you the gift of immortality. Have you forgotten this, Desidra?"

One of the shadows solidified and stepped forward. "No, I haven't, but I ask you to consider my opinion." Almost as tall as Romano, Desidra's gaze was unflinching, her dark eyes challenging him. She pushed her long red hair away from her face, saying, "Soldiers and sailors pound the streets over our heads. War threatens our way of life. We can't just sit by and watch, so I say we take action."

"What better place for a vampire," Romano sneered, "than on a battlefield of blood!"

"That isn't what I mean. I'm talking about protecting our home and this city."

Romano scowled. "Immersing ourselves in mortal affairs would threaten our existence, risk discovery. Vampires in a human war? Preposterous!"

Desidra shook her head and set her jaw stubbornly. "We're already involved in human affairs. To exist we must feed on them."

The falcon stretched its neck, and a thick drop of blood fell from its beak. It emitted a piercing cry. Its small predatory eyes were fixed on Desidra, as if measuring her.

Desidra wasn't finished. Watching the falcon apprehensively she said, "The Japanese are all over the Pacific theater. If they attack Seattle, bombs will destroy our cherished underground quarters and perhaps us as well."

A shadow emerged beside her, this one a young male of the clan, fair-haired and slim but muscular. Bowing his head slightly toward Prince Romano, he said, "My dear sire, I agree with Desidra. War is descending upon us in ways we may not be able to handle. There are so many soldiers and sailors on the streets that our hunting is made difficult. They move in packs through every alley and byway. Only two of the Kindred found prey last night. I caught nothing."

"You're a poor hunter, Christopher," growled Romano. "When I sired you fifty-two years ago, you were an effete boy of eighteen, spoiled by wealthy parents and then, when they learned of your sexual preferences, they thrust you into the world without money or love. I saved you from mean-spirited humans, took you in when they turned their backs to you."

The falcon on Romano's shoulder released a wild cry, and as it stared at Desidra she saw it tense, as though it was about to spring.

Romano yawned. "I've seen countless wars during my two thousand years of tenure. How many vampire years do you have, Desidra? A hundred, a hundred and ten? You've seen comparatively little."

She cried out, "You Elders are all alike: ancient men filled with fear and petty control impulses, keeping the rest of us in bondage."

Suddenly a hot and violent wind arose, wrapped itself about Desidra's body and slammed her backward into a storefront. For a moment she was dazed by the impact, but she steadied herself and stepped away from the building. It had not been the falcon's magic; Romano had utilized other forces. The heat of the wind frightened her. Was he trying to immolate her as he'd done to others who displeased him? Would her status as his favorite save her, or had she gone too far?

Romano's anger lifted her once more and hurled her violently to the ground. As she rose painfully to her feet, the Elder resumed his attack. Like a puppet dancing at the end of its strings, her body moved in rhythm to the will of his anger. He shook her one way and then another.

The falcon swooped in her direction. She struck it with her hand and deflected its thrust.

Romano whirled a dust devil at Desidra, a tornado of dirt and debris that sucked her into its center and spat her out again. From somewhere nearby the falcon screamed. She smelled its anger, its ravenous hunger for her.

Bruised and bloodied, she exerted all of her own powers and Romano's wind weakened slightly. The falcon let out a cry, as if in pain.

I've done something, she thought. *But I'm not strong enough, Not yet.*

The sire struck again with his wind-force, staccato blows that rammed her against deteriorated storefronts, then lifted and bounced her across their faded surfaces.

"Out!" he screamed. "I banish you, Desidra, until you learn humility!"

"Don't count on it," she shouted, and she braced herself against another onslaught that sent her tumbling away down the underground street.

Desidra needed a place for her recovery far from her sire and the clan. Lying on the underground street she saw Prince Romano and the Kindred in the distance. He was speaking to them, with his back to her.

I'm too close now, she thought. *He could reach me.*

At this moment, she had barely enough energy to heal herself, and though her powers of recuperation might be rapid, her ability to fly was temporarily limited. *I need blood to speed the healing process*, she thought. *I must go above.*

Painfully, she crawled through the dark and dusty corridors of the underground city, dragging herself inch by inch until she was well away from Prince Romano and the rest of the Kindred. On impulse, she entered one of the dilapidated storefronts and curled up in a corner. Not the safest place, but it would have to do until she'd rested for a few moments. Despite the lack of light, her eyes, acute as a cat's in the darkness, took in her surroundings.

She found herself lying beside an ancient chamberpot. The broken remains of a cot and table rested against one wall, and on the opposite wall hung a faded certificate. She scanned it quickly: "Doctor P. Blackstone, General Practitioner."

Laughter bubbled in her throat. How ironic. A doctor's office. Now it was no more than dust and rot and eternal

5

darkness. As *all of us are*, she thought, and lay back on the hard, uneven floor, her arms folded across her chest.

She steeled herself against the pain of her wounds, maintaining silence, knowing with certainty that Prince Romano was capable of killing her. How would death come? Through fire? Or would he chop her into little bits of flesh and bone that could never be patched together again? Her "life" could be ended under certain conditions, despite the fact that she and others of her kind were referred to as the Undead.

Vampire tradition spelled out who could be the destroyer, and Desidra recited it softly from memory: "The right of destruction belongs to the sire of his clan, the Elder. He shall be the only one to spill the blood of a vampire. Only the creator can unmake."

Prince Romano was proud of his lineage. He'd sprung from the Tremere clan, and the influence of their rigid hierarchical system had molded his character. He had punished her to let her know who was in control.

The punishment had been harsh.

If I had the power, I'd kill him!

Then she sighed, suddenly uncertain of her feelings. It was Romano who'd given her back her life, or a facsimile of it, on the day she'd turned seventeen. She'd been mortal, then. A fever had ravaged her all through the night, and she'd heard her mother crying and a minister chanting. Candles sputtered at the ends of her four-poster bed. She could smell her own impending death, a sour odor.

"Let her go in peace," the minister had said, or perhaps it was a doctor who'd spoken. One by one everyone had slipped from the room, leaving her alone.

She'd wanted to scream after them, "I'm not dead yet! Hear me! I want to stay with you!" But she was unable to make a sound or exhale a breath.

While she lay there frozen with fear, a giant void had opened and invited her in, but before she could step across its threshold, a dark creature had suspended itself over her bed. Slowly it lowered itself onto her body and softly kissed her. What was this thing? An angel come to take her to heaven?

She clung to its comforting presence, but pleaded to stay. "Don't take me yet."

The entity held her, growled, and sank two sharp fangs into her neck. She was in agony for a while, but then a feeling of sensual intrusion and ecstasy overcame her. Slowly and voluptuously the vampire drank her blood and made her drink some of its own.

On that night Prince Romano had redeemed her and doomed her forever.

My sire has great powers, she thought, *developed over the centuries. If he wants to destroy me, he can do so at any time. Does he expect me to apologize and plead for reentry into the clan? Never!*

She thought about Romano's attempts to keep her under strict control, and her refusal to cooperate. An insect buzz caught her attention, and she watched a fly as it passed by her face and landed on a wall. It scratched itself, apparently oblivious to her.

I'll consult with my mortal friend Kweca, Desidra thought. *She'll help me.*

She released a deep groan. *I need blood. Enough to give me the energy to crawl out of this hole.*

A thump!

Something coming her way.

Romano? Have to move. Have to get out of here!

She lifted herself to a seated position, slowly and with pain. Something there . . . in the dark shadows. It moved, and she saw that it was a giant rat watching her from a safe distance, its glistening, black eyes fixed on her. Behind it emerged another rat, and another, and more. All waiting.

They smell my wounds, she thought. *They're waiting for me to die. Waiting to tear into my flesh.*

"We'll see about that, my little friends," she whispered. "I'm a predator, too."

With smooth movements she removed a large woolen scarf from her waist and, despite her wounds, slid with deceptive speed toward those who'd come to dine. She tossed the heavy scarf across her prey and quickly suffocated half a dozen of them.

It wasn't much sustenance, but it gave her some

strength. She wiped her mouth and walked up a stairway to an exit.

Outside, the day greeted her with a Seattle-gray sky and rain as soft as baby skin. A dark day, a good day for a vampire to be outside. If the weather remained this way, she could walk safely down the streets in her human form to find a satisfactory hiding place. With one problem. The tattered chiffon dress she wore and her bare feet would draw unwanted attention.

With difficulty she formed herself into a shadow shape. The smell of gasoline and smoke and the rich stink of burnt meat floating from small restaurants tickled her nostrils. She slipped past the public market and ragged beggars and watched the fishermen unload their cargoes of silver-pink salmon and giant green crabs. Along First Avenue there were signs on telephone poles and inside store windows. One in particular intrigued her. It displayed a red-headed young woman clutching papers and directly above her a message: "Get A War Job—See Your U.S. Employment Service."

Moving south, down the alleyways that lay behind various government buildings, she reached the Federal Building and in the shadows of that structure found a large trash container. A small sign on its side advised that pickup days were Wednesday and Saturday.

Today was Tuesday.

Lifting the lid, she saw that the container was full of cardboard and papers. She bent over and allowed her body to slide into the bin, then burrowed beneath the debris and waited for nightfall when she could escape safely. *I'll be stronger then. Able to fly.*

Her body would restore itself.

In the warm darkness she passed time reading the bits and pieces of the paper that covered her. There were canceled purchase orders from the Army Engineers, discarded blueprints, a list of building materials headed for Alaska, and job announcements, quite a few of them: *Senior Engineers, Pipe Fitters, Telephone Clerks.*

Suddenly the lid was lifted, and light filtered through the debris.

Desidra lay motionless.

Voices.

Something heavy clumped above her, perhaps a box.

"That's it for the day," a man's voice said. "I'll be glad when this war's over and we hire a janitor. I'm supposed to be middle-management, and here I am hauling out garbage."

A woman's voice: "Janitors make more money building airplanes. That's where they've all gone . . . to the factories. So are most of the housewives."

"Goodie for them," said the man with a note of disgust. "Even at my age I'll probably get drafted."

The trash container lid slammed shut with a loud clang, and she heard the voices recede as the mortals left.

Desidra rose to the top of the trash and inspected the new contribution. It was a large cardboard box, with the name of an office supply store stamped on one side. She rummaged through papers in the box. Mostly business letters and advertisements. But here was something interesting. A job application, coffee-stained and crumpled: "UNITED STATES WAR DEPARTMENT—Clerk-typists for positions out of the United States. Apply Federal Building, Room 200. Applicants must be citizens of the United States, at least 18 years of age."

She examined this with great interest, and a plan began to form in her mind. One that Prince Romano would not like.

Desidra burrowed deeper into the container until she reached its metal bottom, and there she slept. When she awoke and poked her head out of the trash it was night. She heard vehicle noises, and at the end of the alley saw a flatbed truck filled with wooden crates clatter by. Other than that, the passing traffic was light.

Her vitality seemed to have returned, at least for a while, and she made herself invisible, entered the Federal Building, and found the War Department offices. A few employees were still at work in one room, but there was plenty of opportunity for a shadow-shape to investigate the other deserted offices.

Desidra slithered into one.

How quiet it was in here. Only typewriters and file cabinets and chairs and desks. No mortals. Exactly the way she wanted it to be. Her gaze focused on a particular file cabinet. She tried one drawer and then another. They were locked.

But locks were easily picked, she knew, and soon she was able to examine the contents of various folders. In one marked "Acceptable for Testing" she located a number of completed job applications and studied them carefully, noting addresses, names, and physical descriptions. Since her vampire experiences would not translate well onto any sort of government form, she looked for an application with background information that suited her and then copied much of it onto a blank application. Selectively, she added certain of her own abilities and education, as well as the fact that she spoke several languages proficiently, especially Japanese.

As for her address? She jotted down an address and grinned as she did so.

From this moment on, she would be, "Desidra Smith." Smith sounded more reliable than her own esoteric family name which originally had been Bathlandor. The name Desidra was a bit exotic, as well, but she liked the ring of it, and it was so intertwined with her identity that she didn't want to change it.

Carefully, she placed Desidra Smith's application in the file of applicants to be tested, then folded the application she'd stolen and tucked it in a pocket of her dress.

It was easy to gain an advantage, she thought. Particularly when all the necessary material was so accessible. Now she knew what the job would be and where: Post Headquarters, the Alaska Department, near Anchorage, in a newly formed cryptography unit.

As for the application she'd removed, the young woman who'd submitted it would assume it had not been accepted.

She repeated her new name and background softly to herself . . . Desidra Smith, a respectable young woman from a working-class family, with nothing marring her reputation. An innocent! According to the application she had no living relatives.

Quietly, she slipped back outside and into the trash container once again. Tearing the stolen application into shreds, she scattered its pieces over the other debris.

By late evening all signs of the beating had disappeared from Desidra's body, except a deep and painful gouge on her shoulder. Rising from the trash she saw the rest of her clan fly from their underground retreat and spread out across the city for their nightly Blood-hunt. As each vampire went its way down narrow dark streets and shadowed alleys, Desidra, a dark bird-shape in the sky, flew in a different direction—northwest across Puget Sound, skimming the islands that split the huge inland waterway into a spiderweb of blue.

A sense of urgency pushed her forward, her desire to see her Indian friend, Kweca. Another rule to be broken, she thought. Romano's law proclaimed that no clan member could fraternize with a human, except for the purpose of feeding.

Images rose in Desidra's mind of how she and Kweca, a Wise Woman of the Makah tribe, had first become friends. The Indian woman had been seated by the water, watching the moon, listening to the pounding surf, communing with her own restless spirit and seeking union with others, those who floated away from their bodies. With startling suddenness, Desidra had appeared before her.

"You are not the spirit I seek," the Indian woman said quietly, "though we are both people of the night. Name yourself, and I will provide mine." The language the shaman spoke was a tribal tongue full of clicks and gutturals.

"Your name is Kweca?" asked Desidra, having read the woman's mind.

The Indian woman had not appeared surprised. She had laughed and switched to English: "Close enough. According to the custom of my people, it is time for me to select a new name, but you may call me Kweca. Are you spirit or demon?"

"A little of both," answered Desidra, and bared her canine teeth.

"Ah," said Kweca without flinching. "Wolf and eagle caught in one spirit."

The memory made Desidra smile. She hadn't been hungry that night, else she might have destroyed a fine friendship before it began. By human standards a long relationship ensued—almost thirty years now. Although their encounters were few, the friendship endured. Each time they met it seemed to Desidra they had only parted the day before.

A whistling wind interrupted her thoughts as Desidra flew over the Olympic Mountains, then down again to touch the snow. She burrowed into a glacier and let it wrap her in its icy embrace before she burst forth into the darkening sky. On the other side of the mountains, the earth was thick with fir and cedar trees. The wind shook the treetops, whipping branches back and forth like waves on an inland sea. Maintaining a slower pace of flight than usual, Desidra dipped down to examine the rain forest. No hurry. No one was chasing her. Her absence wouldn't be noticed until dawn.

The Hunger, the need for the crimson elixir, reminded her that her body was not completely healed, that it needed blood to make her whole again. But she pushed the message aside.

A sense of freedom caught her, a deep release from all that bound her or attempted to do so. Kindred traditions. And Prince Romano with all of his rules, damnable rules. Moving upward again she assumed another shape, this one less birdlike, more like a dark cloud flowing with the air currents.

The wind blew against her with ferocity, and she welcomed its cold breath as she might have accepted a lover, opening herself to the sensual pleasure as it played across her body. She filled herself with the wind's force and for a moment was buffeted about in oneness with it, a feather of matter in the currents that pushed her. Then she steadied herself and pursued her northerly course up the Olympic Peninsula.

Below her, in waning light, several Canada geese flew with their long necks stretched forward and great wings beating in what appeared to be effortless motion. It was late for such birds to be flying. These were stragglers, no doubt trying to catch up with a larger formation. She watched them swoop toward land, and she flew closer to view them.

How beautiful, she thought. *And how alive. Not Undead, as I am*.

A huge military plane flew overhead, and she reminded herself of her mission. The war. She had to explain her desires to Kweca, seek advice from her.

The Strait of Juan De Fuca came into sight, a broad

inland channel between Canada and the United States. At the northernmost tip of the peninsula she recognized Cape Flattery and nearby Neah Bay, a community on the Makah Indian Reservation.

Down she went through the night sky, over the tops of small tattered buildings and long communal lodges and immense whaling canoes carved from cedar logs. The odor of dried fish and the salt smell of the strait blended in her nostrils. Still invisible, she picked up Kweca's scent and moved rapidly across the ground to find her.

As always, Kweca sat by the water, this time on a huge, half-buried log bleached white by the salt air and seawater. Light cast from a nearby shack revealed she had aged. Her body looked leaner and there were dark shadows under her eyes that had not been there when they'd last seen one another. Nonetheless she was still Kweca, her hair shining black, face unlined. Despite the fact that most Indians donned the clothing of their conquerors, Kweca wore a skirt of shredded cedar bark edged by a fringe of the same material. A coarse black-and-white blanket hung from her shoulders.

"You come again," said Kweca, her voice as melodious as always, her gaze fixed on the saltwater in front of her. Waves advanced and receded against the beach, deep throbbing sounds that pleased Desidra's senses.

"You always know when I'm here," answered the vampire, and she solidified into her human shape.

With a stick, Kweca made designs in the sand. Intricate configurations that were of unknown meaning to Desidra. "It's been a long time," the Indian said.

"Only two years."

"By your standards a few moments. Time turned meaningless when you became a vampire."

"I haven't forgotten mortality," Desidra said. "I will age, too, and not so gracefully as you. The oldest vampires are often quite ugly, their features twisted by their own rapacious natures."

"A strange thing to say about your own kind."

"I am outcast now."

"Oh?" Kweca said. "Do you want to tell me about it?"

Desidra shuddered and ran fingers through her long hair and across the smooth skin of her face and her full red lips. Without filling in details, she said, "Sometimes I wish I were not Kindred. The joys, the sensuality of being Undead are offset by the latter centuries of our existence. We become wasted and wrinkled and filled with cruelty and fear. One day I will behave like my sire, whom I abhor."

"There's something you need of me?" asked Kweca.

"Your advice. You've heard of the war in the Pacific?"

"Yes, it's out there now. Boats beneath the waves, sleek and fast as seals. And great birds in the sky spitting fire and thunder. White man's war!"

"The Japanese are not white."

"White or otherwise, they behave in the same manner, conquering and subjugating."

"You are a Wise Woman," said Desidra, "a wizard of your people. Do you see war machines in your visions?"

"No," Kweca said with a smile. "I hear about them on the radio. There is a honey-voiced Japanese woman who is most informative. Tokyo Rose. She entertains us daily when there is nothing else to listen to."

"I know of her, but she stretches the truth."

"No more than any other political animal. What is it you want from me, Desidra?"

"My sire is angry with me, because I wish to go to war for America. I need your counsel."

"Have you been in battle already? I see wounds upon you."

Desidra touched her injured shoulder. "It's almost healed. You saw me favoring it?"

"No, I felt your pain." Kweca rose and moved toward Desidra. In the dim light the Indian's dark eyes glistened. "I sense from your thoughts that you might have been killed. Was it the Elder, Romano, who injured you?"

"He could have done more damage, but he held his power in check. Once I was his favorite, but I've fallen from grace. Forever, I fear."

"Nothing is forever, except the wind and the heavens."

"I must confess something," Desidra said. "I've applied

for a job with the War Department, and I used your postal box number on the reservation for a mailing address. Do you mind?"

"No, I think I can share that much with you."

"What do you think of my decision?"

"Follow your own spirit, not mine. Yours is a good one and the reason we're friends."

"I'm a vampire. Do I have a spirit? A soul?"

"I don't know about others of your kind; perhaps some are empty vessels. But I sense otherwise about you."

"I hope you're right."

"You are a predator," Kweca said, "but that is not morally wrong in itself. You shouldn't feel shame."

"We're both savages by the white man's standards," Desidra said.

Kweca looked at her, and in the low light the Indian's features appeared to be chiseled from marble. Then she laughed, and her features softened.

Desidra explained, as she had to Romano, about the need to protect vampire territory, and that she had certain skills that would be helpful to the American war effort. "I have a knowledge of Japanese history, culture, and language. Romano allowed me to have an extensive education before he took us into the underground city some years ago. After that time, he lost his charitable nature."

"You wish to be a soldier?"

"A civilian, not a soldier. Too confining for my taste. I've broken into government files and filled out an application. The written test won't be a problem, but the physical exam will. It includes a blood test. Whatever's in my blood that makes me a vampire will be revealed."

"Wouldn't they detect only the last drink of blood you've taken from a human?"

"Yes, but vampires are not entirely bloodless, Kweca. A small quantity of mortal blood flows in my veins. I hope that my latest feeding will mask whatever nonhuman chemistry I possess."

"So you shouldn't feed from diseased or dying human vessels before the physical?"

Desidra nodded. "Normally we live well on such fare, but this time I need uncontaminated blood."

"I see another problem. Your vampire body is cool. What if they take your temperature?"

"Not a concern. I allow my imagination to remind my body of the joy of fangs in flesh, warm blood flowing. That warms me."

"A strange revelation," Kweca said.

"Nonetheless, it is so. When I allow my imagination to expand, my body temperature rises. The content of my blood, however, is a different matter. What shall I do, Kweca? You're a medicine woman, can you conjure up something for me?"

"Make blood, you mean? I'm not the Great Spirit. I can't create living matter, only the illusion of it. I'm a medicine woman. White men call me impostor; they don't believe in my herbs or potions or visions. No, I can't make blood for you."

"And I can't return to the Kindred until I succeed at what I intend to do."

"Don't let your ego get in the way of your good sense, Desidra. Don't do something foolish just because you've made a public announcement."

"It's more than ego."

"Something you have to prove to yourself?"

"Perhaps."

Kweca hesitated for a long moment as she considered the problem of her friend. She etched more designs in the sand.

"What do your sand drawings mean?" asked Desidra.

"Little prayers for your safety."

"A prayer for a vampire?"

"I don't pray to the white man's God, I pray to mine. My God is tolerant of animals."

Desidra laughed. "I need all the help I can get."

"You'll need identification papers. I can arrange some, if you tell me what you need. I know a clever man who will do it for you. And remember, if you want to join humans, you'll have to behave like one. Can you do that?"

"It shouldn't be too difficult."

"When is the written test?"

"In a day or two."

"And the physical exam?"

"Shortly thereafter."

"Blood is your main obstacle?" Then Kweca asked, "Is there a way I might give you some of mine?"

"Too dangerous. I've warned you about that."

"And you've told me many times that you're able to drink blood from a human without turning that person into a vampire or causing death. You said it's only in the exchange of blood that transformation occurs, when the human takes in vampire blood."

Desidra shook her head. "Those are just technicalities. The truth is, the Hunger might overtake me. I could draw too much blood from you and you'd die."

"I'm your friend. You'd control yourself."

"When the Hunger takes over, I'm transported backward in time, across ancient, dark eons. Whatever human compassion I still possess vanishes for the moment, and I become what my sire is, what each of my kind is and will always be: a carnivore, a wild beast. The Hunger is master, and we do its bidding."

"You won't let that happen. I'm strong and healthy, and my blood is as pure as the spirits of my ancestors. I want to do this for you. Now!"

"You don't understand. It's a blood-lust, and I'm captive to it."

"We have blood rituals, too. Some of our people still cling to a custom white men have outlawed, the Kloqually. It's the local dance of war, a celebration that involves burning coals and blood-letting. Watch." Without warning, Kweca pulled a tiny knife from her skirt and slid the sharp blade quickly across the side of her neck. A trickle of blood stained her light bronze skin.

"Come," Kweca said. She leaned back on the large, white log and presented her neck to the vampire.

Desidra tried to turn away, but the rich, warm scent of blood was more than she could bear.

I must have her!

Again her conscience came into play. *Fight the urge,*

you've done it before. This is your good friend. Your only mortal friend. Remember that.

But the humanity still clinging to Desidra was washed away by the Hunger. The sight of Kweca's blood on the length of her graceful neck was a beacon welcoming Desidra home after a long journey. It offered sustenance and the warmth she lacked and craved. It would heal her completely. She knelt beside her friend and licked a small amount of the dark fluid from the neck, then a little more until the bleeding stopped.

Kweca lay motionless.

Like a doe listening to the sounds of a hunter, thought Desidra, and the Hunger assailed her. Its primitive impulse drove her into the abyss she'd tried to avoid. She grasped her friend tightly with both hands and sank fangs into flesh, drinking slowly at first and then with increasing lust.

I need, I need, I need.

All of her senses were sharpened now, and the sweet pleasure intensified and carried her down the Hunger's dark path. Strength returned to her injured shoulder. It no longer pained her. She lifted her head for a moment and stared into her friend's eyes. They were glazed and filled with fear.

"Don't kill me," Kweca pleaded. "Please don't kill me."

The threads of human conscience that were still part of Desidra began to weave themselves together. *My friend, I can't kill my friend!* She released her hold on the human.

"I love you Kweca," she said, still savoring the taste of the Indian's blood. "Please trust that I could never hurt you." *Am I becoming like Romano, a beast?*

Unsteadily, Kweca rose to a seated position. She touched the small puncture wounds on her neck. "I trust the human in you, but the predator needs a muzzle." She grasped Desidra's hands. "You have the spirit of me now. Make good use of it."

"Friends?" Desidra asked as she rose to her feet.

"Eternally. Will you need more of my blood before you take your tests?"

"Courageous of you to ask that."

Kweca smiled.

"No," Desidra said. "The test is only a short while off, and I'll never do that to you again. But I'll need clothes. I'll probably have to make an overnight trip to a department store."

"To steal?"

Desidra shook her head. "To borrow. I always repay my debts. When you live two or three thousand years it's easy to fulfill obligations. You take from one place this day or month or year, then pay the debt by taking from another, and it continues, in endless succession."

Kweca laid her hand on Desidra's arm. "I won't judge you. No more than I'd question the wolf in pursuit of the lamb. But stay with me and I'll drive to town in the morning to purchase what you need. The owner of the white man's store will be surprised to see me buying a new dress. My people usually wear what your people have discarded. He might even think I'm becoming civilized."

"I can get money," Desidra said.

Kweca set her jaw stubbornly and shook her head. "Let me do this my way."

Desidra agreed, and it was done Kweca's way.

At the appointed time Desidra mingled with half a dozen people in the hallway of a medical facility, applicants who had passed the written government test. Dressed in a cotton, short-skirted suit and white blouse with her long red hair twisted into a loose knot at the nape of her neck, Desidra looked like a beautiful mortal female. But she didn't feel mortal. The written test had been almost too easy, the questions childish. Still, it was surprising how many mortals had dropped out of the examination during its first hour.

A thin woman in a white uniform approached. She had dyed black hair and a pinched expression. The humans surged toward her.

Desidra watched.

"One at a time, one at a time!" the woman shouted, and the group slowed to a halt. "You first." She beckoned to Desidra and led her toward the clinic.

Sickly little thing, thought Desidra. Employing her animal instincts she analyzed the potential prey and wondered if anyone at this medical facility had noticed the woman's bloated stomach or heard the growl of her irritable colon. Too many vegetables in her diet, not enough protein.

"Undress," ordered the woman. Handing Desidra a white cotton garment, she added, "Put this on and sit in the waiting room until I call you. You'll be seeing Dr. Cooper."

When she completed the change, Desidra seated her-

self on a bench beside a man with a bandaged finger.
Blood! She could smell it. Congealed blood and fresh
flowing blood.

"Did you cut yourself?" she asked politely.

"To the bone. On a band saw."

"Sounds painful."

He grunted affirmation.

Wondering if she sounded human enough, Desidra
considered charming, useless, human civility. So common
in their petty affairs. Animal ways were better, more direct.

She sat quietly, all of her senses drinking in the man's
blood odor. The recent feeding from Kweca had left her
still yearning, and she had a strong desire to dispense
with polite behavior and take the man. Perhaps she could
coax him into a closet, kiss his finger, kiss his mouth, and
move from there to the thick, throbbing vein on his neck.
Not enough to kill him. Just enough to enrapture him.

An imaginary newspaper headline surfaced in her mind:
"Vampire Attacks Patient in Doctor's Office!"

Predator, get control of yourself. Select your target and place!

The man smiled. "I appreciate your sympathy. Most
people don't care about pain, unless it's their own."

She smiled in return, moved closer and ran her fingers
gently over the bandage. "I wish I could heal this for you."

"You're sweet," said the man. "I wonder if . . . "

Her short relationship with the stranger was terminated
by the black-haired nurse, who exclaimed, "In here, quickly!
We have a lot of people to process."

Desidra smelled the woman's agitation, saw drops of
sweat on her forehead, and she whispered to the nurse,
"You ought to eat a little raw meat. It might help your
stomach problem."

A seeming impossibility occurred. The pinched face
became even more so, and half-phrases sputtered from
the woman's thin, bloodless lips.

Desidra stepped past her though a doorway.

In contrast to his assistant, the doctor seemed full of
good will and chatter.

He checked Desidra's temperature, which she elevated
immediately through thoughts that lingered on the

bloody-fingered man in the waiting room. Perhaps he'd still be there when she left.

Dr. Cooper checked her pulse. Desidra adjusted it to human normal. "Is it too high?" she asked, though she already knew the answer.

"It's fine, far better than mine."

"You've been under stress?"

"The good kind," he answered. "Tomorrow I'm marrying the most wonderful woman in the world. We're both thirty-seven, getting hitched for the first time. Going to honeymoon at Snoqualmie Falls, renting a cabin. Have you been there? Spectacular . . . all that water. Higher than Niagara, you know."

Desidra simulated a human breathing pattern.

The doctor made entries on a clipboard. "There ought to be a nurse doing this," he apologized. "But we're short-handed. The war and all."

He cleaned a spot on her arm with alcohol, thrust in a needle, and drew blood into a vial.

As far as Desidra was concerned, this was a convenient way to get blood, but without the rapture. She licked her lips and listened while his words spilled forth without pause. She could almost taste his agitation.

"My fiancée works on the Boeing assembly line," he said, "riveting warplane parts. She's picked out a house for us and is talking about paint and wallpaper and drapes and I can't keep up with her. We're understaffed here, and the paperwork keeps getting heavier and heavier. Keeping up is impossible. Ah, here we are . . . finished."

He removed the needle and pressed a cotton pad against her arm. "Keep this on it for a few minutes."

Desidra's eyes were fixed on the vial of blood he held. She watched as he wrapped laboratory instructions around the tube and secured them with an elastic band.

"We should have some answers from the lab in a day or so," he said.

But he bobbled the vial. It slipped from his fingers and flew toward the floor. Desidra knew she could catch it before it hit, but only if she revealed herself for what she was—something inhuman.

The vial exploded on contact, spraying blood and shards of glass on the doctor's white lab coat and the floor.

"Oh God," he said. He looked at his watch. "And I've got about thirty more patients to see today. Would you mind waiting while I clean up and get some fresh equipment?"

"I have another appointment," she lied. The spilled blood was exciting her, and she needed to get away from this office quickly, before something nasty happened, before . . .

Kweca's blood, mixed with her own, was splattered on the floor, and Desidra wanted it back, despite the glass shards.

There was another option.

The doctor bent over the spilled blood and made an ineffectual attempt to wipe it up with a towel.

Desidra stared at the throbbing veins on his temple and neck, blood pumping through his body at a fast rate. She wanted to sink her fangs into one of those fat veins.

Not here, she reminded herself. *Later, somewhere else, when it's dark.*

"This is terrible," said the doctor. He looked up at her apologetically.

She knelt beside him and met his gaze, fixing him with a seductive, hypnotic stare, as a cat might transfix a bird. Her dark eyes were large and of an ancient depth. They drew him toward her, until he was only inches from her face.

He stopped his feeble attempt to clean the blood and glass.

"Must I take this foolish test?" she asked in a sultry voice. "I'm quite healthy, as you can see. Why waste your time?"

His voice was slow, his eyes glazed over: "You know, you're right. I'll sign your health release right now, and you can be on your way to that appointment." He glanced briefly at the towel in his hand, then stood up and tossed it in a hamper. At a sink he rinsed his hands, then found Desidra's papers and filled them out with false information.

"Sorry I fumbled things," he said. "Guess I've got too much on my mind. War and marriage. So much to think about." He handed her a carbon copy of the completed form.

"I understand," murmured Desidra, stuffing the paper into her purse.

As she left, she stepped over the spilled red liquid on the floor. Such a waste and how ironic. All the worry and taking blood from Kweca had not been necessary—might even have killed her friend.

Though she could usually remain outside in daylight for a few hours at a time, the medical clinic had taken its toll. The Hunger must be satisfied, but not until after dark. She returned to the old hotel near the Seattle waterfront, where she'd reserved a room for temporary use.

Upon entering the lobby, she saw that the privacy and quiet that had first attracted her to the place had been disturbed. Uniformed police officers milled about, talking to the desk clerk and pounding up and down the shabbily carpeted stairs. The word "knife" punctuated their conversations.

In the corridor on the first floor police stood by the open doorway of a room. The smell of fresh blood was strong in Desidra's nostrils, filling her pores, actuating ancient urges. Instantly all her senses were alert, her eyesight keener, her hearing fine-tuned, her sense of smell at its optimum.

Several pairs of official eyes focused upon her. "You staying here, miss?" one of the officers asked.

"She checked in last night," the hotel clerk shouted from the check-in counter.

Desidra's mind raced. She didn't have her identification papers in order, if the police demanded them. A supernatural escape might be necessary, and could lead to complications. She stared into the young officer's eyes and said softly, "I'm afraid I can't be helpful. I've been at the War Department all morning." She gave him a brief, sweet smile. *Perhaps he'll tell me what's going on, and I don't need to read his mind.*

The young officer weakened. "We have the assailant,"

he said, and added, with a note of bravado, "Domestic discussion turned nasty. Wife stuck him with a knife—then claimed it was no worse than he'd have done to her. The guy's done for, but we called an ambulance."

Desidra licked her lips: the smell of blood was stronger! She tried to control the tremble of emotion that passed through her body. With a shake of her head, her red hair loosened and swung back and forth in a slow ballet of movement.

The policeman's heart and breathing were accelerating. She saw his eyes go over her figure, pausing on her breasts when he didn't think she noticed.

Good! she thought. *That ought to distract him.*

"Is it all right if I go to my room?" she asked in a voice choked by her blood desires.

"Her room's on the third floor!" the desk clerk shouted.

"Nosy devil," said the officer. "You go ahead, miss."

Desidra hurried upstairs. The stairwell and hallway were narrow and stank of urine and stale cigarette smoke. Only the poor and degraded resided in this desolate place. None of the other hotel residents had made an appearance during the commotion downstairs, and she wondered if they had too many problems of their own to involve themselves in the travails of other humans. Were they fearful of the world outside their rooms?

Her own room was bleak and tiny, no more than a dark closet. Its amenities were limited to a narrow bed and a yellow-stained wall-mounted sink. She settled down on the bed to wait for night, but the Hunger, unabated, rose within her like a ravening beast.

She hugged herself. *Don't let go. Think about something else.*

But she couldn't.

A bloody body, barely alive, lay waiting in a hallway only two floors below!

Sometimes she loathed such urges and felt shame for them. When they swept over her, she often thought of how something important was missing from her existence, of the emptiness inside since she'd become vampire. In her former mortal state she'd been in love and engaged to be married—a relationship that ended with the dominance of Prince Romano.

In the years since she'd been Kindred, approximately a century, she'd hoped to find someone with whom she could spend her eternity. None of the vampires in her clan fulfilled that need. There was Christopher, but he was more like a brother. She needed someone to share her passion. Was she destined, like most of the Kindred, to haunt the dark passageways of time in unending loneliness—searching, always searching for mortal love again?

The instinct that could not be denied spoke to her wordlessly. The vampire Desidra became invisible and rose from her bed. A door opened and an unseen wind whistled softly down the corridor and two flights of stairs.

In the dim light of the murder room, two policemen were gathering evidence, inserting it into containers. Off to one side sat a distraught woman in handcuffs. Desidra approached her, dragged cold vampire-fingers across the woman's throat and pinched.

The woman screamed.

Both officers moved away from the body and ran toward the hysterical woman.

Exactly as Desidra had intended. She crossed the room and lowered herself onto the dying body, pressing her lips around a large slash along the man's neck. Her tongue probed the flesh; her canine teeth dug deep into the carotid artery. Fresh, warm blood flowed out of the body and into Desidra.

One of the officers looked toward the murdered man. "Jesus!" he exclaimed. "The damn body's white as chalk!"

The faces of the officers were a mixture of horror and fascination. They knelt over the body and touched its pale contours.

"It's cold in here," one of them said. "Is a window open, or a door?"

"I don't know, and I don't care," said the other officer. "Let's finish and get the hell out of here."

At five minutes past midnight Desidra returned to Neah Bay.

Kweca looked up from the small fire she'd been building on the sandy beach. She tossed a few dry sticks on top of it and flames blazed upward. The sudden light from the fire emphasized the strong lines of her nose and cheeks and turned her black eyes into glittering jewels. Suddenly Desidra saw something new in her friend, the likeness of a fierce Mongolian female born centuries earlier superimposed on her face. The flames subsided, and the strange image disappeared.

"The wind has returned you to me," said Kweca. She examined her friend. "The suit I bought you is stained with blood."

"In a worthwhile cause." Desidra paused, thinking about the dead man in the hotel room. "I can always get more clothes, if I need them."

"And your new job?"

"War Department paperwork says I'll be assigned as a cryptographer at a new Signal Intelligence unit in Alaska. It will augment the Allied cryptanalysis facilities at Pearl Harbor and Washington, D.C."

With these few words Desidra had revealed more than she intended. Still, she wasn't worried. Kweca, even with her professed dislike for the ways of white men, would never betray the American war effort. She often referred to herself as "the original American," and genetically she was exactly that, representing all that was good and true in her race. Desidra could think of no better friend to have.

Kweca stretched her hands forward, palms up, as though offering Desidra a gift. "Indian languages are ideal for code-talking. Knowing this, your government has made code-talk from Choctaw and Comanche and Navajo and other native tongues to convey messages by telephone. In the Navajo tongue there is the matter of timing, slight pauses before certain words are spoken. Word stems change many times, depending upon the object being acted upon. Knowledge and intent can change a word. My Makah language is equally difficult to interpret."

"A great problem for any enemy," Desidra said. "Such languages are not widely known and are traditionally unwritten."

"That is true," said Kweca. "When do you report?"

"November. They haven't actually told me yet, but I know anyway. Guess that means they're well-organized, getting the personnel chosen while the facility is still under construction. Technically I'm awaiting assignment."

"Months from now," Kweca said thoughtfully. "So what do you do in the meantime?"

"Maybe I'll refresh my knowledge of Japanese history and language. Think I'll make a side trip to the Pearl Harbor cryptography unit, too, and probe around a bit. Get a preliminary education from the code-breakers."

"Pearl Harbor. Where the Japanese sank the great war canoes. I saw pictures of the firestorm. Why are you going into such danger? Stay here where it's safe. You've told me fire can mean death to a vampire. If you stay with us, my family will build you a cabin, your own place."

"Why would they do that?"

Kweca smiled. "Because I would ask them to."

"I couldn't accept a gift of that magnitude."

"A fine animal skin tent, then? You could live in the traditional Indian way."

After a pause, Desidra replied, "Perhaps. Thank you."

Gently, she cradled her friend's face in both hands. "You are a wise, kind woman, Kweca. You've never questioned my shape-shifts into animal or bird. You don't mind that I see you at odd times without warning or invitation, and you ignore the fact I'm vampire and not human. I've learned much from you and trust your advice. But I can't stay and hide. Something important beckons me."

"Then you must follow your spirit. I pray that you will return unharmed."

"Of course," promised Desidra, and she disappeared quickly into the night.

A short time later, an invisible entity sailed past a guard, through two locked doors, and down into a cellar office. Desidra had arrived within the well-secured facilities of the Naval Combat Intelligence Unit at Pearl Harbor, one of the key Allied code-breaking facilities.

I'm here! she thought, feeling a rush of excitement and anticipation. Papers on the floor and on the tops of desks rustled as she passed by.

A thin blond man seated at a desk asked his bearded companion, "Dick! Did you feel that? Cold air blowing in."

His companion grinned. "Maybe a ghost. A Japanese ghost-spy."

Desidra enjoyed becoming the wind, suggesting to superstitious mortals that another entity might be present, one they could never hope to explain. It made for interesting reactions.

The blond man tugged at his earlobe. "It wasn't my imagination. Dammit, I felt something."

"You've been down here too long," Dick said. "Your frustrations are showing. Cheer up. We'll have the Japs on the run before too long."

"Think so, huh?" said the blond. "We work our tails off to crack their naval code and what happens? The Japs bomb the shit out of Pearl Harbor."

"Yeah, but we're building up a head of steam now," Dick said. "They'd better watch out."

"I try to be optimistic, but even when we figure out

their codes, we only understand a small percentage of what they're talking about. What are they going to do next?"

Dick slapped him on the back. "Look at it this way: they're having the same problems we are."

"Not quite. They've had more military victories than us. Look what they did in the Philippines. The Japs showered leaflets on the Filipinos telling them to desert the island, and MacArthur retreated to Australia."

"Trust me. All this data we're collecting is adding up to something."

"But what?"

"I don't know, but they're up to something big. Yamamoto is about to make a move. I sense it."

"Yeah, but where? Toward India? Australia? Hawaii again? Where, dammit?"

"I wish to God I knew." Dick sighed. "Basically I'm a crossword puzzle freak working on codes. Let's just do our jobs, okay, and leave strategy up to the high brass. Otherwise we'll go nuts."

"We may go nuts anyway," came the retort.

The men returned to their work. One tapped the keys of a machine, while the other studied a thick report.

Desidra reveled in her freedom of movement. Despite the man with heightened awareness, no one here really *knew* she was present. There was no one to whom she had to bow or yield, in contrast with her association with Romano. How delicious to be able to stand in the shadows and eavesdrop on the code-breakers' conversation all by herself!

There were papers piled everywhere with no obvious order she could discern. It was apparent to her that ordinary military rules were not heavily imposed on this small group of men. Perhaps the commanders felt as she did, that their talents would be suffocated under too much control.

She felt a fellowship with them, looked forward to her own duties.

They'd spoken of Admiral Yamamoto. If he was their nemesis, their frustrating rival, perhaps it was time for

Desidra to head for Japan and discover for herself what the devil was up to.

She took flight.

The night was clear and the vast Pacific Ocean calm. Desidra skimmed across its surface and dipped down to enjoy its salty touch. She'd learned a great deal this night, but much more remained to be revealed, in the company of Yamamoto.

She headed for Japan.

She flew south from Tokyo toward a group of offshore islands where key elements of the Japanese fleet were anchored. It was there that Desidra expected to find Admiral Isoroku Yamamoto, Commander in Chief of the Imperial Japanese Navy, the brilliant military officer admired by the Japanese people and revered by his men as a godlike figure. What was it about the man that inspired such devotion?

After making the decision to go to war, the ministers of Japan left the naval strategy to Yamamoto. From all Desidra knew about him, he liked it that way. He was a man who preferred to make his own decisions.

As I make mine, thought Desidra, and a bit of admiration for him crept into her thoughts.

Yamamoto knew a great deal about America, she recalled from a secret document she had seen at Pearl Harbor. He'd attended Harvard, had been a naval attaché in Washington, D.C., and had done a lot of traveling across the United States. No doubt he'd digested substantial information that would aid his current war plans, and she was here to discover those plans and undo them.

The Japanese were a well-disciplined people, thought Desidra. Their codes of manners and ways of life were laid out in an orderly fashion. They'd learned to live in crowded harmony on the collection of islands that made up Japan. And they did this by following rules without question. To do otherwise might lead to war among themselves.

A shiver of anticipation ran through her vaporish body as she entered the quiet harbor on the island of Hashirajima where Yamamoto's 68,000-ton flagship, the *Yamato*, lay at anchor. The surrounding islands looked like a collection of green velvet hassocks. They were lovely, but Desidra spotted antiaircraft batteries atop most of the islands

The Japanese are masters of preparation, she thought as she passed by the myriad ships that occupied the dark mirror of water below her.

Silently, she thanked Prince Romano for the extensive education he'd allowed her in years past. He might be a monster now, but in their early days together Romano had been charitable and supportive, encouraging her to learn a number of languages, insisting she have a good background in mathematics and history and human psychology. Now, ironically, he had become her oppressor . . . or worse: her enemy. From some perspectives the turnaround in their relationship seemed dramatic, but it occurred to her now that perhaps he had never been her friend or benefactor—and that what he had done was really not for her benefit but for his own, for the enlargement of his personal circle of power and influence.

On the flagship *Yamato*, Admiral Yamamoto stood erect in his starched white uniform, addressing a dinner gathering of officers. Yamamoto's wide face was expressionless, as if carved from stone. His round cheeks and high collar gave him a boyish, almost impish appearance, but his close-set eyes revealed the essence of the man: a samurai of the highest order. A tough, hardened warrior, he held a cup of sake in his hand as he spoke. It was an inspirational speech, filled with exhortations and energy.

Dozens of uniformed officers listened with starched attentiveness. In addition to Yamamoto, Desidra caught a glimpse of another important individual whom she recognized from photographs: stern-visaged, frowning Vice Admiral Nagumo, the man who had carried out the attack on Pearl Harbor under Yamamoto's direction. The others were captains and staff officers, as indicated by their insignia.

Unseen, she slipped between tables, weaving snakelike through the assemblage, listening to conversations, drinking in the sounds of beating hearts, rushing blood. She loved the music of human arterial systems, and the ones she heard were rich and full of juice, heightened by the excitement of war.

She stopped to listen to one man in particular, a heavy-lipped man with little expression in his closely spaced eyes. His conversation indicated he was a medical officer stationed in the Kuril Islands. "I have a method for punishing prisoners," he whispered to another officer. Desidra listened to the gruesome details for a moment and then, sickened, she moved on.

I won't forget this bastard, she thought.

Filled with warm sake, the officers cheered their leader and toasted recent triumphs. They chattered as they ate tai, rice balls, sushi, and other foods almost too artistic to devour. The military certainly lived well.

It surprised Desidra to see what looked like chocolate truffles on a small plate in front of Yamamoto. Then she remembered reading he had a sweet tooth for American confections, developed while he attended college in the United States.

"We've won victories in Manila, Malaya, Bali . . . everywhere!" shouted a young officer. "Americans are feeling the edge of our sword!"

Another man added, "They won't admit they've been beaten, yet they black out lights at night and cower in their houses. Weaklings, cowards!"

"Don't underestimate them," warned Admiral Yamamoto. "I've lived among Americans and seen their industrial capacity. They can be extremely productive and energetic when they realize what they have to do. America is a sleeping giant, and before it awakens we must draw its Admiral Nimitz out of safe harbor into a massive, convincing defeat."

Desidra knew of that admiral, commander of the U.S.

Pacific fleet at Pearl Harbor. Her studies of human military affairs had taught her the names of its celebrated men and women, and Nimitz was one she particularly admired.

"The most important objective," Yamamoto said, "is to finish what we have begun: crush the U.S. fleet."

The men surrounding their naval leader cheered him, and gazed upon him as if he were more than human.

"America is a giant without teeth!" Vice Admiral Nagumo said.

"The teeth are growing back," said Yamamoto. "We must tempt Nimitz out by attacking something important."

Desidra read Yamamoto's mind. Unlike the almost religious fervor of his men, his thoughts were pragmatic, stoical. They spoke to her: *Make this war quick and victorious. Get in and get out.*

"It is time to set the bait," Yamamoto said.

Desidra suspected that the admiral's military moves would be perfectly planned, with little chance for error. He was a brilliant military man, but none of his plans contemplated the intervention of an American vampire!

She was surprised by her own fervor, considering that her original reasons had been to protect vampire territory and blood supply.

An American patriot? she mused. *Is that what I'm becoming?*

She had discovered long before, that the Japanese language was filled with shades of meaning. Nevertheless, she had no trouble reading the paperwork the military men spread out in front of them. The great operation to destroy the rest of American naval power would unfold in a few days. There would be diversionary raids in other parts of the Pacific and Asia, including an attack by their northern force on Dutch Harbor, Alaska, and the westernmost islands of the Aleutian chain.

Where was the real target? She waited for Yamamoto to reveal it in thought or speech.

On impulse Desidra leaned over one man and pressed a cold kiss on the back of his neck. He shivered, looked behind him, and saw no one. When he turned back to his original position, she licked his cheek. He rubbed it and looked around nervously, but didn't cry out.

Doesn't want to draw attention to himself, she thought. *It would be undisciplined. What a delicious game this is!*

The man pushed his meal aside and from a briefcase brought forth a sheaf of papers. Some of the other officers did the same. Messmen in white uniforms cleared away plates and utensils.

Moving about in her invisible state, Desidra was able to see the papers clearly. One held a coded message, which she found similar to the Egyptian hieroglyphics she'd studied years before. Reference was made to *AL* and *AO* and *AOB* and *AF*.

Cryptanalysts at Pearl Harbor had already determined that the first three groups of letters referred to Alaska's Aleutian Islands. But *AF*? Japanese messages picked up by the Americans had never designated *AF* as a specific place, though it had been mentioned often. They were shipping a lot of materials in that direction, so wherever *AF* was it must be important.

And the bait of which Yamamoto had spoken? She perused his thoughts. No answers there. *Wait . . .*

"Midway will be the bait," the Admiral said. "It's important to the Americans for several reasons, most significantly its location, only eleven hundred and thirty-six miles from Pearl Harbor."

He laid out the battle plan. The Combined Fleet in cooperation with the Japanese Army was to occupy the Midway Islands and other key locations far to the north. They would take the entire South Pacific while the Americans were diverted to Japanese occupation of portions of Alaska.

Drunk on sake and their own triumphs, the military men cheered wildly. They had the ships, the planes, the submarines, and the fighting spirit to accomplish anything. Or so they believed.

Suddenly the room fell silent, and the object of everyone's attention became a young lieutenant who had tipped over his cup of sake, spilling it on a set of plans.

"A bad omen," someone said.

"That's archaic thinking," another officer answered.

But Desidra saw concern reflected in the faces of the

men, and this gave her further insight into the psyche of this enemy. Despite their meticulous planning, the Japanese were as superstitious as anyone else.

Quietly the young lieutenant slipped out of the room, and the upbeat tempo of the gathering resumed. Unseen by the participants, Desidra lingered a while until she had thoroughly memorized their battle plan.

A short time later she entered a small Japanese message center, stood behind the radio operator, became corporeal, and pressed a nerve on his neck. He slumped unconscious in his chair. Quickly, Desidra sent a radio message in Japanese over an airwave that she hoped would be intercepted by the American military. The message was directed to a Japanese military outpost, one that existed only in her own imagination. With a number of carefully selected words and phrases she was confident that the brilliant American cryptanalysts at Pearl Harbor would decipher her meaning, understanding that Yamamoto's target was the coral atoll, Midway, and that his battle plan encompassed not only the South Pacific but Alaska as well.

Still dazed, the radio operator stirred and moaned in his chair.

7

On the morning of June 4, 1942, Desidra rode the tailwinds of Japanese Zeros and followed the wake of Japanese warships, part of the great armada headed for Midway. Invisible, she danced across the tops of destroyers and cruisers and battleships and carriers. She dove beneath the waters of the Pacific Ocean and watched Japanese submarines head for the area between Hawaii and Midway where they could observe and report U.S. fleet activities.

The amount of equipment the Japanese had thrown into the conflict was astounding, thought Desidra. Far more than the Americans had. She wanted to do more to help, but the scale of the operation was too large, even with her enhanced powers.

She'd forewarned the Americans to the best of her ability. But how could they fight effectively without the battleships that had been disabled or destroyed in the attack on Pearl Harbor? The American war industry was gearing up at a feverish pace, but big ships could not be constructed overnight.

Underwater, Desidra watched a Japanese submarine. Nearby, a pair of hammerhead sharks swam lazily, despite the activities around them. For a few moments Desidra became an immense shark, and to amuse herself she swam toward them head-on, as if she were a submarine and they were enemy craft. Startled at her size and behavior, the real sharks veered off and swam away.

Underwater, Desidra moved as rapidly as the Japanese submarine, circling it and interfering with the ship's sonar, until the captain altered course for a time.

Then, to upset him even further, Desidra assumed her human shape and erupted from the ocean. Rocketing skyward, she passed through a cloud and changed to invisibility. She heard the buzz-drone of airplane engines, and as she emerged from the clouds she saw a formation of American warplanes, dark blue Navy Hellcats and others, all with the insignia of American stars on the undersides of their wings. Desidra flew upward and attached herself to the undercarriage of a dive bomber.

I *must taste this war*, she thought, *feel its pain, know its rage*.

The man inside this plane had little or no wartime experience. His equipment was in need of repairs, his fear palpable.

He *wonders if he'll die*, she thought, and she felt a rush of compassion. This man, no more than a boy, was ill-prepared for battle with an enemy who'd planned with such precision and cunning.

Desidra listened to the Americans' brief communications with one another, then heard excitement as they spotted a Japanese carrier. The pilots exchanged anxious messages.

The American formation dove into battle, with Desidra unseen and unnoticed. More American planes appeared, diving in from different directions, and Desidra found herself in the midst of a violent dogfight, with bullets passing near her and even through her, harmlessly. Always ready to break free in the event of impending flames that could kill her, she was thrilled by the conflict and enjoyed being on the edge, between unlife and death.

Miraculously, the plane to which she was attached survived, and as the battle raged she found that the Americans had qualities the Japanese military had not foreseen. Faced with the impossible, the Americans improvised, buried their fears, dove into hell, and fought in creative, unexpected ways, appearing where they should not have been, skimming the waves and maneuvering their planes in a manner that was bewildering to the enemy.

The Japanese became prisoners of their own well-laid plans.

Desidra left the bomber and watched from an American carrier. More American planes joined the conflict: fighter planes and dive bombers. A nightmare of flames and billowing smoke filled the sky. Planes dropped like comets into the cold sea and ships burst into bonfires. A giant Japanese carrier was transformed into a raft of fire.

The American bombers were slow . . . the Japanese Zeros swift and lethal. Desidra saw an American pilot sitting in his cockpit, waving one arm as though in greeting, and in the next moment he was hidden by a sheet of flame. And gone, like a match lit and blown out.

Manmade thunder and lightning rushed across sky and sea, immolating ships and planes and lives without discretion or discrimination. No one was safe from the battle's raging appetite. The planet itself seemed vulnerable, and Desidra shuddered, touched her eyes and found she was crying. Vampire tears, blood tears. This was not survival-inspired hunting, a necessary business. This was carnage. Mortals were worse than vampires, she was coming to believe. Vampires killed to satisfy the Hunger, while mortals killed for reasons she couldn't understand.

She watched, and out of the hellfire emerged a result that surprised and pleased Desidra: the Americans had won.

Newspapers later announced that the Americans had lost a single carrier, the *Yorktown* and one destroyer, the *Hammann*. As for aircraft, one hundred and forty-seven American planes were destroyed. In contrast, five Japanese carriers were sunk and three hundred and thirty-two of their aircraft lost.

For a long time afterward, Desidra wondered about the humans who had manned those ships and planes. Did anyone estimate the value of their lives?

It was a Friday evening, shortly after the victory at Midway. In human form Desidra strolled along Alaskan Way, a thoroughfare that ran the length of Seattle's busy waterfront. A familiar area, a place where the Kindred frequently prowled for blood. She missed the company of her brethren but knew she must avoid contact with them.

Banished!

Any one of them who sought her out would be punished. If they saw her on the street or flying in the dark skies over Seattle, they'd have to ignore her. She recalled Christopher's vocal but nonphysical defense of her wish to join the mortal war effort. He'd undoubtedly received his share of Romano's harsh discipline as a result.

A young human couple strolled by hand-in-hand, gazing out at the dancing lights of ships and boats in the bay. The man wore a heavy sweater and wool cap, and his beard and hair were long. A fisherman, probably. He spoke cheerfully to his companion, and in response she giggled and whispered something in his ear. Desidra envied them their relationship, and wished again she might find someone to warm her. A vampire's extended existence was too long to spend alone.

Yet mortals, despite the love they often found in one

another, had unwholesome opposite traits as well. She'd
seen the ugliness of human alley-beatings and warfare—
and other deadly pursuits they followed. Was human existence no more than a cruel and pointless game?

She brushed the suit she wore, the one Kweca had
given her. The bloodstains that had marred its surface had
faded into the soft brown fabric. The garment was still
grimy, but this part of town had its share of derelicts, and
so she blended right in.

Great cargo and military ships were moored at the
docks that jutted into the bay, and out of those ships
spilled the seamen who worked them. They walked the
streets in small groups and larger packs. Some were
from big cities and quickly learned their way around any
town in which they landed. Others came from small
communities and farms and looked at the city with anxious eyes. When strangers spoke to them, they stared at
their feet.

Walking at a leisurely pace, Desidra rounded a corner
and came to an abrupt halt. Two sailors in uniform
blocked her path. Their faces looked eerie in low illumination from a streetlamp.

"Hey, baby," one said. "How's about a little action
tonight?" Tall and angular, his breath came in a gurgle of
sound, as if he were submerged in water. He was obviously
inebriated, as was his short companion, who leered at
Desidra drunkenly.

She recognized them, having seen them only a short
while before on another street where the large one had
whistled and made suggestive comments to her.
Apparently they had circled the block to overtake her.

"I don't fraternize with strangers," Desidra answered in
a quiet voice.

"Frater-what?" the shorter man said. He could hardly
stand. Suddenly he bent over to one side and retched
onto the sidewalk, a mass of steaming yellow vomit.

Glancing around, Desidra saw several civilians, older
men, carrying on an animated conversation on the opposite side of the street. She considered calling to them for
assistance but hesitated. She could employ her own pow-

ers to make short work of the drunken sailors, but that might not be appropriate under the circumstances.

Suddenly she was amused. *What if I tell these two nitwits I don't drink more than one bodyful of blood a day? Or I could say that I don't have anyplace to keep their extra fluid and anyway, it doesn't keep well. Only fresh blood will do. I have my standards, after all.*

She met the gaze of the big man, and thought, *Shall I tell them the Kindred refer to each human prey as a 'vessel of blood'?*

To the Kindred, humans were like intelligent cattle, a resource to be nurtured and drawn from—not wasted. A source of energy for vampires. The supply. The resource. Innumerable terms were used to describe the significance of humans to vampires. Mortals and vampires were, in Desidra's mind, symbiotic.

The big man taunted his companion. "Man, you used to be able to drink me under the table. What the hell happened to you? Here we got this sweet baby to play with and you're layin' down on the job."

The tall man reached out, seized Desidra's wrist in a tight grasp, and twisted her toward him.

Without flinching, she brought her knee up sharply into his crotch. He crumpled to the sidewalk clutching himself and cursing. "Bitch!" he shouted.

"It wasn't my idea," protested the shorter man. "It was Dave's." He pointed toward his fallen companion. "He ain't even a real sailor, couldn't get in the navy like I did. He bought that suit at a surplus store, so's he could pick up girls."

"Shut up," shouted Dave. Then, looking at Desidra he vowed, "I'll get you, bitch."

Laughter came from the men across the street. "Big tough sailors!" one shouted. "America's finest, beat up by a girl!"

"God help us if that's what we're sending into war!" bellowed another in a bassoon voice. "Hey, miss. Join the war and kick some butt for us!"

"I did!" she answered, and then thought, *Let them wonder what I mean.*

She waved to them and left her would-be attackers to

console one another. Fortunately for them she hadn't been forced to reveal all of her strength. If they only knew how close they'd come to death.

Pausing, she gazed out on the bay. A passenger ferry approached, its lights illuminating the water with a warm glow. Kweca would be on the next ferry. Desidra looked forward to good conversation with her friend. She was anxious to tell Kweca about Midway, of the horrors that lingered in her mind. She wanted to rid herself of them and share her discoveries about the dark side of human nature, the war-frenzy and utter folly of it. Still, she was pleased by the American victory in the great battle. The Americans had not started this war, but they were going to have to finish it.

A human might have enjoyed receiving credit for a contribution made to the victory, but not Desidra. Public recognition would only come if her vampiric identity were exposed. She was not participating for personal glory; she was doing it to preserve her homeland, the habitat of the Kindred. Her goal was to prevent a rain of Japanese bombs and resultant fires that might annihilate her brethren in cities along the western coast of the United States. All vampires were vulnerable to fire.

Her eyes took in all of the night's details and her ears picked up the smallest of sounds. Someone scuffled in the alley behind a nearby tavern. She followed sound and scent.

Inside the black corridor of the alley an old man struggled with a large, familiar male who waved a knife. It was Dave, the make-believe sailor she'd encountered earlier.

"Please," said the paper-thin voice of the old man. "I got no money."

"You better have," his attacker raged. "Where'd you hide it? In your shoe?" He held the knife against the old man's throat.

In a blur of motion Desidra reached the scene and knocked the weapon away. It clattered across cobblestones, and she helped the old man to his feet, a vagrant in mismatched shoes and a tattered overcoat that was several sizes too large. His body beneath the coat felt to her as if it were all bones.

She barked to him, "Get out of here. *Now*, while you can."

He took a couple of steps back, tripped over his coat and fell, then struggled to his feet and ran. He disappeared around a corner.

Desidra turned to his attacker.

"You again, bitch?" the big man asked. His voice was filled with bravado, but she saw uncertainty in his eyes. He was turned a little sideways to her, apparently to avoid another kick in the groin.

The ancient Hunger rose in Desidra, drowning out everything, filling her with a desire so strong it threatened all semblance of sanity. Fangs descended, and she smiled at the counterfeit sailor.

He turned to run.

Desidra was a fast and powerful wild beast. She pounced on her prey, turned it over, and sank fangs into the neck.

"What the . . . !" gurgled Dave. He struggled briefly, but when realization came over him he froze like a deer caught in headlights. His pulse, which had been racing, slowed.

She drank until there was no more to take, and satiated, she left the corpse in the alley. Someone would find it in the morning and give it a decent burial. More than Dave deserved.

From a telephone booth several blocks away she called the restaurant where she was supposed to be meeting her friend and left a short message for Kweca: "Apologies. I'm running a little late."

To regain her composure, Desidra lay on the cold cobblestones of an alley. It bothered her to lose control, but she rationalized that she'd rid the earth of another kind of predator—the worst kind.

Far worse than she.

Human nature, she was beginning to realize, contained layers of darkness, and it seemed to her that this side— the side that murdered and stole and caused wars and performed an infinite variety of unsavory acts—was far more complex and better able to conceal itself.

Entering the shadowy interior of a department store as

a wisp of smoke,she cleaned herself as much as possible in the restroom with liquid soap and paper towels. Then she went to the clothing section and "borrowed" a new outfit from the racks: dark skirt, cream-colored blouse, and a long, unlined red coat.

When she finally appeared at the restaurant where she'd promised to meet Kweca, her friend laughed and said, "You have a price tag on your blouse." Reaching across the table to remove it, Kweca asked, "Your usual shopping method?"

Desidra nodded.

As Kweca dined, Desidra half whispered the remarkable events of recent weeks.

"It almost makes me want to join you," Kweca admitted. "But I'm too old for that much activity."

The comment brought mixed feelings to Desidra. Her Indian friend was human and couldn't live the two or three thousand years of a vampire; she'd probably be gone in another twenty. Desidra couldn't bear the thought of losing her, but turning her into a vampire was out of the question: Kweca didn't wish to become a vampire, and had made that clear.

I *must abide by her wishes*, Desidra thought sadly.

On the edge of the Makah Indian Reservation, Kweca and a handful of her tribal members put up a temporary shelter for Desidra, a rough tent where she could hide from the summer sun and from Romano. She was left in privacy, which they knew she wanted. No one questioned her strange sleeping patterns, or the lack of cookfire smoke.

In repayment, when the weather was cool and gray, Desidra gathered clams and mussels or helped the Makah women launder clothes in a creek that flowed through their camp. Sometimes she went out alone in one of the tribe's long cedar canoes and fished in the Strait of Juan de Fuca.

In November her official assignment to Alaska came through from the War Department, and Desidra bid Kweca good-bye.

"Stay safe," said the Indian woman. "War is a dealer of death and even you, with all your power, face danger."

"I'll be careful," answered Desidra. "I won't be on the front lines. Mostly I fear Romano. His rage might lead him to kill me should he discover that I've revealed the Masquerade to you, letting a mortal know I am vampire. If he ever finds out, he will come instantly to destroy me, along with anyone I've told. I alone among his subjects could veil thoughts from him, but not all thoughts. I'm not in complete control of the power, so we must worry."

"I don't think he knows, or he would have taken action sooner."

"Perhaps. Unfortunately he's able to conceal all of his own thoughts, and that worries me. He may be biding his time."

On a cold day in November, Desidra took the patriotic oath and stood at attention like a loyal American mortal. She almost fell into the spirit of the event.

"It's important to keep silent about your occupation," said the officer who swore her in, a square-jawed man who seemed incapable of a smile. Telling her only that she would be working with the Signal Corps under War Department authority, he admonished, "You are not to tell anyone about your job, what you do, how you do it, when you do it, or where you do it. You are not to say you are tired or busy. That sort of talk could reveal excess activity in the signal center, possible troop or fleet movements. Do you understand?"

"I do," she answered.

"If you tell anyone outside the Signal Corps about your job you could end up in federal prison for twenty-five years. Even though you will remain a civilian it will be under War Department rules and regulations. They apply to you as much as to any soldier." He handed her an identification card. "This states you have a rating equivalent to an army corporal, and you're to be treated accordingly."

Desidra fingered the card. It was white with black lettering. It seemed that humans had as many rules as vampires, except the rules for humans were codified and written down.

"You'll be boarding an army Liberty ship," he said. "You won't be advised where it's headed until you're well out to sea. In a matter of days—you won't be told how long—you'll reach land. A train will transport you to a final destination that will not be revealed until your arrival."

He passed tickets to her.

They boarded the Liberty ship at dusk. Good timing for a vampire, thought Desidra. A hint of early winter hung in the air, and a chill wind blew across Elliott Bay. Far to the north lay Alaska with its long winter night—months on end with only an hour or two of light each day. She looked forward to it.

Her ship wasn't nearly as large as ones she'd seen at Hashirajima several months before, and this craft had little protection from attack, only comparatively small guns fore and aft.

She recalled wondering at Hashirajima how the Americans could possibly oppose such a powerful adversary as Japan. Her experiences at Midway had answered that question. Despite the fact they possessed only a third as many carriers as the Japanese, no battleships to speak of and inadequate shore defenses, Americans had won a tremendous battle. Was it, as some U.S. officers and men had suggested, due to the American people, the finest example of the human spirit?

If so, humankind seemed peculiar to her for its polarities of achievement on one hand and its limitless and utter perversity on the other. War had a way of bringing out both extremes.

She leaned over the ship's railing and watched a contingent of soldiers as they boarded. The line coming up the gangplank seemed endless, a variety of men, many of them obviously frightened. She could smell the fear that clung to their sweat. Seagulls swooped and dove above them like the fighter planes she'd seen in the Pacific theater. The cries of the birds were wild and melancholy, as if to warn the soldiers that death was imminent.

Other than herself, only a handful of civilians were aboard, people returning to their homes or making necessary visits. A number of women and children had been evacuated from parts of Alaska in early summer, following the Japanese occupation of the small islands of Attu and Kiska at the far western end of the Aleutian chain.

For Desidra, the mortals onboard represented a smorgasbord, and as she saw each one she found herself wondering what its blood would taste like. That one at the top of the gangplank, a stocky young man with hair the color of hers, reminded her of a man whose blood she had thought would be sweet, but which was in actuality exactly the opposite, and it had nearly made her sick. Ever since then she had avoided humans of similar appearance, for even the sight of them made her gag. Her gaze shifted.

Ah, the tall, dark man on the deck. He was a different case altogether, with jet-black hair and high cheekbones. She could almost hear the sweet, pure blood coursing through his veins, even at this distance. Yes, in her enjoyment of the variety on this ship she would stop to partake of this soldier. Following him up the gangplank was another soldier of nearly equal interest. A bit older and heavier, this one had pale blue eyes and a way of moving that revealed to the hunter-vampire the quality of his body chemistry.

As the ship pulled away from the dock, Desidra went astern and watched the churning, frothy wake. She wondered if Japanese submarines were ahead of them, somewhere deep in the Pacific Ocean—waiting.

She found a purser and, after producing her identification, asked him about sleeping arrangements. He led her to a cabin.

"You'll share it with one other woman," he said, opening the door for her and handing her a key on a metal ring. "There's two bunks," he said, "upper and lower. You have a sink, but no toilet. Have to use the public facility down the corridor."

"Where do I bathe?" Desidra asked.

He shrugged. "The cabin next to you has a shower, but a warrant officer occupies that cabin."

No matter, she thought. She could dive into the ocean or fly through a rainstorm or wash herself in fresh snowfall. But this purser would arrange something better for her. She'd see to that. She tickled his mind.

"We have two supper sittings on this ship . . . first and second," he said, scratching his head. A perplexed expression formed on his face.

"And which will be mine?" she asked, her tone bolder.

"I'll assign things so you can take a shower in the officer's cabin while he's at first sitting. You'll have second sitting."

"Thank you." *Most convenient,* she thought, *since I don't eat human food, only human blood. No one will ever notice which meal I attend or whether I eat or don't eat, and the Masquerade can be maintained.*

She entered her cabin and surveyed the new environment. A barren little crypt, the room was small and dark, with a dirty porthole that gave no glimmer of the sea and only a little light. The bunk beds filled half the available room space. There was a tiny closet for clothing and the diminutive sink the purser had mentioned. At least there was privacy here, cool and dark. She lay on the lower bunk. It sagged.

The cabin door opened and a woman entered, limping slightly and listing to her left.

Desidra absorbed her essence: middle-aged and fearful, clothing cheap and colorful, odor of peroxide in her blond hair. Her skin was thin and badly wrinkled, and not even her heavy makeup could conceal premature aging. Little blood in this one, for she had been squeezed of most of her juices.

"I guess we're roommates," the woman said. "I'm Petal,"

"I'm Desidra, nice to meet you."

"I'm a movie actress," Petal announced.

How transparent humans are, thought Desidra. This was a faded female with a bad leg, trying desperately (and not very well) to look young. How easily the Kindred would hunt her down, if they wanted to do so.

Smiling at Petal, Desidra swung out of the lower bunk and offered, "You can have this one. I don't mind climbing up on top. Are you going to work for the army?"

"No, I have a little money and want to entertain the troops. You know, read a little poetry and dance for them."

A sad little female, Desidra thought. *She has nothing to give but herself, so she'll sleep with soldiers or sailors or the purser. And she'll keep fading until she disappears completely.*

Petal held up an object that was lightly covered by a piece of cloth. She removed the cover, exposing a cage and a small yellow bird. "Meet Whistler. He sings with me sometimes. I hope it won't bother you."

"No problem."

She stepped outside and left Petal to her unpacking.

A lone soldier paced the deck. Taking notice of her, he said, "Don't light any cigarettes, miss. There's a blackout onboard when the sun goes down."

She engaged him in small talk, the kind humans often employed when speaking to strangers. He was from Alabama. His watch lasted until midnight, and then he'd awaken another soldier to replace him on deck. In turn that man would awaken another at two A.M., and so forth.

Vigilance all night long, he assured her.

He was naïve. Only one guard at a time to protect hundreds of people through submarine-infested waters? Night was a time of danger, when predators prowled.

"What will you do if you see the enemy?" she asked.

"I'll sound the alarm!"

Desidra said little in response to this, but mused, *And the mortals will die awake, instead of in their sleep. What difference will it make?*

Several days passed and the vampire's contact with Petal was minimal. Only the little yellow bird remained in the cabin on a regular basis. While Petal was busy pursuing the purser, Desidra prowled the decks restlessly. She'd given up taking showers the second day out upon discovering the warrant officer hiding in the shadows of his bunk, watching her bathe. Thereafter, she did her bathing at night in the pleasantly cold ocean.

I'd enjoy making a meal of that sneaky lout, she thought.

On deck the sixth night at sea she again encountered the soldier from Alabama, whose name turned out to be Sam. They talked until it was nearly time for his relief watch to appear.

"Dick's a deep sleeper," Sam said. "Hard to get him moving. He's late for everything. Fun guy, though. Stick around till midnight and you'll see him. Has an eye tattooed on the back of his right hand. He likes to spook folks with it."

At midnight Sam finished his duty hours and bid her good night, adding, "Dick will be along soon."

Desidra waited, but the replacement soldier didn't appear. She finally decided to take over the watch herself.

She didn't need much sleep, and if necessary could go for days without any. She laughed aloud and the winter wind howled with her. Desidra, a vampire, was standing watch on an American Liberty ship!

She waited. Dick never appeared.

Just before dawn, she crept down to the level that served as sleeping quarters for the soldiers. They lay slumbering, a pod of men. She walked invisibly among them, coveting their bodies and listening to the beating of hundreds of hearts. So many of them, and all hers if she wished.

For now there will only be one, she thought.

After a few minutes she discovered the man who had missed his duty call. His hand, with its tattooed eye, was easy to find. Bending over his bed, she slid her sharp canines gently into his throat, only a fraction of an inch, no more than a mosquito bite. She withdrew enough blood to make him feel pain the following day. Punishment for his selfish lack of responsibility.

In rapture, Desidra thought of the eternity remaining to her and again longed for a companion. This one? He had good blood, but had proved himself unreliable. She drew back from her prey. The man continued to snore gently, Desidra picked up the sweat-stench of him. He wouldn't make a good companion, she thought, not someone she'd like to turn into Kindred.

She surveyed the other men in the area. Their dream thoughts revealed their strengths and their weaknesses, yet not one of them seemed satisfactory. Maybe it was her mood.

A sense of melancholy fell across her momentarily.

Still, she sensed someone was out there for her Dark Kiss, the embrace that would remove the pain of her loneliness. Was he elsewhere on this ship? Or waiting for her in Alaska?

10

As Desidra walked along an upper deck of the ship the following morning, she saw Petal behaving in a suspicious manner, looking over her shoulder as though someone was following her. When Petal noticed Desidra, she smiled weakly, in apparent embarrassment, then slipped into the purser's cabin.

With an inward smile, Desidra entered her own cabin, picked up a book, and floated to the top bunk. She was halfway through a Steinbeck novel, *The Grapes of Wrath*, and intended to finish it before evening. The hardcover book had come from a small library onboard ship.

A pattern had been developing in which Desidra and her roommate kept much different schedules. In the daytime Petal cavorted with the purser, a square, mustachioed man, while Desidra remained in the cabin, ostensibly sleeping, as far as Petal knew. At night Petal sometimes used the cabin but more often didn't, and Desidra roamed the decks as she pleased.

It wasn't that Desidra couldn't go outside during daylight hours. She had, in fact, a good tolerance for light, at least for a vampire. Most Kindred had no tolerance for sunlight at all, while a few such as herself could spend hours in it. Some could even tan, although she was not one of those.

She turned a page of the book, then paused to listen to the throb and drone of the reciprocating engines, which made her think of a giant heart beating inside the ship. Beneath her on the lower bunk Petal's canary sat in its cage, twittering in rhythm with the motors. An interesting, noisy little creature, it had learned to trust her and gradually she was able to hand-feed it.

How fragile he is, she thought, *yet his tiny heart beats and his blood circulates; he's more alive than I am.*

She stretched her long legs the length of the bunk and tried to sleep. She would have preferred to sleep in the trunk that accompanied her on this trip, but it was stored in the hold of the boat. Still, she thought, there would probably be ample opportunity when she reached Alaska. She always slept better inside the trunk, where she felt less vulnerable.

The night before, a hard blast of seawater had cleaned the outside of the porthole, and now gray light filtered through it, light that was beautiful not only for its lack of color but for the subtle gradations within it . . . shadings and great, melding streaks that alternately approached and receded from blackness.

There was a change in the regular motions of the ship. The seas were getting rougher.

Desidra pressed her face against the thick glass of the porthole. Whitecaps did a devil dance on the water, and sea spray spattered the outside of the porthole. With her predator's eyesight she could see a great distance in limited light. Something was out there on the water. Another ship. It rose high on the waves, came crashing down, and spun sideways. She was awestruck at the ferocity of nature, the way the seas tossed a large ship as if it were no more than a matchstick.

A Liberty ship similar to the one in which she traveled, it appeared to be in serious trouble. It was listing to starboard. Waves crashed over its decks.

The wind had turned vicious.

Leaving her cabin, Desidra hurried down a long companionway and made her way past other passengers still in their nightclothes, gathering to see what the problem was.

By the time she reached the upper deck, the ship's crewmen were congregated there, viewing the stricken ship through binoculars.

"It split in half!" one of them shouted.

One of the halves was tipped up on end and beginning to sink. The other portion, still afloat, held several people.

Desidra's ship shuddered and its bow rose, then it slid down the side of a thirty-foot wave.

The wind continued to whistle and shriek its fury.

Desidra's ship groaned and creaked, but it headed on a steady course toward the stricken ship.

This was another kind of war, the ocean's war. Not one easily won by mortals.

"We could go down, too!" a little Irishman cried, a civilian passenger Desidra had noticed on deck several times. On those occasions he'd been full of good cheer and good whiskey, but today he was sober and deadly serious. "Jesus! The hull broke on the weld line!" he said.

Desidra recalled reading that Liberty ships were constructed quickly and inexpensively for the movement of wartime cargo and personnel. They had welded hulls, not as strong as the riveted variety. Based upon the design of a British tramp steamer, the Liberty ship only had a life expectancy of five years.

How old was the one she traveled on?

The deck rumbled under her feet.

Hurriedly, Desidra stepped behind a bulkhead and made herself invisible. Then she flew out across the raging sea, directly into the wind, motivated, ironically, by what remained of her humanity—an urge to help humans in need.

Half of the sinking ship had sunk beneath the waves and the remaining portion was going down fast. Men in lifejackets bobbed in the waves, only their heads above water. They reminded her of a flock of fat ducks.

Nearby were three lifeboats full of men and women. These survivors had rowed well away from the wreckage, far enough to avoid being sucked into the whirling funnel of water swallowing the remains of the ship.

A solitary crewman in dungarees clung to the nearly

vertical deck. He wore no lifejacket. The sea rose toward him rapidly as his craft, his floating world, slipped into its grave.

Desidra hovered above the man, an unseen presence. There was blood on his forehead, but the sight didn't arouse the Hunger in her. This hapless creature needed her help and compassion.

It was not so different from the experience in the alley behind the Seattle tavern, when she saved a vagrant from death. She lingered over the memory of that scene for a moment. The old man's attacker had provided her with a fine, bloody meal that night, exactly what he had deserved.

This time, however, the attacker was the sea, and it offered no prize.

She hesitated.

At the last possible opportunity the crewman jumped free of the remaining piece of the doomed ship. He splashed into the whirling, angry water and struggled to stay afloat.

Suction was pulling him down into the belly of the sea. In seconds Desidra saw a change in him, from desperation to passive acceptance of his fate.

She dove in after him.

Her invisible form displaced water, creating the configuration of her shapely body. The churning sea was cold and stimulating, but she avoided diving too deeply. Like any of the Kindred, if wounded, she could sink to the bottom but wouldn't die, unless her body fell prey to sea life or deep water pressure.

The man was only a few feet beneath the surface. Beneath him Desidra saw a massive shadow, the last section of the dying ship.

It was difficult for her to move as rapidly in water as she did in air, but she crawl-stroked her way to the seaman and wrapped her arms around his chest. Then up she swam. His eyes seemed to be staring at her, although he was semiconscious and could not possibly see her.

She plunged into his thoughts. They were almost blank, apparently waiting for death.

No! she thought. *You won't die!*

Reaching the surface of the sea, she guided the man toward her ship, pushing him along the choppy surface as if he were floating. Lifeboats were rounding up survivors, but Desidra skirted those areas.

She brought the seaman in a wide arc around the ship and flew carefully up over the stern and onto the aft deck. She was invisible, but he was not. Who could explain a man who looked half dead rising from the sea and floating to the deck of the ship? Luckily, the deck was unoccupied.

When the man was safely onboard she heard his heart beat.

His eyes fluttered.

She stood back and let others take over.

Moments later, two crewmen appeared and helped him to a seated position.

"A mermaid rescued me!" he exclaimed in answer to their questions.

They stared and scratched their heads thoughtfully and brought him hot coffee and blankets. "How did you get back on this ship?" asked one of them.

"I didn't see any of our crew helping you."

"The mermaid rescued me," repeated the half-drowned man.

"He must have hit his head," said the other crewman.

Back in her cabin, Desidra stripped off her wet clothes and tossed them in a laundry bag. The canary twittered.

A *mermaid*, Desidra thought with a smile as she lay back on her bunk. *Mermaids are only myths, but vampires are real!*

11

The train proceeded slowly from Seward to Anchorage. Snow and ice blocked the rails and periodically had to be shoveled or brushed away by train personnel as well as passengers. By the time they reached Anchorage, the snow had ceased and the sky was clear and full of stars. It was two o'clock in the morning. Most of the passengers were half asleep, while others stared out the windows like children waiting for Santa Claus to come riding over a snowy hill, reindeer and all.

Petal, appearing pale and more faded than ever, bid Desidra good-bye, and added, "My friend on the ship rented me a room in Anchorage. He says there are all sorts of good opportunities here for my theatrical career."

"Good luck," said Desidra, and meant it.

The vampire stepped from the train into a white world. Seven-foot icicles hung from the eves of the train station like gigantic swords waiting to be grabbed and taken into battle.

An amusing thought occurred to her: an international war convention should declare frozen icicle swords as the only acceptable and legal weapons of combat, and when those weapons melted the fight was over. Yes, she liked that idea very much, for it seemed to her that blood should not be spilled needlessly.

She wondered what her ultimate place would be in the much larger picture that encompassed all life and unlife, and what she would find here at the top of the world. What material effect could she have on a war between nations of mortals?

A soldier in a jeep pulled up and stared in her direction. "Are you Desirée Smith?"

"Desidra," she corrected. She handed him her identification.

"Oh, okay." He handed it back. "Let me help you with your suitcase. I'll be taking you to the post."

At the army post where Desidra would be quartered, they drove past rows of buildings painted with camouflage colors, each dimly lit structure identical to the one next to it.

"NCO quarters," said Desidra's escort. "For noncommissioned officers."

The driver escorted her to one of the buildings, and within that structure to a small one-bedroom apartment. He opened the bedroom door and set her suitcase next to her metal trunk. The trunk had arrived earlier.

"You're one of the lucky ones," the driver said. "Most people have to get by without their luggage for at least a week. Report to the Signal Center tomorrow morning at eight. The lieutenant in charge of your shift will brief you on your responsibilities."

He handed her a card with an address. "The buildings on this post are numbered. You have a watch?"

"Yes, thanks." *An internal clock and it keeps perfect time.* "Do you have keys for me?"

"Sorry, they don't allow locks on NCO quarters. The brass makes unannounced inspections. For security."

After his departure, Desidra examined the apartment. Other than her suitcase and trunk, the bedroom contained little except a cot made up with a pillow and some gray blankets that were imprinted "U.S. Army."

The crude outline of a dresser had been printed on one wall. A broken mirror hung above this peculiar artwork.

In addition to the bedroom, there was a small living room and kitchen. More space than she actually needed.

She turned out all of the lights, then closed the bedroom door and lay down on the cot, wondering what to do with herself for the next few hours.

Someone entered the apartment, a soft shuffle of sound on the other side of the bedroom door.

Romano? No. He would have appeared here beside her, raging and autocratic, not scuffling about in another room.

She opened the bedroom door and peered into the darkness. An odor assailed her. A human female had come and gone. Strange. Human patterns were difficult to translate into any sort of logical meaning.

Desidra climbed into her trunk and pulled the lid shut. It had no inside lock, which meant she couldn't secure herself inside, and someone . . . anyone . . . could jerk open the lid at any moment and discover her sleeping, unbreathing form. It would make for an interesting confrontation, which would undoubtedly lead to a psychological evaluation of her, or worse still, a physical examination.

If it happened, it happened.

She yawned, burrowed under clothing in the trunk, and slept until dawn.

When her internal clock told her it was time to rise, she took her usual cold shower and was about to step outside in a cotton dress. Then she reminded herself she was playing the role of a warm-blooded mortal and that any lightly dressed mortal would freeze. She slipped into a sweater, donned a heavy sheepskin coat, and headed for her appointment.

The building she was to work in was an oversized Quonset hut, fabricated of metal that reflected the white of its surrounding environment. It more resembled an igloo than a high-security structure, making it difficult to identify from the air as anything of great significance.

A guard at the entrance of the hut examined her identification. After being allowed in, she looked around for the lieutenant she'd been told to contact. Finally she asked a sergeant for help.

"You'll have to settle for me," said the round-faced soldier. "I'll fill you in until he gets here."

Desidra looked around. The floor was made of wooden planks and was none too level. Snow drifted through cracks between the boards. A rusted potbelly stove sat in the middle of the structure dispensing heat for no more than five or six feet in any direction. Soldiers, seated at more distant positions, periodically rose from their workplaces to warm their hands at the stove.

An *ideal climate for me*, Desidra thought. But *obviously not for mortals.*

"Here's where you'll be working," said the sergeant, who identified himself as Miller. He led her past another guard into an enclosed area at the rear. "Lead walls," he said, patting one of them. "We call it the 'vault.'" He gestured to a group of soldiers working at machines that looked like oversized typewriters. "You'll be operating one of these. This equipment is one of the most closely guarded military secrets on our side, I'd guess." He paused, and almost whispered as he said, "The Sigaba."

She hadn't heard of it, and felt a rush of excitement.

Within a few hours she had learned something about the ingenious rotor machine that prevented enemies from breaking down enciphered American messages. The technology was simple, but the code system highly complex.

Because of her earlier Egyptian studies, Desidra knew that humans had been using codes for centuries. Around 1900 B.C., in a town on the Nile River, a master scribe had carved the life story of his master, Khnumhotep II, on the nobleman's tomb. The scribe had used, in addition to the normal symbols of the time, his own hieroglyphs. In doing so, he gave birth to cryptology.

Secrecy depended upon the key list used for the code. The enemy might know something about how a cipher worked, but security depended upon the means of access. She also knew that in the present world telegraphy and radio-telegraphy were used for military communication, and no system was acceptable whose cryptogram characters could not be sent via Morse code.

Mortals were remarkable creatures, *thought* Desidra. But in spite of their wonderful inventions and large brains, they couldn't figure out how to avoid deadly wars with one another.

Sergeant Miller interrupted her thoughts. "Hope you won't mind the hours. Seven days a week and four long shifts, some overlapping."

"I don't need much sleep," Desidra answered, knowing that few mortals could be deprived of rest for long, though she'd heard of one who required only a few minutes each day.

Taking a seat in front of her workstation, she attempted to place her feet against the wall. Something was in the way. She looked down and saw a cylindrical object resting in a small metal hammock. The object rocked in its receptacle.

"It's a bomb," the sergeant explained. "We're under orders to destroy cryptographic equipment in case of enemy invasion."

Obviously the personnel were expected to sacrifice their lives along with the equipment, Desidra thought. In an explosion a vampire might escape, but probably not a human.

When she returned to her apartment that evening, she discovered that most of the lightbulbs had been removed. Although she needed no illumination to see, it was a curious circumstance to consider. A scent lingered in the room. The human female had made another visit.

Mortals were strange creatures.

12

Late November.

Using magic unknown to the rest of the Kindred, Prince Romano enlarged himself to twice his normal size. Because he was sired into the Tremere clan, Kindred who'd been strongly influenced by the infiltration of magi a millennium earlier, his magic was strong. When he subsequently formed his own clan he did not share this knowledge and used it instead to enforce his rules.

Now he loomed three times the height of Christopher, glaring down at him. Romano's familiar, the ferocious falcon, was proportionately larger and sat on the prince's shoulder in its usual position. It appeared to be ready to tear the flesh from Christopher's body, as it had done to other members of the clan who'd fallen out of grace with the prince.

No vampire could control or defeat this creature, with the exception of its creator, this sire who had expertise at magic.

"You have displeased me," Romano said. "When you spoke out in support of Desidra, you did so at your own peril."

Christopher said nothing. He stared up into Romano's red eyes, fully expecting to be killed at any moment. Over seven months had passed since Desidra's expulsion.

During that time, Romano had avoided him, looking away whenever he was present, speaking over and around but never directly to him, as if Christopher had died.

But now, Christopher thought, after weeks of terror the other shoe was about to fall. He almost looked forward to the punishment, for it would relieve him of the anxiety that had clung to him like a parasite.

He felt his sire ransacking his thoughts, turning them over and looking for the ones Christopher was attempting to conceal, albeit involuntarily. The old vampire was like a burglar opening drawers, emptying them, looking for something of value. Defiant thoughts, Christopher realized, but he didn't care. There was nothing he could do to save himself. Absolutely nothing!

"Ah, but you are wrong," Romano said, his voice modulated and almost pleasant.

Christopher didn't respond aloud, but his thoughts spoke to Romano: *How?*

"Bring Desidra back," the prince commanded.

I don't think she'll come. She's stubborn!

"You defy me?" Romano leaned close. The falcon's beak touched one of Christopher's eyebrows. The terrified young vampire looked into the fierce, dark eyes of the bird. Shining eyes. No compassion there, only deadly readiness.

"No, of course I don't defy you, you're my sire," Christopher said, finally speaking aloud. "I only meant . . . "

"Do you like her?"

"She's a good friend."

"I'm sending you because I also care for her."

"Sire?"

"If I go after her myself," Romano said matter-of-factly, "I'll kill her."

Christopher took a step backward, away from the falcon. "My sire, you say you care for her, that she occupies a special place in your . . . "

"In my heart?" Prince Romano laughed. "I have no such organ! As sire of a clan, I have no time for sentimentality. There must be order, observance of rules . . . respect for the Elders, the ancient traditions. Desidra has challenged me, and I can't permit that. It undermines my authority, and if I permit it, another of the Kindred will step forward, and then another. I will not tolerate that!"

"I'm sure she didn't mean to displease you."

"She humiliated me!"

Elder and falcon had pressed forward again, into Christopher's face. Once more the young vampire retreated, two steps this time.

"You will bring her back," Romano said, his tone steady and menacing.

"Yes, my sire." Trembling, Christopher listened as Romano told him where Desidra had gone. Then the gnarled, old vampire said in a level, deadly tone, "Don't return alone, Christopher, unless you've killed her."

Christopher's eyes widened.

The prince smiled. "I see in your thoughts that you fear her. She has great powers for her youth, although they are no match for mine."

"I'd rather not kill—" Christopher said. He caught himself. "If she won't come, isn't there a better solution?"

The sire's tone became gentle, but no less threatening. "You don't want to disappoint me, do you?"

"No."

"Then do as I say!"

"She is too powerful for me."

"I'll teach you a way, one you must not disclose."

Christopher stood silently, his head bowed in respect. He tried not to think defiant thoughts. Still, they continued to surface, like rebellious children within his psyche.

Romano described one of the ways to kill a vampire, a method requiring no weapon. "Come up behind her and jab this into the nape of her neck." He extended a long, sharp fingernail, and with it touched the upper portion of Christopher's neck, just below the occipital bone. "A quick thrust and penetration here followed by a twist destroys an important part of the brain. The vampire dies instantly."

Christopher shook his head. "Like all of the Kindred she can read my thoughts and would know instantly what I'm up to."

"That's the next trick I'm going to teach you. The way I

am able to keep my thoughts from other vampires. First understand this: I will instruct you in the manner of veiling your thoughts from all but an Elder."

Was he telling the truth? Christopher wondered.

"Pay attention!" Romano said. "The method must be done properly."

Christopher listened and learned, and then was sent on his way. He rose high in the air over the city of Seattle, and as he ascended the air grew cooler. Presently, with distance from Romano, he began to feel more comfortable.

He flew north. In the direction Desidra had taken.

13

The steamer trunk was sealed as tight as a coffin and inside, not breathing, slept Desidra. She dreamed of a time long before, when she'd been a small human child carrying a lunch pail and a strap of books, on her way to school.

A boy walked just ahead, and she ran to catch up with him: Jamey Stossel.

Smiling, he said, "Morning 'Sidra." He had small blue eyes and a broad face covered with freckles. Jamey was nine, a year ahead of her in the one-room schoolhouse they attended. She liked him.

Gallantly, he carried her books.

In her dream-vision the years passed. Desidra grew taller and her figure filled in. She was seventeen. Jamey's body had grown hard and his wide face had become square-jawed and handsome. His light brown hair was combed straight back, with a tonic sheen to it. He bore with him the musky smell of the tonic, aware that she found it appealing.

Desidra's long red hair, tied with a ribbon, still reached the small of her back. In another few months, when she turned eighteen, she'd wear it in coils and braids the way her older sister did. A passage into womanhood.

Desidra and Jamey spoke of love and of marrying soon.

Jamey wanted to be a doctor and Desidra a teacher. They would work in the small town in which they'd been born, and planned to live in the old Lambert house, a Cape Cod with a white picket fence. It needed fixing up, but they looked forward to the task. The place had many rooms, and verdant grass and fruit trees. An ideal spot in which to raise children.

Suddenly the happy time turned bleak. Desidra fell ill and reached the brink of death, the candle of her life almost extinguished. Pneumonia.

Then Prince Romano appeared and administered the Dark Kiss, a treatment not found in any medical text or doctor's bag. Sensing her death he gave her, by his standards, a great gift: not life, but something more powerful.

As far as humans knew she died, and an undertaker placed her body in an open casket. Aware but unable to move a muscle, she felt the warmth of Jamey's lips on hers, their final kiss. "Good-bye, dearest," he murmured. "Good-bye." All the while Desidra's eyes had stared straight ahead, unmoving, not revealing the consciousness that remained. She wanted to touch him, but her arms were paralyzed. Dead arms, dead fingers.

And now in her dream, going backward in memories after so many decades, Desidra heard the coffin lid close and spadefuls of earth thumping against the casket.

Finality.

The end of human existence.

Later that night her sire came for her and dug her from the grave with his own hands. She'd clung to Romano, needing him, wanting him with an aching passion she'd never felt before, not even for Jamey.

Within the steamer trunk, Desidra stirred and came to awareness. Detached from the memory chamber of her human past, she sensed a presence nearby, one that could read her thoughts.

Vampire.

Lifting the lid, she sat up and gazed into a familiar face. "Hello, Desidra."

It was Christopher, his blond hair sprinkled with flecks of snow that also dusted his eyebrows and clothing.

Christopher, who'd gone briefly to her support during her battle with Prince Romano. She had mixed feelings about this young clan member, gratitude for the courage he'd displayed, but disappointment that his courage had limitations. What was he doing here?

She perused his thoughts and was surprised to find them blank. *Be cautious,* her instincts told her.

"You've come to join the army?" Desidra asked.

He laughed. "No. Prince Romano sent me to retrieve you. He wishes to pardon you for your youthful indiscretions."

"I'm older than you!"

"And more impulsive! He wants you back."

"Subject to further punishment, I suppose?"

"I'm sure he'll be reasonable, if you return right away."

"Can you guarantee his forgiveness?" she demanded.

No answer came, for both of them knew that nothing could be guaranteed when it came to the arrogant, old vampire.

In the manner that he had been instructed, Christopher sprinkled false thoughts through his brain for her to gather if she looked again. Observations about the beauty of Alaska . . . an aversion to being away from the clan . . . a collection of innocuous old memories. True thoughts, actually, but they formed an impenetrable layer over the workings of his brain he wished to hide.

He noted that after an initial attempt to read his thoughts she'd been distracted. She was wondering about Romano now, with considerable suspicion.

"I like being here," she said, "This place enables me to see things more clearly. Prince Romano keeps us in thrall, not unlike a vampire keeping a mortal in such a state, forever captive to do the bidding of the master."

Christopher improvised. "Would you return, if you could be his favorite again?"

"My taste of freedom is too sweet. I don't need to be anyone's favorite."

Christopher sat on the floor by the trunk, so that they were both at eye level. "You're hardly free," he said. "The human military system has you captive now, under a system of rigid rules."

Stretching her arms and yawning, Desidra said, "I can leave any time I wish. Invisibility, shape-shifting, any means I choose."

"But you defied Romano because of his rules, and what happens? He tosses you out and you fly straight into another set of rules, another structured situation."

"All human activity is structured during a war."

Frustrated by his inability to sway her, even after reading her thoughts, Christopher said, "You've placed yourself under the command of inferior beings who are no more than cattle to the Kindred. We feed upon humans. We don't follow their dictates!"

"They are intriguing creatures. I join and leave them at my discretion. It's the same with Romano. I'll return to him if I choose to do so."

"What are you talking about? He banished you!"

"I made him do it, pushed him to the edge."

"Intentionally?"

"Maybe."

Christopher laughed, then grew serious and said, "Our sire deeply regrets the confrontation, feels he should have handled it better."

"He said that to you?" asked Desidra.

"Not in so many words, but I could tell. He truly misses you." Christopher planted false thoughts to support this, but noted that Desidra didn't venture into his mind.

"Then he'll continue to miss me," she said. "It pleases me to make him suffer!" She looked away. "No, I don't mean that. I wish him none of the ill will he inflicted upon me. At first I revered him, but that was before I began to pay attention to his obvious flaws. Wouldn't you agree he is less than perfect?" She leaned close to her visitor and said, "Come on, Christopher. You can tell me."

"The prince gave me an extended existence," Christopher responded in a hollow tone. "I don't speak against him."

"Good-bye, then," Desidra answered. She lay back in the steamer trunk and grasped a handle inside the lid to close it.

Christopher held the lid open. "You must come with me," he said. "You must."

"Never."

But Christopher detected weakness in her tone and in her thoughts. She missed the Kindred, and maybe even Prince Romano a little. It seemed that she was only refusing out of pride and stubbornness. Perhaps with a little more time, he could convince her.

He tried one more ploy. "Where do I join?"

"What did you say?"

"The army. Where do I enlist?"

"How foolish you are."

"Prince Romano would want me to protect you, and what better way than to remain near you?"

"I can take care of myself."

"Then do this for me, helping me to follow the wishes of my—of *our* sire. He'll be displeased with me if I return without you."

Truth. And understatement.

After a long moment, Desidra said, "He'll punish you, right? Maybe kill you if you don't bring me back. Isn't that correct? You're playing a dangerous game with me, Chris."

He felt a tickle in his brain as she dabbled at the thoughts he had left lying about. Finding them of no interest, she left.

"It's not a game," he said.

"You've never been able to deceive me, Christopher. But if you truly want to enlist in the army, you'll need an identity, a history. Give me a few days to put something together for you. Stay out of sight, make yourself comfortable somewhere."

She pulled the lid of her trunk. Just before it thumped shut he said to her, "I'll sleep in a snowbank."

As Christopher stepped outside into a snowstorm, he felt the stinging lash of a thousand bits of ice, and Romano's words returned to him, "Don't come back alone, unless you've killed her."

14

Shortly after Desidra began working in the Signal Center's cryptography unit, she watched a burly officer stride in. He brushed snowflakes from the arms of his uniform. From her desk, Desidra observed that he held his nose high, as if something didn't smell quite right in the building. He cast disdainful glances left and right, barking terse commands and greetings to subordinates. His square body was held as tight as a steel rod, his fleshy face filled with hidden anger.

From a hundred feet away she read his thoughts, and they revealed mental imbalance—an overwhelming, contagious rage, a paranoia without boundaries. He hated people, especially those he considered to be slow or dimwitted.

If he'd been a vampire, this one would be possessed with a terrible, uncontrollable blood urge, beyond anything condoned by the Kindred.

Pausing at Desidra's desk the officer stared at her with pale blue eyes. "You're the new cryptographer?" he asked. "I'm Herkle, captain of this operation." He thrust out a thick, red hand and grasped hers firmly enough to let her know that he was the only authority in this place. His hand was clammy.

"I need to discuss your duties with you," he said.

"Everything has been explained to me," she said, intentionally provoking him a little.

"By whom?"

"The sergeant and my co-workers."

Herkle's voice tightened. "We're under high security restrictions, and I need to make sure nothing is missed." He glanced around the crowded room. Then his pale eyes returned to hers. "There's no place here to have a conference," he said. "I'll meet you at your quarters, end of this shift. What's your NCO address?"

She gave it to him without bothering to read his mind. Herkle's intentions were patently obvious to any female with a brain.

After Herkle's departure, she asked Sergeant Miller, "What kind of man is he?"

Hesitation. "Well, he's a fanatic about details and regulations. If you break any rules, or he thinks you have, he'll ride your back and stay there until you learn his way of doing things. We're kind of lucky. He doesn't come around often, and the lieutenant is a lot easier to get along with."

"What's Herkle's connection with this unit? Is he some sort of cryptography expert?"

"Naw. He's strictly security, a watchdog. He doesn't understand most of what we do. Likes to swing his weight around, but don't worry about him. Two weeks from now there will probably be someone else in charge. Everything's in a state of flux."

She peered into Miller's thoughts and learned that Herkle was a nasty-tempered human with many enemies, foes who were not of the Japanese or German military variety.

After work she slogged through the mantle of white on the ground. A steel-gray sky sifted snow over the land, covering everything, concealing the earth's secrets. Desidra's heavy coat and boots, unfamiliar to her, hindered progress. Each step was an effort, a struggle against an environment that refused to acknowledge or give in to the presence of humans.

Or vampires pretending to be human, she thought. If only she dared fly now, throwing off her heavy coat and boots, she would skim over the landscape and commune with the snowflakes.

Some other day, perhaps. She had assumed loyalty to a human cause and would direct her energy toward it.

Alaska was beautiful, but it was also a wild, dangerous country and mortals should not take it lightly. They could build their airfields and garrisons and little houses, but bears broke into their trash cans and storage sheds, and at night the land was ruled by predators. It was a hostile environment for mortals, but Desidra, like the other predatory animals, loved it.

Herkle was waiting for her when she reached her quarters. She ushered him into the kitchen, the only room with a lightbulb. Lifting her head, she sniffed. The mysterious female had been around again. For what this time? The apartment contained nothing of value.

The captain sat heavily on a chair and leaned forward. His pale eyes lacked warmth, but his ruddy complexion gave a hint that an inner fire had been lit and was about to burn out of control.

He sat back, as if attempting to calm himself, and said, "I want you to understand how tight security must be in the Signal Center. I cannot overemphasize how important it is that you limit your friendships." He looked around. "Anything to drink here?"

She brought him a bottle of Coca-Cola, not what he had in mind. As he took a reluctant sip Desidra inquired, "Do you think I'd fraternize with spies?"

"You're no different from any soldier on this post, and you'll follow regulations the same as they do. While we're on that topic, I don't want you to date any enlisted men."

"If that's a regulation applying to civilian personnel," she said, "I'd like to see a copy of it. No one mentioned it during my orientation."

"There's nothing in writing. It's one of *my* rules."

"For your soldiers perhaps, and since I'm not one of them I'll continue to use my own good judgment." She smiled, with more than a hint of defiance. "I was warned by the military in Seattle what I can say or can't say, and I'm well aware of the need for security. I won't answer intelligence-related questions or anything I suspect is improper. If I make a wrong move, I expect to be punished, perhaps even sent to federal prison."

Ha! she thought. *As if they could keep a vampire behind bars*!

The captain seemed startled at her boldness, and his silence enabled her to continue: "In the meantime, I'll continue to live my life as I always have."

I *mean my unlife*! she thought.

"The best advice I can give," he said, "is don't trust any-one except me. And follow the rules, or someday you'll be *very* sorry." He rose and headed for the door. "I'll see you again. *Soon*."

The door slammed.

Another Romano! she thought. Not as powerful and filled with weak human emotions, but like her vampire sire he demanded passive acceptance from her.

It seemed to her that this captain was a fool. He had no idea she could read his puny mind, so consumed was he with thoughts of grandeur and his obsession with her. She licked her lips, anticipating the possibility that she might taste his blood when the Hunger next struck her.

Perhaps in the middle of the night.

Herkle was someone she'd have to watch carefully, for he could easily explode, like the bomb suspended directly beneath her workstation.

15

"You understand this isn't our usual procedure," Captain Herkle said, examining the identification documents that Christopher had submitted. "Normally enlistees' papers are sent up from the States." He sipped coffee from a chipped mug, set it next to a sandwich. "You're a volunteer?"

"Yes, sir."

Herkle flipped through the documents. The sandwich, which lay half-eaten on a piece of waxed paper, captured Christopher's attention. Rare roast beef, very moist and red. He looked away, tried not to think about it.

The papers had been falsified by a friend of Desidra's, in exchange for cash—money that Desidra had "borrowed" during a midnight visit to a bank in southeast Alaska.

Much of the information before Herkle was correct: Christopher T. Wilson, born in Akron, Ohio, the son of James and Patricia Wilson. Height, weight, hobbies, scholastic interests . . . all were correct. The papers showed a birthdate of 1924, however, making this applicant for military service eighteen years old. His actual birthdate was 1870, but by vampire standards it wasn't much of a difference. Half a century was hardly anything to an entity whose life span was measured in thousands of years.

There was no written record of his "transmutation," of course, from mortal to vampire.

"It says here you went to Lowell High in San Francisco," Herkle said. "Went to Galileo myself, not a scholastic kiss-ass school like yours. I suppose your mommy and daddy had money." Herkle's tone had become increasingly unpleasant. "What did your daddy do for a living?"

Christopher's mind raced as he tried to think of the name of a business in the city where his father might have worked.

"He was in real estate," Christopher answered and left it at that.

"I see you got your physical from Dr. Robbins in Seattle. Haven't heard that name before, and I'm familiar with most of the army doctors."

"He's a recent volunteer. He gave me clearance on everything."

In actuality the doctor had written a clearance on a regular army form, but in the shaking hand of an alcoholic, immediately after receiving a wad of cash from Desidra.

"I'm ready to serve, sir. A buddy of mine was killed at Corregidor, and ever since, I vowed to do my part as soon as I was old enough."

Following these untrue, extemporaneous comments, Christopher bored into the thoughts of the captain to see how they were being received. No sign of suspicion there. No narrowing of the eyelids, no intense stare.

"I lost a buddy at Corregidor," Herkle said.

"Sorry to hear that, sir."

"The weather in Alaska is dismal, Wilson. Over the long winter we go for months in almost total darkness. Drives some crazy. Not many females here either, you know."

"I can take it, sir," Christopher said. As *if I care*, he thought. I *thrive in the cold and dark, and as for females, they've never been of interest to me. Not in the way he's suggesting.*

"I've heard it said that men who volunteer for Alaska duty must be crazy," the captain said. He studied the cleverly forged psychological profile included with Christopher's papers, then looked across the desk at the youthful-appearing applicant. "Are you mentally off center, Wilson?"

"No, sir. That report says I'm fine."

"I don't give a damn what it says. Now you listen carefully. If I learn anything strange about you, you're out! I already have my doubts."

"I can handle it here, Captain."

"And you're completely sane?"

"Yes, sir!"

Herkle's expression became hard and unyielding. "Don't bull me, soldier. Sane people don't volunteer for Alaska duty, and even if you happen to be sane you won't be for long. One of my men went crazy last month and wrapped himself around a power transformer. Shrinks said it was loneliness. But I know better. The man was weak."

Christopher shifted uneasily on his feet. He wanted to get away from this man. Either that or kill him.

A cruel smirk worked at the edges of Herkle's mouth, and he added, "Transformer toasted his ass."

"That won't happen to me, sir."

"You never know," said Herkle. "Strange things happen when men don't fit in."

Initially there had been thoughts in Desidra's mind of spending time with Christopher and discussing ways in which they might collaborate to help the war effort. Such hopes were soon dashed.

"You know I didn't come up here to be a military man," he said to her, as they sat naked on a hillside, immersed in the cool whiteness of a snowbank. Only their heads were exposed. "I came up here to watch over you."

"And take me back to Seattle!"

"Only if you want to go."

"You're a poor liar," said Desidra.

Christopher pushed closer to her and grinned. "I only lie when I'm trying to protect myself."

"You're a bit of a bastard," she said. "But a charming one."

Below them Elmendorf Field was darkened, a safeguard against attack by the Japanese. "Do you think they'll bomb us?" she asked Christopher.

"They associate death with noble deeds," Christopher

said. "The worst kind of death becomes sublime in their minds, so they take chances with their lives."

"Americans have a little of that in their own souls," Desidra observed. "So do some Muslims, who believe there is no greater honor than to die in a great *jihad*, a holy war."

In the distance lights twinkled in the town of Anchorage. There was a blackout in effect, but some people always forgot the rules, especially with the high level of drinking that went on in this cold land.

Anchorage wasn't much, thought Desidra: a clothing store, a grocery market, some taverns and restaurants. Not many houses, although many of the men in the Alaska Communication System lived in quarters there—some in houses, others in apartments over the mercantile operations.

"Have you ever thought of living off the post?" Desidra asked. "They allow some soldiers to do that instead of crowding them together. It would make things easier for you."

"I might request it," Christopher answered.

Desidra continued to look in the direction of Anchorage.

She knew one of the restaurants there served country-fried chicken and another specialized in chili. Both restaurants had an unwritten addendum to their menus: firm young Eskimo girls and a few white ones from the States. Men lined up for blocks waiting to be served food and girls, but thus far Desidra had seen none of the men with whom she worked standing in line.

Lucky for them! she thought. It angered her that girls so young were misused.

To Desidra, human nature was a study in contrasts and contradictions. Within each mortal were unpredictable, inexplicable tendencies, individual actions and broad sweeping events that seemed to come out of the blue, without apparent foundation or purpose.

She sighed and looked out on the vast Alaskan wilderness, an infinity of mountains, rivers, and snow beyond this oasis of civilization. So much beauty. Did any of the army personnel take time to explore this magnificent country, instead of standing in line to take advantage of unschooled girls?

"You really should return to the clan," Christopher suggested.

"What are you talking about? You're enjoying this new environment and freedom from our sire as much as I am." She didn't bother to read his thoughts, preferring to allow others to their privacy whenever possible. It was a game to her, trying to discern thoughts and intentions from speech and facial expressions. In particular, the eyes spoke. They rarely concealed the truth, if you knew what to look for.

"You miss the clan," Christopher said. "And even our sire, a little."

"Very little," she said, realizing suddenly that Christopher had slid into her thoughts quite expertly. "Get out of my head!" she demanded.

"All right, all right, but you're being stubborn."

"I'm not going back. This job is something I have to do. Can't you understand that?"

Christopher didn't respond.

Desidra gazed out on the white wilderness. All times of day and night melded into the long Alaskan winter—month after month of darkness without end. Humans got up in the dark, went to work in the dark, got home in the dark, made love in the dark. One of Desidra's co-workers had said that wintertime in Alaska often induced strange "out-of-synch" feeling in humans, without the usual barometers of life found in the Lower Forty-Eight.

But ideal for vampires.

Her present behavior, sitting here inside a snowbank, was carefree and youthful, not unlike young mortals who went skinny dipping in a local swimming hole with little concern for one another's naked bodies. She thought about Jamey, whom she had loved in her youth, a time long past, never to return, but still vivid in memory.

Love. Would she ever experience it again in any form?

How unfulfilling to be alone with a vampire who had no interest in her yearning sexuality. Most vampires had a tendency to be bisexual, their passions aroused equally by females and males, but Christopher's Blood-hunts only involved men, a carryover from his mortal life, he had told her.

Something touched her arm.

She looked at Christopher inquisitively and resisted an urge to read his thoughts.

Fingers were against her ribs, tickling her.

She giggled like a mortal child.

Christopher dove into the deep snow and disappeared from view. Then like an underwater swimmer, he moved around her without touching her, making small noises that revealed his location, but only for brief seconds. Suddenly he burst from the snow and shot up in the air. She saw his naked form, a shadow against the moonlight, hovering there.

"It's time for the Blood-hunt!" he called to her.

She followed and they became dark bird-shapes that swept over forests thick with evergreen trees and encrusted with snow, over rivers that were full and wide and slicked with ice, and over high mountain lakes that were the color of opals. They danced on the top of Mount McKinley, the highest point on the North American continent. Then, abruptly, they descended.

There was something below them in a clearing: a log cabin with traces of smoke rising from the chimney. Down the bird forms swooped, hesitating by the entryway of the structure.

"Ladies first," Christopher whispered.

She entered, leaving him outside. In the shadows she saw a human form wrapped in blankets and hides. Two rifles hung on a wall, and a box of ammunition rested on top of a chair.

A *hunter, as we are*, thought Desidra. *Only tonight he is the prey.*

A large dog huddled close to the figure, while three other dogs slept separately on the opposite side of the cabin. Some of them snored as loudly as their master.

Desidra assumed her human shape and leaned over a bearded, rough-textured human male.

The dogs awoke and detected her presence, but she gave them a silent command to remain still. Animal commanding animal. A message of dominance. The dogs whimpered, fell silent.

She sank her fangs into the soft, yielding flesh of the

man and took a deep drink, but did not forget Christopher. She consumed only half of what she might normally have taken and moved aside.

Her vampire companion moved in and took her place.

The human stirred.

"Not too much!" she whispered to Christopher.

The large dog began to move, but seemed unable to rise, as if it were held down by a weight.

Christopher stopped drinking and his fangs retreated.

The man awoke and cursed. He extended a large hand from his covers and scratched the dog's head. "Keep still, King! Go to sleep."

The dog whined a protest, but did as commanded.

The vampires slipped through the walls and flew away.

"It was a good hunt," said Christopher. "And we didn't go for the kill."

"You did well," Desidra said. It was grand to be in the company of another vampire on a Blood-hunt. She had missed the camaraderie.

In the days that followed, within the darkened army barracks where he slept, Christopher visited the beds of his sleeping companions. From each he took a controlled quantity of blood, but never enough to awaken them or do harm.

Army life was rather enjoyable, he admitted to himself, and he hoped Prince Romano never learned of his feelings. If that ever happened there would be a price to pay. While Romano had not set a deadline for bringing Desidra back or otherwise dealing with her, the sire could send someone to check on progress at any moment—or he might come himself. He was unpredictable; it was one of his carefully honed defense mechanisms.

By the end of the first week of duty, Private Christopher Wilson lay in bed, feeling his vampire pulse quicken. Not only was he Kindred; he was homosexual. An interesting secret to withhold from his military commander! He could hear blood pumping in the veins and arteries of the sleeping soldiers all around him.

He made himself invisible.

The sheet and blanket over him slid away, and like a wind he slipped out, remaining at bed level as he floated down the aisle between the beds, headfirst. He was supine like a sleeper on his back but without a bed or apparent body.

Tonight he'd leave his own barracks and visit another, spread his pleasure around. Quickly he moved to an adjacent building, quietly unlatched the door and slipped inside, still supine, as if he were on an unseen gurney.

The Hunger was rising in him now, heightening all of his senses. Which victim would he select tonight? A sleeper in the back of the room caught his attention. The breathing was smooth, the heartbeat faultless, rhythmic and strong.

Closer the vampire floated. He felt himself being drawn like metal to a magnet. As he neared he saw in the shadows that it was a beautiful young man, barely past shaving age and unsuspecting of an animal presence.

The predator lay beside its victim now, but on air instead of a mattress. An ancient pain arose from within, a feeling associated with the Hunger. It was only by satisfying the Hunger that Christopher could release the pain.

With practiced motions, the vampire turned toward his victim. Fangs erupted from Christopher's mouth, cutting his lower lip as they passed by it and giving him a taste of his own blood, like an hors d'oeuvre. It was intentional, a trick taught to him by his sire.

Sharp teeth sank into the young man's smooth neck, and Christopher took a deep draw of blood, then a longer one, and more still. Extreme pleasure replaced all pain. The sensation was almost overwhelming, but at the height of ecstasy he pulled back, lest he kill the human.

The young man turned over, sat up, and said in the most civilized of voices, "I don't know your name, but would you mind doing that again?"

Christopher gave him his name.

"I'm Lance Flynn," said the other man. "Private First Class."

Someone in a nearby bed moved restlessly in his sleep.

Christopher put a finger to his own mouth to indicate that they should speak more quietly.

"We both have a secret," the man whispered. "Am I right?"

"Absolutely, but there's a distinct difference. I'm vampire and you're not."

There, it was out in the open for the man to accept or reject. Christopher was tired of hiding his truth. And anyway, who'd believe this soldier, if he announced that a vampire had kissed him? They'd send him to the psych ward.

"You're kidding, of course," came the response. Unable to see the wound on his neck, he rubbed it.

Parting his lips slightly, Christopher bared his long canine teeth and let his eyes shine red.

Lance began to shake. "Oh, God! Don't kill me!"

"Generally we only kill humans with terminal ailments, or those who haven't learned how to live in harmony with others of their kind. I am Kindred, a fallen angel some would say. Still we have our scruples, and I have no intention of harming you."

"Your eyes . . . so red . . . how?"

"Tapetum lucideum. A reflective layer in the eyes of predators."

Lance continued to tremble, but had the courage to ask questions. "Were you born like this?"

"My sire made me this way," Christopher said. "I didn't ask for unlife. But now that I have it, I've learned to enjoy it. I'll live for thousands of years, and quite well if I wish. Or I can live like a bum. I can be whatever I choose to be." Christopher omitted important details, including the purpose of his trip to Alaska.

Lance's eyes were wide with wonder, like a child's showing fascination for a juicy horror story. "I wish I could be the way you are," he said at long last.

"I can take care of that," said Christopher. "If you want the transformation."

His new friend sighed softly. "I think I do. It has to be better than the way things are now."

16

January.

Christmas came and went. The new year arrived without a great deal of celebration. There was too much to do.

Desidra sat in the small, lead-lined compartment at the rear of the Signal Center. A simple shelf ran around the middle of three walls. Twelve wooden chairs were stationed along the shelf. On the shelf in front of each chair was a Sigaba, the rotary code machine Desidra had been told about. Code-breaking tools! And now, she was operating one.

She was the only woman on her shift. This night, a heavy flow of messages passed through her hands: ships sunk, lives lost, families destroyed, amputations and blindness, jungle rot and pestilence, suicide, and madness. Desidra wondered how humans survived so many tragedies. They didn't heal rapidly from their wounds as vampires did, and their prolonged pain must be unbearable, but perhaps they were hardier than she'd thought. She'd heard many stories of mortal courage, instances in which severely injured mortals eventually returned to their feet and went about their business without too many whimpers.

Hearing a murmur of sound, she turned in the direction of the soldier seated next to her. His mouth moved in a strange little harmony with his fingers.

He was a serious soldier named Frank, a young man too frail to be fighting a war, even from behind a desk. Though there was little conversation in this heavily secured section of the unit, Frank was even more quiet than the others, lacking even the social skills required for a pleasant good morning or good night.

Now his fingers flew over the Sigaba keyboard, inches above it, never touching anything.

Mental breakdown, Desidra thought, and she sneaked into his brain—an undetectable intruder. He had grown ill from the overload, stemming from an inability to process all the negative data that was going through his brain. She closed her mind to everything but his thoughts. They rambled:

Can't stand it, the unhappiness I read ten hours a day at this machine. Have to do something for the hurt ones, the sick ones, but what? I'm only one person. Can't do anything. Can't. No place to go except here. No escape. Wish I were in combat—then I could really do something. Hide from the hurt, back there in that dark place. Yes . . . there! Now they can't get to me, can they, Mama? Mama, do you hear me?

"Frank!" Desidra said, and she tried to call him back from the dark place. But he was gone, carried by his memories of a gentler world.

She withdrew from his mind.

No one else in this small room seemed to notice Frank's retreat from reality. Each soldier continued doing his task without looking right or left.

Desidra called one of the soldiers who guarded an outside door to come and help her with Frank.

"Something's wrong with him," she whispered, when the guard arrived.

"Another one gone loony," the guard replied without lowering his voice. "Some do. It's the inactivity and pressure of details. Little scraps of paper with words on them. Critical words—no room for mistakes."

That might be part of it, Desidra thought, but she'd read more in the man's mind, an intense need to take some physical action. Instead he could only sit there and read about horror.

The guard took Frank's arm. "Come on, fella. We'll get you to the hospital."

Frank stood up and allowed himself to be escorted toward the door, face expressionless, body rigid.

Desidra went to another guard who'd been watching and asked him, "What will they do with him?"

"Put him in with all the other nuts."

"Then what?"

"Who knows? Discharge, maybe. Or he could get well enough to come back. A few do. From the look of him, though, I'd say he's a goner."

The following morning, after Desidra completed her shift, she hiked through snow to the post hospital. A black sky curved down to meet the earth, a darkness that would last until noon, then would turn steel gray for an hour or so, then back to ebony once more. It was all part of this time of year, when night was relieved by a stark white cover of snow that glistened in the moonlight.

As a vampire, she enjoyed the nocturnal atmosphere. But how did it affect mortals? She'd read that virtually all of them suffered from the lack of light to one degree or another, and in the most severe cases they grew depressed and sometimes suicidal.

Vampires could not endure the sun; humans could not stand a lack of sun. Each with a burden to carry.

Inside the hospital she floated silently and invisibly down a maze of long white corridors and found the door to the psych ward. She passed through without opening the door and entered a huge room walled off from the rest of the hospital, as though the men inside were contaminated.

There were dozens of patients in this large ward, most seated on their beds, men who rocked back and forth, staring at nothing. A few paced restlessly with a similar lack of emotion. She was appalled by what she saw and what she read in the remnants of their minds. They were beyond despondence. This was acceptance, numbness, a terrible form of unlife. A common pattern emerged, brief glimmers of conscious thought. Americans were dying in the war, and the men here could do nothing to stop the killing.

I'm more alive than these men, Desidra thought, with deep sorrow. It was a remnant of her humanity.

That same afternoon, Christopher engaged in war game maneuvers with his unit, dubbed the "Green Army." Into his breathless body he drew in the Alaskan winter, reveling in the cold edge to the air and the dark skies. He wondered if Desidra sensed its pleasures as he did.

The men accompanying him were shadow-shapes, their flashlights flickering on and off to illuminate the way. Dressed in white camouflage uniforms they hiked in snow-shoes, with full backpacks and rifles with fixed bayonets.

Some of the soldiers grumbled complaints of physical pain and fatigue, but Christopher felt strong and filled with joy.

A soldier came running back from the head of their column and spoke in low tones to the lieutenant in charge. Christopher overheard the message: "Enemy movement, other side of the hill."

It was a reference to the "Blue Army, not a real enemy, for these were only practice maneuvers, training for what might come. Everyone, even those in the communication service as he was, had to learn to defend the post and its secrets. This wasn't a child's game, this was war.

The men in his unit had built up a keen competitive edge, and bets had been made on the outcome of this mock battle. Excitement rippled through the ranks, and with his heightened senses Christopher could smell a feverish odor. Feigning, he sucked in air and then out, allowing it to vaporize in the cold air so that he appeared to be breathing.

"On your bellies and up the hill," the sergeant said to the nearest men. "Pass it on. Lights off."

The men repeated his command, until all flashlights were dark and the entire unit was crawling up the hill in moderately deep snow.

On the right flank a few yards away from the others, Christopher came to the top of the rise and saw movement behind a cluster of rocks.

"You're dead, Christopher," a voice whispered suddenly. Something hard and cold pressed against the back of his head. "Or should I say double-dead?"

"Lance!" Christopher whispered.

Turning, Christopher ran his fingers across his lover's neck. "Careful," Christopher said. "You haven't been a vampire very long and I can still teach you tricks."

"I think I'm falling in love," Lance murmured, a comment that went without response. The vampires moved apart and rejoined their units.

Flashlights flickered on and blank shots were fired, leaving red dye markings. Those who were hit fell in the snow and lay there pretending to be dead soldiers on a bloody field of battle.

Christopher's Green Army was victorious, and they took survivors as simulated prisoners of war—among them Lance, his hands up like his companions. His eyes glowed faintly red for a moment in Christopher's direction, then dimmed.

Christopher was happier than he'd ever been before. At last he'd found someone truly compatible. It didn't matter that they'd only known one another for a short time. Their future friendship was a certainty and would provide the stability that Christopher had craved.

But in making Lance a vampire through the exchange of blood, he knew he was in violation not only of the rules of Prince Romano, but a cardinal rule of the Kindred: no human could be admitted to the society without the consent of an Elder. In Christopher's case this meant the consent of Prince Romano.

He tried not to think about the danger in which this placed him. He'd heard of Elders granting their blessing after the fact, but only in rare instances. The prince was not likely to be sympathetic, particularly since the transmutation had occurred while Christopher was supposed to be carrying out an important assignment.

Romano would only grant his blessing if Christopher could get back into his good graces, but under the circumstances, there appeared to be only two ways to do that . . .

Bring Desidra back or kill her.

17

The lieutenant in charge of Desidra's shift was upset. She could smell the biting odor of his anger.

"Some idiot in this unit sent out a high-security message over the radio," he fumed, "and now the brass are coming down hard on us." He paused and looked around sternly. "All right, which one of you did it?"

No one responded.

"All right, play it that way," he said. "I'll take the blame for all of you."

He turned and with a dissatisfied grunt walked back to his desk.

"Good man, but he's pretty riled up," Sergeant Miller told her as soon as the lieutenant was out of hearing range. "Captain Herkle came in early and gave him hell. Laid out a pack of new regulations to follow."

"Maybe they're justified this time," Desidra suggested. "I mean, if somebody sent out a high-security message over an unsecured radio wave . . . "

"The contents of that message didn't amount to squat," the sergeant said in a low tone. "High security? The message was supposed to be directed to a nearby base, asking for a supply of pens and pencils. I don't know why it went out over the air, but it sure wasn't a high-security item."

"If we're low on writing instruments it's a sign of how

busy we are, and we're not supposed to let the enemy know that."

"Hogwash," Sergeant Miller said. "Maybe someone just forgot to order them or enough of them. I know one thing: Herkle will use this as a cause célèbre, an excuse to come down hard on us."

The sergeant bit his lip, looked around uneasily. "Just a while back, one guy committed suicide. Hugged a power transformer because he couldn't take it any longer. Tried to do everything right and still got blamed for doing it wrong. Herkle would tell him to do one thing and then bawl him out the next time for doing exactly what he'd been told to do. The captain likes to select one man from the herd and pick him to death, whipsawing and confusing him. If he senses any weakness, he moves in for the kill."

"He sounds like a dictator. Our own little Mussolini or Hitler."

Sergeant Miller whispered to her, "Herkle takes men out on maneuvers, calls them names, and tells them they were born without brains. He insults their wives and kids and says 'Stupid attracts Stupid, and Stupid breeds Stupid.' Then he marches the whole squad up mountains and down into icy rivers and if they complain God help them because he makes them remove their heavy outer clothing and march in thermal underwear. That doesn't give much protection from the wind, but Herkle says he does it to toughen them up. Trouble is, they end up in the infirmary with frost-bitten toes that have to be chopped off, because they had to slog through ice in their socks. Herkle's tough."

"Not tough," Desidra said, shaking her head. "*Weak.* Weak men have to tear others down in order to feel stronger."

The sergeant grinned. "I like that philosophy. Maybe I can add something to it. He's a bastard, too."

Desidra laughed. "Well, there are a lot of those around." She thought about Romano and some of the Elders, whom she considered to be abusers of authority.

Two tall officers entered. "They're here," said Miller. "Let's watch the lieutenant go out of his friggin' mind.

When they get done questioning him, he'll be a basket case."

"So," Desidra said, "do you know who sent the radio message?"

"Yeah, one of the fellows on second shift. Poor sucker," Miller said. "He'd been on duty for forty-eight hours straight. Herkle was punishing him for not having his shoes properly shined. Now, the guy is in deep crap. No one's ratting on him, not even the lieutenant. It's kind of an unwritten law with us."

"Include me in," she said. "I heard people talking about the man yesterday, that he was so sleep-deprived he could barely stand up."

"Right. His brain wasn't working. The pattern is, Herkle causes problems that never would have existed if he hadn't gotten involved, and then he slips free of blame and crucifies some buck private."

"May I ask a question?" Desidra said. "I'm a civilian, but I hold the equivalent of corporal rank. In case of capture by the enemy, what would that classification mean?"

She wasn't actually concerned about her own capture, which she felt was nearly impossible, but the question intrigued her.

"Not much," came the response. "You'd get shot along with the rest of us, and since you're female, I'll leave it to your imagination what they'd do to you first."

She shuddered and was glad she was a vampire.

As she was about to leave her workstation, she saw Captain Herkle come in through the outer door. He stopped in front of her and said, "Remember what I told you?"

"I haven't forgotten."

An eyebrow arched. "See that you don't. I'm watching your performance and behavior very closely." His mouth turned up on one side in what was supposed to be an intimidating smile but looked more like a physical deformity. "I have a special interest in your case."

You are a bastard, Desidra thought.

18

The spring of 1943 arrived. Snow remained on the ground and the earth was frozen, but temperatures reached a comparatively comfortable forty degrees Fahrenheit. More daylight was beginning to appear, and the humans in Alaska looked forward to warmer days, when they could expose their bodies and lie in the sun.

Desidra knew she would have to take special precautions when the sun reappeared—more inside responsibilities, less time outside. Perhaps she could arrange to work the night shift on a steady basis, and as the days lengthened into summer she would spend more time in her steamer trunk. Thus far, while she was inside it, no one had examined its contents during routine building inspections.

Vampire luck, she supposed.

The loathsome Captain Herkle had walked into her apartment several times. She'd smelled him there. But she'd remained buried beneath clothing and blankets inside the steamer trunk, listening to his heavy footsteps as he drew closer and then moved away.

As for Christopher, he'd moved into a small house in Anchorage with a handful of other Alaska Communications soldiers. How would he fare? Quite well, she expected. He seemed fully at ease, as if some magic in this far northern place was nourishing him. That, and a new love in his unlife.

Desidra sighed. Christopher was fortunate, finding Lance and converting him to a vampire. So what if Christopher violated the rules of Kindred in doing that? She didn't care much. In recent days she'd seen them together and witnessed the way they looked at one another, behaving as if no one else existed in the world. She envied their silent communion.

So far Christopher had said nothing to her of the transformation of the mortal, although it was obvious to her what had happened. She could smell a vampire from a long way off.

In the months since she'd been here Desidra had absorbed a great deal. Among other abilities, she'd learned to repair the hand-operated code equipment, and as a result a lieutenant colonel offered her a transfer to Nome with more responsibility and a higher rate of pay. There were no white females in Nome at the time, he told her, so she'd be what he called "the Snow Queen." He went on to jabber something about an old Russian folk tale. She declined the position, responding to his banter by quipping that she had no desire to play royalty.

Actually she liked her present assignment. It was interesting and worthwhile, and she didn't need a promotion or a power base. That was for small minds, like Herkle's. He was no more than a figurehead, handling more than his ability or experience permitted. It shocked and dismayed her that a man of his emotional instability had been given so much authority, and she hoped this was the exception rather than the rule in the American military.

Lieutenant Gresham, who was in charge of her shift, gave her some hope. Good-natured and competent, he treated her with affable charm and genuine respect. Sergeant Miller seemed capable as well, as did most of the men.

Such odd twists and turns in human character and decision-making, thought Desidra. What would she have become if she'd lived her life out as a mortal, if she'd never gotten sick and Prince Romano had not whisked her away from the brink of mortal death?

Desidra used time off from work to fly out over the cold northern sea. It was late afternoon, and the wind was relatively light, breathing no hint of an impending storm. This disappointed her, for she savored the violence and ice-cold heart of the weather in these latitudes. She set course for the remote Alaskan island of Kiska, toward the extreme west end of the Aleutian chain.

Although the U.S. Navy patrolled the waters between Japan's Kuril Islands and the American Aleutians, Japanese forces occupied western portions of the Aleutians. They had built an airstrip and garrison on Kiska populated by 7,800 soldiers. This island, like most in the chain, was treeless, rocky, and irregular in shape. The shoreline, with few exceptions, was comprised of rock cliffs that jutted out over a raging, frothy sea. Aleutian weather was considered the worst in the world, and Kweca had told her that the Aleuts, Eskimos who lived there, warned: "Never speak of the wind, for if you do there will be a storm."

Hovering in the dark sky over the military installation on the small island, Desidra saw a section of shoreline illuminated by light. A small motor launch, buffeted by waves, was headed out toward a Japanese submarine that waited just offshore.

She saw evidence of recent heavy American bombings. The charred remains of a building still glowed with the embers of fire, and there were deep holes in the airfield. Japanese crews worked briskly, beginning to clean up and repair the damage. The sound of generators could be heard. Several soldiers stood outside a barracks building, examining a chart spread open on the hood of a jeep. Other men appeared to be checking antiaircraft guns.

On the opposite side of the island, Desidra found a desolate stretch of unoccupied rocky land. She crossed it without difficulty, skimming the surface in a manner that intentionally allowed her bare feet to feel the sharp scratch of the rocks. By nature she craved a physical connection with the earth. Waves crashed against the shoreline and cold wind whipped her hair and blew ice-water in her face. The weather was changing.

She saw something on the ground ahead of her.

Women's clothing was scattered here and there, and behind a rock, two naked bodies, lying on their stomachs. Turning them over, she saw they were young Asian women, and from the condition of their flesh judged they'd been dead for at least a week. The cold air had kept them reasonably preserved.

A few yards away she found a third young Asian woman. And two more in another location.

Five young women in all, shot through the heads.

Murdered.

With care Desidra moved the bodies into a small, low cave. She placed them side by side and smoothed the hair off their faces. Then she stood there a moment, showing quiet respect for the dead in the manner she'd learned as a mortal child. Finally she went back outside and collected smaller rocks, which she piled over their pale, naked bodies.

Who could these unfortunate young females be?

Too young to die!

It seemed odd to be feeling such compassion for mortals. She was a predator after all, and fully capable of savage behavior, with the capacity to rip human flesh and suck blood from it. Thus far in Alaska she'd limited herself to small quantities of blood, taken from sleeping inhabitants of the Alaskan wilderness and from Japanese soldiers as they slept. Sometimes during such forages she picked up bits of military information from the Japanese, which she brought back to the Signal Center and filtered into the intelligence stream, so that American authorities would be sure to see it.

Sometimes she took blood from hibernating bears. Enough to keep her going. To keep her . . . undead, but not enough to kill those magnificent creatures.

Thus far she'd been able to control her Hunger, but at times she sensed an otherness deep within, one she might not be able to control forever. It was a presence that lay in waiting, deep in the soul of every vampire. It spoke to her wordlessly.

The cough of a motor and approaching headlights interrupted her thoughts. A military truck moved slowly across the rocky surface. It stopped, and she heard the staccato of Japanese chatter. Two soldiers emerged from the rear of the vehicle, carrying bundles in their arms—dead human bodies, from the odor Desidra picked up. Female bodies. When they reached the edge of the cliff they tumbled the corpses into the sea.

What sordid activity was this?

The soldiers inspected the nearby territory and began to speak anxiously. They were confused. Despite a howling wind, Desidra picked up parts of their conversation. They were looking for other bodies, the ones she'd hidden.

The vehicle turned around, and its headlights illuminated something near Desidra. A glint of metal. Invisible, she moved toward it and retrieved a small brass box with Japanese lettering inscribed across the top, a name: Toyokuni.

The truck rumbled away.

Inside the box Desidra found a letter-sized envelope. A ruby-red battle ribbon with a golden sun in the middle was pinned to the envelope. She moved away from the wind, into the cave.

A piece of rice paper lay in the bottom of the box. It bore a message in uneven Japanese characters: "I am dying."

Desidra opened the envelope and unfolded a letter. It was written in the same uneven script and flecked with spots of blood. Apparently it had been written by an injured mortal. Her eyes scanned it.

My dear wife:

I know I shall never see you again. The Americans bomb us, and I sense that my remaining days and hours are few. You are far from me, my darling, but I am comforted by the knowledge that you are safe on the estate of my honored father, and that each day you gaze upon the sun rising over sacred Mount Fujiyama.

Some of the officers have brought captured women to this desolate rock called Kiska. Korean, Chinese, and Philippine women who were taken prisoner in conquered territories. As the Americans move closer to the destruction of this garrison, our highest-ranking officers have ordered the killing of these unfortunate women. Some are thought to be enemy spies, but evidence is lacking.

Those who control our destiny fear the Americans will soon take back this island, and there will be retribution for the many enemy soldiers and sailors we have killed. Know this, my beloved, I have never been unfaithful to you and have taken no part in the murders of defenseless women.

Desidra continued to read. The letter went on to describe events in the life of the writer, including the poor quality food he and other men had been eating, and how he missed the ceremonial tea his wife had served him on special occasions. It was signed by Lieutenant Mitsuo Toyokuni.

Touched by the letter, Desidra held it to her breast. The lieutenant must have died or been seriously injured, or he wouldn't have abandoned the brass container and its contents. A kindly man, it would seem, unsuited to the horrors of war.

Considering human behavior, she wondered why mortals believed vampires were vicious beasts. The Japanese military's misuse of young girls was rape, and when the soldiers were finished ravaging the females, when they had no further use for them, they murdered them.

She'd observed this sort of conduct during other wars, but this kind of violence could not be veiled or forgiven for any reason.

She thought about a few high-ranking American officers who regularly had their mistresses imported to Alaska for liaisons that their wives would never discover. And about the kind of officer that Captain Herkle represented. It seemed that the Japanese had no monopoly on misbehavior, and that in human society power was often abused.

The image of Romano came to mind, and she drew comparisons. Vampires, even with the abuses of some Elders, were still superior in this respect, for they generally followed old, proven guidelines of the Kindred, taking actions in times of emergency that benefited the whole and not the individual.

Romano, of course, was an exception.

She replaced the letter in the brass box and took it with her to a section of the island that bore no evidence of war. There she sat on the shoreline, watching the relentless, dark sea, listening to it and feeling the eternal breeze against her face.

Her heart went out to the Japanese lieutenant who had written with such compassion. They were not the words of a warrior, but of a man who'd been carried far away by his sense of duty and the maelstrom of human conflict.

How long would this conflagration last? Japan had actually begun its dreams of expansion years before. From Desidra's earlier studies, she knew that there was a mystical belief by the Japanese people that their emperor was the bodily representation of heaven on earth, and that it was the emperor's divine mission to rule the entire world. Primitive Japanese religions spoke of "the Heaven-Shining," which created the first ancestors of Emperor Hirohito, who ruled today.

Japanese soldiers were driven to give up their lives in combat. It was considered the supreme sacrifice and the most honorable thing they could do with their lives. Had the lieutenant been driven by such motives? She suspected otherwise.

Gripping the box, she wondered what to do with it. If she left it on the island the message might never reach the Toyokuni family.

Toyokuni.

An impressive-sounding name, it seemed familiar to her. Perhaps there would be information back at Elmendorf.

Desidra was a firm believer in the predestination of each life form, be it noble or otherwise. A feeling came over her that fate had caused her to find the letter. A mortal encountering this letter might have tossed it in the sea, while another, perhaps unable to read it, might have passed it along to his superiors. In that event the eyes of strangers would intrude upon the private thoughts of the unfortunate lieutenant, and some might laugh at his perceived softness, calling it weakness.

He deserved better.

For now she had to report back to work in the cryptography unit, and the little brass box would go with her.

19

With the memory of the murdered Asian women haunting her, Desidra soared high above the clouds, trying to forget what she'd seen. She'd witnessed the aftermath of human crimes before, and usually it helped to let her mind go, seeking solace in her imagination. Now she took on the shape of a fantastic creature that could both swim and fly, with broad stingray wings and a narrow bird head. There were white spots on her gray belly and back, and her long thin tail snapped back and forth, making crisp, popping sounds. She smiled inwardly. Any warplane pilot who saw her would likely go into a panic.

As the vampire dove into the dark green water below her, it seemed to her that there were many similarities between fish and birds and between the environs in which they lived. Currents of water or air flowed over and around both, and it was on one of those currents that she soared upward and out of the water, rising away from the surface of the earth and then bending back toward it again.

She realized she shouldn't concern herself with the plights of mortals. Prince Romano had taught her this, asserting that humans deserved no pity since they were continually falling into unfortunate situations they'd created.

"The human stock is a blood source," he said. "Suck but do not allow them to suck you."

He went on to say that fraternization was prohibited between vampire and human, and that vampires were also forbidden from venturing into the psyches of these lesser creatures. Such ill-advised efforts would drain the energy base of the Kindred, the prince taught.

Nevertheless, Desidra was determined to do her bit for the American war effort. Although she didn't breathe, the cool air seeped into her pores and renewed her energy. She flapped her broad wings rhythmically, and her speed picked up as she headed for Japan.

Penetrating a thick cloud, she caught a glimpse of the curved mass of islands that made up this mountainous country. She descended. Directly below her lay a row of windowless gray buildings built low to the ground. Antiaircraft guns were arrayed on a hillside, and Japanese fighter planes were parked irregularly around a landing field, apparently in order to make the facility an awkward target for enemy air attacks.

From War Department reconnaissance photographs she recognized the gray buildings as her destination.

Descending further, Desidra shape-shifted in order to avoid detection. She reduced her size. Into a ventilation duct a tiny creature fluttered, seeking the light ahead, her wings trembling against a rush of air. Down went the creature, through a duct system and out into a brightly illuminated room. Looking somewhat like a gray-brown moth, she hung from the top edge of a camera located in one corner of the room, just beneath the ceiling.

The room was filled with a machine pulse and the beating hearts of twenty-three Japanese humans.

Although Desidra could have made herself invisible, she had opted for shape-shifting and compression. The severe reduction in her size required the expenditure of great energy, even more than that required for invisibility. Compression involved a diminishment of mass, a microcosm of what occurred when a star crushed in on itself, ultimately becoming a black hole. It was a secret known only to the Kindred.

She could remain this size for no more than an hour, and then the compression would begin to reverse itself automatically. If that happened, if she forgot to change back in time, control of her body would be removed from her for the period of the metamorphosis—up to an hour—leaving her without the vampire powers of protection and making her as vulnerable as a human mortal. Poison gas could paralyze or kill her. Bullets could stop her heart. A knife in her belly could cause her to bleed to death.

Still, she did it this way out a need for risk-taking, a powerful desire to test the limits of vampire invulnerability. The desire was impulsive; she didn't know in advance when the urge would overtake her. It was exhilarating, like the surprise gift of a lover, except this gift came from inside.

The moth-creature saw several rows of cipher machines known to American cryptanalysts as "Purple" and to the Japanese as "97-*shiki O-bun In-ji-ki*," or for simplicity of purpose, "J."

The equipment looked simple, thought Desidra, but she knew it was an extremely complicated machine cipher. Code-breakers in the Army Signal Corps had solved Japan's enciphered messages, figured out the mechanism, and painstakingly duplicated the Japanese machine using a jumble of parts.

Once the Americans had the "Purple" machine, decoding became less difficult. They built several more of them and supplied the equipment to their allies.

Here in the Japanese station, the "J" machines were contained in drawer-sized boxes placed, ironically, between two American-made Underwood electric typewriters and connected by numerous wires to sockets on a plugboard. A white-uniformed man sat at each machine, typing rapidly, copying from sheets of paper clipped on little stands. Desidra was certain they were transmitting messages to other Japanese intelligence facilities.

Teletype machines were set against another wall, throbbing as they received messages. Instead of spilling paper onto the floor, these units processed the paper, cutting and carrying it by a conveyor mechanism to wire trays.

A guard stood at an open doorway, and for an instant

Desidra saw him glance in her direction, almost subconsciously. Just a moth on a camera.

She flew to one of the receiving trays and clung to its wire edge. Using her knowledge of cryptography and Japanese she read the messages. One concerned the travel plans of Admiral Yamamoto, who was scheduled to fly to the Northern Solomon Islands on April 18, 1943, for an inspection of Japanese military facilities there.

Desidra's wings fluttered excitedly. That was only weeks away.

The guard approached her with a rolled newspaper in his hand, and Desidra fluttered upward and across the ceiling. He paused to follow her flight, but soon lost track of her. She was behind him now, clinging to a gray sign that camouflaged her own coloring.

With a curse the guard gave up and returned to his station.

Desidra's flight from Japan to Alaska was swifter than the rockets that Hitler had under development. She passed Japanese and American reconnaissance planes and a squadron of American B–25 bombers. Something was brewing and she wanted to know what, but was due back at work. She continued on her way, and at 6:25 A.M. arrived at her apartment. She bathed, dressed hurriedly, and walked into the Signal Center two minutes before the start of her 7:00 A.M. shift.

"Hi, Jerome," she said to the guard at the entrance.

"Hi, right back at you," he said.

After clocking in, Desidra went to her workstation. The code-breaking soldiers with whom she worked were already present, with their heads down and fingers moving rapidly across the keyboards. She said a quick hello and went to work typing a fake message and setting her equipment to produce a simulated printout in code. When she'd finished, it looked no different from any other intercept coming in from American intelligence sources.

Marked across the top in uncoded red letters was a warning: "DO NOT DECODE. PASS IMMEDIATELY TO YOUR SUPERIOR OFFICER." The coded message below these words described Yamamoto's travel plans.

In Washington, D.C., the message was received and decoded. One of the cryptanalysts let out a whistle. Was this a ruse by the Japanese? Had they used phony radio signals to cover some other military move of theirs? To throw Americans off the track? They'd used that kind of deception previously, from the attack on Pearl Harbor to other incidents in battle.

"We've got to fly with it," said one of the officers. "If we don't take action, and the message is authentic, we're in big trouble!"

The officer in charge placed the original message and its written translation into a briefcase which he snapped shut, locked, and secured to his wrist. "I'm off to pass the word along," he said.

Admiral Yamamoto, Desidra learned, had a reputation for punctuality. Obsessed with being on time, he kept complex schedules to within a few minutes. This obsession, she believed, would be his undoing.

The intercept that she had forwarded to Washington had, in effect, become the death warrant of a bold and imaginative leader of men. American intelligence rated him as quick-thinking and highly capable. On a lighter side, in the 1920s, he had enjoyed playing poker with Americans. Two fingers were missing from his left hand, a war injury from a 1905 battle, but he played cards with the dexterity of a full-fingered man. He was also an accomplished chess player, another game of strategy.

Desidra's message was delivered to the highest levels of American intelligence, and she, the vampire and secret observer, followed its course. She overheard American military leaders arguing about Yamamoto's fate, debating whether to take advantage of the situation. Should they proceed with his "execution"? They argued pro and con. What kind of leader might replace him? Finally it was decided to proceed with the attack on the supreme commander of the Japanese fleet, in the hope that it would demoralize his followers.

On April 18, 1943, Desidra sat invisibly inside a Japanese bomber at the rear of a long compartment. The plane had crossed an expanse of ocean and now approached the island of Bougainville in the Northern Solomon Islands. It was a Sunday morning, seventy-one weeks to the day after the destruction of Pearl Harbor by forces under Yamamoto's command.

Four Japanese men sat forward of her, speaking rapidly and excitedly to one another. She identified the dignified man in the simple naval pea jacket as Admiral Isoroku Yamamoto. He asked questions of the others, and then responded with information concerning Japanese forces on the islands. An unsmiling, small-statured warrior with a shaven head, Yamamoto wore a samurai sword but no military insignia or decorations.

A Zero escort plane flew alongside the bomber. Nine other Zeros accompanied them as well as another plane that carried Yamamoto's chief of staff.

She would need to leave quickly once the attack started. As with all vampires, fire could kill her. Desidra knew that American planes were lying in ambush at high altitude, waiting for the *bête noire* who had planned the infamous sneak attack on Pearl Harbor. According to intelligence reports, Yamamoto had not made the decision to go to war with America. He had argued against it. But once the decision had been made by his superiors, he was resolved to strike hard against an immensely powerful adversary.

Gunfire shattered the vampire's thoughts. She saw a squadron of American planes approaching!

The Zeros veered off to meet them.

The Japanese officers changed. Their conversation became higher and more agitated, and with a fluid motion the admiral drew his samurai sword. An odd gesture, thought Desidra, and she wondered if it was involuntary or a preparation for *seppuku*, the ritual suicide known to Westerners by the more common term *hari-kiri*. The officers stared out a window to the right.

The bomber veered off and flew over the rugged, densely foliated jungle of the island, just above the treetops. Percussive explosions filled Desidra's ears, and she saw multiple bursts of light in the sky as planes in the skirmish were hit.

20

Back in Alaska, Desidra's mind was filled with the images of war. What drove humans to wars of agonizing, lingering destruction? Part of her knew she shouldn't concern herself with such questions. She had other things to worry about, such as her own survival.

Occasionally a vampire was destroyed by an Elder for breaking rules and traditions, as she might be punished by Romano. Justice was swift and clean in Kindred society, but she bore no fear. She was ready for whatever happened to her.

Her thoughts flitted to the letter and brass box she'd found on Kiska, which she'd tucked away in an compartment of her steamer trunk. The Japanese soldier who'd written it might have been one of those thrown into the sea. She vowed to deliver the letter to his wife. She would go to his father's home and ask where the poor woman was.

She'd researched the lieutenant's father, Kanji Toyokuni. A famous man known as adviser to military men and prime ministers, he claimed to consult with the gods for wartime strategies. A visit to his house would be an opportunity to secure information about Japanese military movements and at the same time deliver the letter.

Desidra missed Kweca, who listened so well and

seemed to hold the knowledge of a thousand years. *If I could speak to her about these matters*, Desidra thought, *she would lead me along the path of human understanding.*

Seeking Christopher instead, she flew across Elmendorf Airfield, but was unable to locate him by scent or sight. Hovering in the dark sky she saw humans and animals moving about below her like black objects on a frosted game board. Odors assailed her, the pungency of mortals and the musk of unidentified animals, but none matching the dry, sweet scent of a vampire.

She remembered Lance, a lanky man with skin the color of milk. Christopher's special friend. Desidra hadn't met him yet, had been awaiting an introduction from Christopher and an admission that he'd created a new vampire. She headed toward a row of army barracks, hoping to catch his trail.

Lance would not be my choice to make vampire, she thought, *but Christopher seems happy.*

Her own preference would be a male human whose ruddy complexions indicated a good source of red blood. Still, appearances were sometimes deceiving.

She picked up a vampire scent, and no one was in sight but Lance, partially hidden by the military truck on which he was working. She landed beside him and reassembled herself into human form.

"Have you seen Christopher?" she asked.

There was no look of shock or surprise in his expression at her sudden appearance. Obviously he was feeling his own power, such as it was at this point in his development.

"Haven't seen him today."

In a moment she'd invade his thoughts, but first she would test his veracity. She asked, "Will you be seeing him?"

He returned his attention to the truck. "Hard to say."

"You seem fond of him."

"We're close."

"Does he tell you much about himself . . . and me . . . about where we came from?"

"Not really."

"Maybe I can enlighten you. Christopher and I come from the same family. Are you beginning to comprehend?"

"No."

"Don't lie to me, Lance. I know who and what you are." she scanned his mind and said, "I'm reading your thoughts at this very moment. This is a test to see if you can be trusted. Speak what's in your mind! I'm much more powerful than you, so, if you persist in your lie, you'll have me for an enemy. I make a much better friend."

He backed away. "I promised him not to tell."

"About . . . ?" She knew what he was withholding, but this upstart needed a lesson.

Perspiration covered Lance's brow. "He told me . . . he was going to tell you . . . "

She lost patience, leaned over and grasped him by both shoulders. "I know you're Kindred, and I want you to act like a good little vampire and tell me at once where Christopher is and anything else you're trying to keep from me. You doubt that I can read your mind? At this very moment, you're thinking you'd like to kill me and drain my blood."

Lance's pale face flushed. "Uh, Prince Romano wants you back any way he can get you. He taught Christopher some magic and ordered . . . Well, he said that if you couldn't be convinced, wouldn't come home, then Christopher should kill you. With a special weapon Romano gave him."

"A weapon? What is it"

"I don't know."

This was the truth. Desidra let go of him and stepped back. New layers of thought in Lance's mind peeled away like an onion, and Desidra learned of Christopher's location just as Lance spoke it: "Mount McKinley."

Within seconds she was up in the sky, riding the air currents, seeking Christopher's trail in the cold moonlight. She located the scent, and when she reached the magnificent mountain known to the Alaskan Indians as Denali, she descended through the mists that veiled its 20,320-foot crown. It would be easy to find Christopher if he was still here. She lifted her head and picked up his scent. Stronger now and closer.

She saw him a few hundred feet below her on the mountain, sitting on a rocky ledge. He appeared to be meditating. Before she flew to confront him, she tried to enter his mind. She nudged a wall that separated her from his thoughts, and it opened, but for only a brief moment. Not enough time to read what lay behind it. She tried again, without success. How did he do that?

She moved toward him.

"Hello, Deceitful One," Desidra said as she approached. She eased herself onto an outcropping that protruded from the frozen snow. In the distant sky, across high mountaintops, the aurora borealis flickered, a rainbow of color against the black sky.

He frowned. "I haven't deceived you."

Her eyes glittered red in the darkness. "Your lover, or should I say progeny, since you created him, told me everything. He told me that Prince Romano sent you to take me back or kill me. I won't go back, so that leaves one option. Let's have it out now. See who has the power."

His eyes flashed angrily. "Lance didn't tell you everything. I never planned to kill you. I thought you'd go back to Seattle willingly, sooner or later."

She probed his thoughts, but again he threw up a barrier.

"I'm never going back," Desidra said, "so what do you plan to do now?"

He lifted his head and cried out. "Nothing!"

"Well, I'm not leaving it at that!" In a frenzy, Desidra flew at him and knocked him from the ledge. He tumbled down a glacier, then burst into the air and flew up at her in a feral rage, extending long fingernails and fangs. He was quicker than Desidra had expected and drew blood from her. Then he veered off and upward, as though preparing for another attack.

She gathered her strength and with her powerful magic held him suspended in the air. He struggled against her, and to her shock made progress and finally broke free. He flew toward her, his eyes blazing red.

"Stop!" she cried. "This is insane. We're fighting like a pair of animals, which is exactly what Romano would want, to separate us with anger and hatred."

"We *are* animals," Christopher shouted back. He circled overhead, warily.

"Sorry," she said. "My suspicions took hold of me, but I'm unable to verify your sincerity."

"A trick Romano taught me," Christopher answered.

He opened his mind to her, and she entered. Inside she traveled the labyrinthine pathways of his brain and felt his agitation and worry and the warmth of his friendship. He'd never intended to kill her.

These are true feelings, she thought.

Sitting on a snow-covered rock, Christopher slumped over and supported his head in his hands. "Romano will come for both of us," he said despondently.

"Not yet. He's counting on you to drag me back to him, like a runaway pet. He'll give you plenty of time." She sat down beside him. "I looked for you, not to punish you, but because I want you to be my confidant. Pretending to be a mortal is more difficult than I thought. Sometimes I dream about my mortal life, but still I don't understand enough about human behavior. Our unlife, even with all of its problems and unending centuries, seems less complicated."

"What is it you wish to confide?" Christopher asked.

She told him of the letter and of her wish to deliver it across enemy lines to Japan.

"I think you should go," Christopher said. "It gives me an excuse, too, in case Romano comes poking around, wanting to know why I haven't brought you back."

Desidra frowned. "Whatever the future holds, we have to be prepared to protect ourselves against Romano. Let's discuss it more when I return from Japan."

"I've already started my defense," Christopher said. "I'm building a private army." He grinned. "A little sip of blood here and a little exchange of blood there. So far I have a half dozen new vampires, and expect to build it up to fifteen or twenty."

Desidra laughed, and the sound was carried on a high mountain wind. "A vampire army?" she said.

"Yes," he said proudly. "We've decided to call ourselves the 'Crimson Corps.' Sounds rather dashing, doesn't it?"

"I like it. It fits you."

Both agreed that it was against all of the wishes of Prince Romano, and then Christopher proceeded to instruct her in all of the secrets their sire had taught him, including the method of veiling thoughts from another vampire.

After imparting this important information to her, Christopher reminded her that an Elder could still conceal his thoughts from her.

She pondered this for a moment, then said "We must never reveal these important methods to the vampire army you've created. We could have difficulty controlling them."

"We?" Christopher said. "It is *my* army! If you want an army, make your own."

"No thanks," she said with a smile. "I'll leave such endeavors to you. I have other interests, and the accumulation of power is not one of them."

The two vampires scampered around on the top of the mountain, discussing many matters. From the highest precipice, they tumbled off. At the last possible moment, before hitting rocks below, they surged upward into the cold sky.

21

Twilight had almost descended, and the remaining daylight was fading into night, blurring the contours of the landscape.

A brownish-gray bird perched in a flowering cherry tree and watched a tall woman approaching on a long cobbled path that ran through maple, pine, and flowering plum trees. The woman kept her head bowed slightly against a misty spring rain. She wore a loose black kimono over another garment of pale blue and white silk, and her glossy black hair was arranged in traditional Japanese fashion. Her face was porcelain white, her eyes outlined with kohl, her mouth painted bright red. This was a geisha, a hired entertainer.

Ahead of her was a lattice gate and gatehouse, and beyond that the lights of a sprawling house. The woman hurried forward.

A harsh cry issued from the bird, and the woman looked up into the branches of the cherry tree. A pair of red eyes in the tree! She froze.

Branches and leaves swayed, and out of the foliage flew a creature with blazing eyes. Desidra alighted in front of the woman, between her and the house. Shape-shifting, Desidra took on the exact appearance of the woman, but entirely naked. In one hand Desidra clutched a small brass box.

Shock and fear covered the geisha's face. Her eyes were open wide and her lips parted.

"I'll have your garments now," the vampire said in perfect Japanese. "And your wooden clogs."

"Fuji-san demon!" the woman screamed. She turned to flee, but Desidra was too fast and blocked the path.

"I won't harm you unless you resist," Desidra said calmly. She repeated her demand for the clothing, and this time extended a handful of gold coins.

The woman's eyes lit up. Her fear, still evident in her trembling body, diminished slightly.

"Think about what you can do with all this money," said Desidra. "You can go anywhere you want, never take orders from anyone again. But you must promise me to disappear, or I shall come for you. Do you understand?"

The woman nodded, and after taking the coins disrobed behind thick shrubbery.

Desidra slipped into shadows and waited.

"May I keep my outer garment?" asked the geisha. "I'll draw attention if I do not cover myself."

"Keep it," said her image.

After the exchange the geisha, wearing her dark outer kimono, hurried barefooted, back down the road.

Her look-alike slipped into the clothing and approached the gate of the Toyokuni estate.

A muscular man stepped from the gatehouse. The sword hanging from a scabbard at his side and his carefully wrapped white garment suggested that he was a descendant of the samurai. Desidra confirmed this by reading his blunt, uncompromising mind. As far as he was concerned she wasn't going anyplace without providing a complete explanation of who she was and why she was there. By nature and training he suspected everyone.

"State your business," he said, holding one hand on the hilt of his sword.

Paranoid, Desidra thought. *As he's supposed to be. Who would want a guard dog that licks the bandit's hand?*

"I am Akiko, the geisha sent from Tokyo," she replied, without knowledge of her specific duties, since the real geisha did not possess this information.

Desidra's acquaintance with Japanese history and tradition had taught her that "geisha" could encompass a wide range of skills, including musical entertainment, food and drink preparation, and storytelling—and talents of the boudoir, if the geisha was agreeable. Despite a misconception by some westerners, the geisha were not "loose women." They were paid hostesses, companions, and entertainers—multifaceted, highly trained women who, if they performed sex, usually did so of their own free will, unlike the activities of ordinary prostitutes.

Desidra held the brass box in one hand.

"What is the purpose of your visit?" he asked.

"To deliver this to the master of the house," she said. She opened the box and he looked at the envelope inside.

"See Mr. Nukazawa," he commanded, pointing back toward the main house. "Side entrance by the shrine."

She bowed deferentially and hurried on her way. Behind her she heard the guard on the telephone, calling ahead to notify others of her presence.

Crossing a patio tiled with flat stones, she came upon a tiny open-air shrine which contained a jade statue of Buddha. Beyond it lay the main house, a harmonious arrangement of clean white walls topped by a roof of heavy red tiles. It was an imposing structure.

One of the doors slid open, and a massive man filled the opening. "You are Akiko the geisha?" he asked.

"Yes." She bowed.

With a sweep of a beefy arm he said, "This way." He stepped to one side, which didn't allow much room for her passage.

Desidra squeezed by him into a narrow hallway. She smelled food: red meat, newly slaughtered. The odor made her dizzy with need. She looked back at him as he closed the door. He motioned for her to go ahead.

The hallway opened into a large kitchen, revealing the source of the food odors. Three men and a woman, dressed in white from their caps to their shoes, were preparing food on long countertops overflowing with pink shrimp and silver fish and vegetables.

Nukazawa led the way through the kitchen, which

opened into another hallway decorated with Hokusai prints on the walls and glazed pottery on small nested tables. Nukazawa turned into another room and she followed. The room featured another Buddhist shrine, this one small and built into a wall. A tatami mat covered a highly polished wooden floor.

"Wait here," he commanded. "The housekeeper will appear presently."

Desidra exchanged bows with him, and he left.

On impulse she knelt before the shrine. The eyes of the little clay Buddha were serene and full of love, and it seemed to her that this mortal must have been a remarkable person—if he had truly existed. Many centuries earlier, the Buddhist religion had been introduced to the Japanese court by the king of Paikchoi, a state in Korea, who gave the nobles scriptures and a sculpture of Buddha as a symbol of friendship. Today, Desidra knew from her readings, there were similar images in shrines and temples throughout Japan.

She laid the brass box on a step of the shrine.

Hearing a noise to her left, she rose to her feet. A distinguished man in a long robe paused in the doorway to survey her. He was, she guessed, around sixty years of age, with long black hair secured in a pigtail. His eyes and mouth were hard.

A *tough mortal*, she thought. *Not one who forgives deception or deceit*. From photographs she identified himself as the famous Kanji Toyokuni, the unorthodox gentleman who claimed he consulted with gods. Before she could confront him, Toyokuni moved on down the corridor, his pigtail swinging. For a brief moment she thought about Prince Romano's white ponytail and whispered to herself, *You'll never find me here, my sire*.

Moments later a middle-aged woman appeared in the same doorway. "You are the geisha?" she inquired.

"Yes." Nodding toward the brass box, Desidra said, "On the road, a man gave that to me. He said there is an important letter inside and instructed me to place it on a shrine before Lord Buddha when I arrived in this house."

"I am Suziko, the housekeeper," the woman said. Short

and stocky, she bore an air of authority. She eyed the box suspiciously.

"The man identified himself as a courier and then hurried off," Desidra said. "I didn't have time to ask questions."

The housekeeper sniffed. "Odd that he would give it to a geisha. The letter must be of little significance."

Desidra protested. "He said it is *most important*."

"Give it to me!"

Desidra hesitated. How much authority did this woman have in the household? Tempted to show her fangs, Desidra instead controlled her anger and said, "It may be a personal letter. One that should go directly to your master."

"I am no ordinary servant," answered the woman. "I screen those people who might annoy or upset my master."

"Including those he has hired? Perhaps this will convince you." Desidra picked up the box and removed the letter. Unfolding it, she handed it to the housekeeper.

Suziko's eyes opened wide, then watered quickly, and tears ran down her cheeks. "This letter is for Mitsuo's dear wife," the housekeeper said. She wiped her eyes and replaced the letter in the box.

Desidra remained silent.

"I'll bring you to my master," the woman said. "On second thought, find your own way. You're highly paid! He is on the second floor, third room on the left."

As Desidra climbed the stairs, she wondered where Toyokuni had gone. Not upstairs, yet that was the direction she was sent. Was the housekeeper playing tricks?

As she progressed upward, she admired the smooth dark wood of the stair railing and the intricate figures and Japanese symbols carved on wall panels. She noted that some of the carvings were intended to impart blessings upon the house, while others described historical events in the Toyokuni family. She recognized the names of Japanese emperors and other members of the royal family.

She wondered if the death of the young lieutenant would be carved in wood one day and what her place in history might be. Perhaps she would be shown as a geisha bringing bad news.

At the top of the stairs, there were several rooms with closed sliding doors. She padded softly to the designated door and knocked. The Toyokuni family symbol was imprinted in broad gold brush strokes on the door. It matched the one on the metal box.

"Enter," a masculine voice said from the other side of the door.

Feigning timidity, Desidra opened the door slowly and poked her head inside.

A man lay on a large bed, an oversized futon that rested upon a broad platform. A younger version of Kanji Toyokuni, he appeared to be tall for one of his race, based upon what she could see of him. His slim but muscular upper body was bare, with a silk coverlet over the rest of a long torso. An open book rested in his hands.

Beside his bed stood a wheelchair and near that a nightstand covered with small bottles. Medicinal herbs, Desidra noted, glancing at the labels.

She identified herself and repeated what she'd told the others about the brass box and its contents. As she stood there staring at the floor, rather than directly at the man, she thought how difficult it was to maintain the quiet demeanor of a Japanese woman, when all of her instincts urged otherwise. Without touching him, her senses had picked up the scent and feel of the man. On impulse she didn't use her vampire advantage to read his thoughts, and in that respect kept herself on a level closer to the human she was studying.

Cautiously, she looked into his eyes. They were brown and filled with sadness, not unlike the eyes of the Buddha. Her emotions were stirred.

The young man stared at the brass box in her hands. "How did you get that?" he asked.

She told him the lie about the courier, then moved with fluid steps to his side, her silk gown rustling. She gave the box to him.

He frowned and reached for it with long, graceful fingers. Desidra awaited his instructions.

"I wish to be alone," he said.

As Desidra closed the door, she encountered Kanji Toyokuni. He waited for her to bow and then nodded with a tiny movement of his head.

After identifying himself, he said, "You have met my son, I see. Ah, that is good. He has been despondent since his wife's . . . "

Desidra looked down at her feet. She didn't dare look into his eyes except for brief moments, lest she reveal her more aggressive nature, which even now threatened to break its leash.

Toyokuni moved away from the door, gestured for her to follow. At the head of the stairs, he said, "Mitsuo's wife is dead. An erroneous message arrived saying my son had been mortally wounded in an American bombing raid. Overcome by grief she jumped from a cliff. We learned a day later that Mitsuo had not been killed, but that he was seriously wounded."

After expressing her regrets, Desidra considered the new information. Mitsuo's wife had killed herself by leaping into space. The poor, misguided mortal. Unable to fly, what did she think as she fell like a rock toward the earth that rushed to meet her? What depth of emotion the woman must have felt for her husband.

"I sent for you to cheer him up," Toyokuni said. "His injuries are severe, but not as damaging to him as the loss of his wife. I fear he wishes to follow her in death. I am told that you have a fine singing voice and other talents."

"They praise me too much," Desidra said, harboring no worries about the adequacy of her talents. Her ability to replicate the geisha encompassed all aspects of the woman.

"Return to my son's room," Toyokuni said, "and give him back his will to live."

"He sent me away."

"It's not good for him to be alone," Toyokuni answered, firmly. He pointed toward Mitsuo's room.

Thinking of her job in Alaska, she said, "I shall do so, but can stay only a few hours and then must leave."

Displeasure etched Toyokuni's features. "I had expected

you to be our guest. The letter from your employer said you would be available to stay in this house. A room has been prepared for you."

Desidra bowed her head and lowered her voice to simulate the submissive nature that she lacked. "I have deep regrets," she said. "There must be a misunderstanding. I can return in a week. Of course, if you don't want me because of this, I will leave with apologies and you will not be billed for my services."

"You're here now," Kanji said, and looked in the direction of his son's room. "Spend whatever time you can with him."

Desidra bowed her head in agreement. She invited Toyokuni's thoughts in, and they poured into her mind. He was extremely concerned about the welfare of his son, If he was upset with what she'd said, he might call the agency and complain. She probed deeper into his thoughts, but was surprised to encounter a barrier.

How can this be? she wondered. *A human able to block his thoughts? This man has more power than I gave him credit for.*

22

On the army post there was the usual flurry of daily activity. The warm air of late spring had melted the snow that previously blanketed the ground, revealing a slimy layer of mud. The living quarters on the post looked like dismal, oversized boxes, and the Quonset huts resembled beer cans with their labels stripped off. In all, the structures looked as if a giant had thrown them about in a moment of pique.

A group of officers slogged through the muck, cursing and laughing at the hopelessness of keeping clean, while mud splattered their boots and uniforms. One was a lieutenant, one a warrant officer, and the third a captain.

The captain looked glum. "You have the addresses of the NCO quarters we're supposed to inspect?" he asked the lieutenant.

"Yes, sir."

"I've added a building to the list, you'll note."

"Yes, sir, Captain Herkle. And I want to thank you for accompanying us today. Nice to have an officer from another division go along on one of our building inspections."

Suppressing a smile at the "brown-nosing" of these lower ranking officers, Captain Herkle said, "I'm interested in the condition of this post. Can't be too certain about the structural integrity of some of the NCO buildings. They're thrown together in Seattle by draft dodgers who think they're helping the war effort by sitting on their butts. I've been down there, so I know what they're like."

"I guess somebody's got to do the construction, or we'd have to pitch tents," answered the warrant officer.

Herkle eyed him suspiciously. "You have a problem with what I said?"

"Sir, no. I mean, it's a good thing there are some guys left down in the States to take care of the stuff we don't do. Manufacturing planes and such."

"They're weaklings!"

The warrant officer fell silent.

They reached the NCO building that Herkle wanted to inspect and walked through the unlocked main door.

"I've been here before," Herkle said. He led the way to the apartment that Desidra Smith occupied, which was also unlocked, according to regulation.

"Don't bother knocking," Herkle said. "You can walk right in, there's never anyone home. I think the woman assigned here is shacked up someplace with a buck private."

His companions said nothing.

They entered Desidra's spartan room. Her steamer trunk sat in one corner by a neatly made up cot. There was hardly anything in the living room and very little in the closet with the exception of a heavy coat, some boots, and several skirts and sweaters.

They looked at the crude painting of a chest of drawers on the wall. Herkle watched the lieutenant peer at it intently.

"I guess someone wanted a homey atmosphere and couldn't afford a dresser," the lieutenant said. "That is, if you could find one in Anchorage. Shipping everything in by cargo plane raises the cost. Ever look at the price of fresh flowers, or fruit? I wanted to buy my wife a blouse in Anchorage, and they were asking four times what it would cost in the States."

"Shall we get this painted over?" the warrant officer asked, pointing to the likeness of the dresser on the wall.

"Naw, we can leave it," the lieutenant said. "Nothing's been damaged."

"Must be where she keeps her panties," Herkle remarked with a gruff laugh, "since I hear she doesn't wear any. Some of the women on this post are no more than whores."

"At least she's not a clothes horse," the lieutenant said. "Not much of a wardrobe here."

"She's not a cook, either," the warrant officer said from the kitchen, as he looked through cabinets and the refrigerator. "Nothing to eat in here."

"I wonder what's in that trunk?" Herkle said. "Maybe we should take a look."

"We have no authority to do that," the lieutenant said. "It's personal property and not part of our review. We ought not to be here at all. This building wasn't even on our list, and we only came here out of courtesy to you, sir, because you wanted to see it."

"I say it's on your list!" Herkle snapped.

"I'm sorry, Captain, but it's not on our list, and it's out of your Signal Corps jurisdiction."

"Shut up!" shouted Herkle. He glared at both men, then stomped out of the apartment, down the hallway, and out into the mud.

As he walked he thought about the insubordination from both men, and of what he would do to them one day if they ever came under his command. An image of the red-headed Desidra came to his mind and he muttered, "Mouthy bitch."

He let his fantasy take him down a dark and lascivious road to a world where he was king of all that mattered and everyone served his every wish. In the most vile and secret chambers of his twisted brain he thought about what he'd do to people who didn't oblige him and show him the respect he thought he deserved. If there was one thing he hated it was defiance, and especially from a woman.

23

Desidra called through Mitsuo's wood slat and rice paper door. She felt a flutter of excitement.

A loud thump came from the other side, followed by another and then his voice, filled with frustration and muttered words she couldn't interpret.

She called again.

"One moment, please."

Another loud noise and something clattered. All of Desidra's instincts sharpened. She placed her fingers against the door and sent her thoughts down and through the paper and wood and into the mind of Mitsuo. Impulsively she allowed his emotions to become part of her own. Entering the minds of humans, getting close to them in any way other than draining their blood, was unauthorized, but she'd learned to do it from another vampire, a brief visitor to her clan.

Pain: she could taste its bitterness. And something else, so dark and ice-filled and endless that she felt as if she were drowning in it, sinking into a freezing pit from which she'd never rise. She withdrew her mind immediately. What had she encountered?

She slid open the door and entered.

Lieutenant Mitsuo lay on the floor beside his wheelchair. The tight expression on his face revealed agony. "My legs aren't ready to support the rest of me yet," he said, and hoisted himself to a seated position.

Desidra hurried to his assistance. The silken clothing she wore rustled and swished as she went, whispering like a living entity. Placing her arms around him, she lifted him into his chair.

Then she bowed, assuming the demeanor of a proper geisha. "Forgive me for my forward behavior," she said in the softest voice she could manage. A difficult role for a predator, and for a moment she wished she was off on a Bloodhunt instead, riding the wind, following the scent of prey.

She felt interest in this human, wanted to draw blood from his body.

"You are a very strong woman," said Mitsuo. "Only two-thirds my weight, I'd guess, but you lifted me easily."

"I exercise each day," Desidra answered. *I fly a thousand miles in the blink of an eye, climb mountains with no effort, and hunt for blood like a tiger in the jungle!*

"I see no muscles, only a lovely woman."

She waved a fan across her face, partially to conceal her smile. "May I offer you the tea ceremony?"

"I require nothing."

"Again, I must apologize. Your father has commanded me to stay with you for a while. Out of respect, I cannot refuse him."

"My father still clings to archaic ways," Mitsuo replied. "He wishes to replace the memories of my wife with another woman. That cannot be." He averted his face.

He refuses to show grief. Yet, it takes him down the road to nowhere.

Mitsuo sighed, more a rattle than a breath. He slumped in his chair and closed his eyes.

Desidra probed his mind again, and the intense cold in this man's spirit and body swept up and over her as it had before. Again, her mind retreated from this thing that threatened to freeze her into position and leave her there for all eternity, like the wife of Lot who'd been turned into a pillar of salt.

It's death, I sense! He's willing himself to die. Death stands beside him patiently awaiting his surrender.

This was a significant difference between vampire and mortal, she thought. The mortal could choose to die by giving in to illness or despair, slipping away without a scream. In contrast, vampires fought the true death with ferocity, even though the long unlife of the Kindred was not always a blessing. Too often it was the reverse.

The wintry Hunger began to rage inside her. This human was dying, and all of her predatory instincts pushed and pulled her to leap and destroy the disabled animal.

Cease! her mind screamed.

She realized she cared about this wounded soldier and had felt this way since first reading the letter he'd written to his wife. She vowed not to let him die. Mitsuo had qualities that intrigued her, and she wanted to know more.

"Let me sing for you," she said, "something soothing." Her voice lifted in melodious song, and became a flute that told a tale of passion.

He opened his eyes. "What's the name of your song?"

She paused, and said, "It's called, 'Bleed For Me, My Beloved.' A song of passion." *Unbridled vampire passion*, she thought, *the kind of loving you've never known*!

"You have sung a strangely erotic melody," he said, "though I fear I haven't the heart to appreciate it. My father expects me to sleep with you, but despite your beauty I don't wish to. You may visit me, as my father desires, and sing to me, but nothing more. Will you keep this small secret from my father?"

"Of course." Then: "I'll return in a week."

"Your schedule is of no concern to me. You work for my father." He turned his face away from her again.

She stared at the side of his neck and licked her lips before hurrying away.

When she left Mitsuo, the unrequited Hunger clung to her like a drug that, if taken, promised to provide her with total release from pain and anger and any other misery. She felt overwhelmed by the call to satisfy the growing demand. The pain was such that it increased with each moment.

It could not be set aside.

She was still in Japan, unable to fly the long distance back to Alaska until she'd taken care of the beast inside her. Her strength came from fresh blood. She thought about how she might start her long flight and end up lying on some lonely stretch of land far from anything that would help her to fulfill her appetite. Although she would not die immediately, she might be forced to lie there for centuries while her body atrophied and shrank into paper-thin tissue and bone. Or she might weaken while flying over the vast Pacific and plunge into its cold waters and sink for miles, into the depths of the ocean. There she would be no more than fish food gnawed to the bone, but aware to the end.

Mitsuo, she called silently, in thought. *Stay alive for me, and I'll stay alive for you.*

She recalled the banquet on Yamamoto's flagship, and the heavy-lipped medical officer who'd bragged about torturing prisoners of war. His conversation had revealed the location of his base, in the Kuril Islands at the northern tip of Japan, not too far from Russia's Kamchatka Peninsula. It was a desolate place pounded by undersea quakes and bad weather. A fitting place for him to die, she thought. The officer was unfit to live, a human monster without a soul.

The Japanese soldiers slept soundly and didn't hear her whisper-quiet body move among them, searching for prey. She half-closed her eyes and floated from building to building and room to room, following her memory of the man's pungent scent.

She picked up the trail.

The odor came from a cement cubicle set a distance from the regular barracks. The officer's quarters. A dark form, she slipped inside and found him. He slept by himself.

The vampire stared down at the sleeping man and listened to his breath puffing from thick lips. An ugly face, one she'd not forgotten. Details of his conversation on Yamamoto's flagship came back, the tale he'd told about dissecting American prisoners while they were still alive, removing their lungs or livers, or portions of brain, all to study the reactions that followed.

This man was the true enemy of all humans. If there were no war, he'd still be torturing and killing for pleasure. All her senses told her this.

"Now it's your turn," she growled, and sank her fangs deep, deep into his neck.

The blood had a foul, human-sweat odor, but this did not deter her in the least. She'd experienced worse. When Desidra had drunk her fill and her victim lay desiccated and lifeless, she uncoupled herself and flew out over the North Pacific, heading north and east.

She felt invigorated, despite a rather unpleasant aftertaste.

24

Desidra took the long route to Alaska, heading from Japan toward the North Pole, intending to loop around to Anchorage. Upon arrival at the pole, she hovered above it and quipped to herself, "I'm on top of the world."

But she didn't feel that way. There was much to consider.

Certain passions had risen in her, and she could do little to eliminate them. A vampire shouldn't be attracted to a human, especially an enemy human. But Mitsuo was in her thoughts and wouldn't go away. She couldn't let him die.

There was a genuine kindness about him, an emotion she'd almost forgotten. It dwelled in his manner of speech, in the way he spoke and looked at her, even in the way he turned his head. His face bore the hint of happier times, and when she gazed upon it she was reminded of her own human childhood and of the young man, Jamey, who'd shared dreams with her.

Jamey. Had he married someone else? During her early vampire years she'd flown back to the town in which they'd lived and searched for him. But under Romano's command Kindred had appeared, forcing her to return to the clan. There she'd had to explain herself in an audience before the prince. He sat on a massive throne-like chair and peered down at her disdainfully. Her story that she'd only wanted a glimpse of her former life had been an obvious lie, one her sire had seen through quickly.

In truth Desidra had been experiencing one of the prohibited feelings, a longing for something lost that could never return.

This was how Mitsuo must feel about his dead wife. He'd been brought up in a wealthy household, given advantages unavailable to other children. He may have started life as a gentle child, but was soon indoctrinated in the ways of a warrior. No doubt Mitsuo had played with wooden swords before he grew to manhood and had held a real one when he learned the sword was the soul of the samurai.

Under the Japanese philosophy of Bushido, he could not allow his grief to destroy him. This was the unwritten code of laws that for centuries had influenced the conduct of samurai warriors, as well as nobles of high status such as the Daimio, the military nobles, and the *kugé*, nobles who were fighters in name only.

Despite the "Westernization" of Japan, Desidra believed that Bushido still influenced present-day Japanese. The code had taught the samurai to be indifferent to death or pain, to face life with great calm, and when death came, as it inevitably did, to embrace it.

She wondered if she could ever find the inner core of Mitsuo and restore it. An impossibility, perhaps, but even if she succeeded would that serve a worthwhile purpose? She and the mortal were radically different life forms. Barring accidental death, she could live two or three thousand years, while he was allotted but seventy or a few more.

Nevertheless, he was a warrior and so was she. She would call upon his fighting spirit and attempt to restore his will to live.

There was magic she could weave to not only save his life, but to make him care for her. Humans were incapable of resisting one of her kind, but she wasn't sure she wanted to force his affection.

The air grew colder, and from one side the leading edge of a snowstorm buffeted her. The icy fingers of the blizzard enticed her in that direction, off course. To avoid the temptation she flew into higher, calmer air, maintaining her route toward Anchorage.

Normally she might have taken a side trip into the storm in order to let her senses fully enjoy its violence. Storms were primal and riveting, demanding her full attention. Today, however, there was too much on her mind. She didn't want distractions.

Do I love Mitsuo? Probably not. It must be the Hunger, a desire to sink long fangs into his neck and draw his life's blood from him, enjoying the ecstasy.

Love is not a word used by vampires.

It was a thought that did not seem to be her own, as if it had been thrust into her consciousness from eons past.

The Kindred professed to care for their brethren and some, such as Prince Romano, even claimed to have favorites. But it was all superficial, all for the primary and paramount goal of the Kindred—the survival of each clan—and for the Blood-hunt.

Supposedly no vampire could feel human love, not even for one of its own kind. The close bonds of some vampires were for need and sustenance, not love. Love was considered a foolish human emotion involving useless sentimentality.

Predators do not feel love.

When she arrived back at the post she slipped into her apartment, climbed into the steamer trunk, and covered herself with clothing and blankets. In the darkness and silence Desidra saw the face of Mitsuo before her eyes.

I love him. Though it defied logic, she was convinced of this. At the first opportunity she would return to Mitsuo and administer the Dark Kiss, the bite and exchange of blood that would give him the eternity of vampire life.

But along that course lay danger, for him and for her.

Nonetheless, it would be the Dark Kiss.

25

"No access for you today," the guard said at the entrance to the Quonset where Desidra worked. "Report to Captain Herkle immediately."

"Why, Jerome?" Desidra asked, surprised. She wore a dark brown skirt, cut below the knees, a white blouse, and a matching brown cardigan sweater.

"I don't know."

She determined that he was telling the truth.

Turning, she crossed the compound to the two-story office building opposite. It had an outside staircase, which she ascended two steps at a time. She rapped on the captain's door.

"Come in, Miss Smith," a voice said. She recognized the raspy tone of the captain.

The office had been painted and rearranged since her last visit, with new file cabinets and framed photographs of Alaskan wildlife on the walls: a Kodiak bear up on its hind legs, a magnificent elk, a polar bear with its teeth bared.

Herkle's uniform was spotless, as if he had dressed specially in order to keep from appearing out of place in the newly decorated office. The odor of fresh paint filled the air. He glared across his gleaming desk at her.

"Where have you been?" he demanded.

"I just came from the crypto unit," the youthful-appearing redhead said. "They wouldn't let me in."

"I mean yesterday. Sit down." He pointed.

Desidra sat in one of two straight-backed chairs facing his desk. "It was my day off," she said.

"And where did you go?"

"Why do you want to know?" She crossed her legs, aware that as she did so the hemline of her skirt slid higher on her thighs.

"Is something wrong with your hearing?" He scowled. "I asked you a question, and I want an answer."

Anger churned inside Desidra, but she forced herself to speak calmly. "I hear you very well." *My hearing is acute, much better than yours, you weak, arrogant human!* "I wasn't aware of any rule requiring that I report my off duty itinerary. I went on a snowshoe hike through the woods."

"Alone?"

"Yes."

She attempted to read his mind but got little input, only a few muddled impulses, mostly concerning visual perceptions: Desidra's clothing, the curvature of her breasts, her long, sensual legs. It was this way with some humans, she'd found. In approximately a century as a vampire she'd encountered instances of human minds whose thoughts were so shallow that they didn't touch the normal range of cognitive powers.

Conventional vampire wisdom said to minimize contact with such humans and not to draw their blood, out of fear that it bore some contagion. His thoughts were like a badly faded map. Right now he was looking at her hips and imagining her in various sexual postures with him. Sickened, she released the probe on his brain. She was far from prudish, but his thoughts were obscene.

I might play games with your body, she thought, *predator games that your feeble intellect could never imagine. One of them I call Run and Pounce and Tear and Shred and Drink and Drink and Drink. It would please me to show you that game.*

"It's not safe to go hiking alone in Alaska," he said at long last. "Snowstorms appear suddenly and you could get trapped."

"I like the cold, and I've always had an excellent sense of direction."

"Do you want to waste the money of the United States government?" he asked. "Is that what you want?"

"Of course not."

"Then don't go on foolish larks on your days off. If you die, we have to retrain somebody to fill your position, and training costs money. You have an important job, Smith, overshadowing your social interests."

"I have value as a—" She caught herself. "As a human being. I'm not just a cog in the war effort. If I die, people will grieve for me. I have family, friends." Small lies, but he would never know the truth.

"I don't have time for your personal problems. On your next day off I'll go to dinner with you. We'll discuss your responsibilities here."

She shook her head. "That wouldn't be appropriate, Captain." This debate was growing tiresome. It was fueling her anger, and even worse, the Hunger. She heard a military plane taking off from the airfield and wished she was in flight, too.

"You want to get ahead, don't you?"

"Not the way you're thinking."

Her rebellious attitude brought Herkle to the edge of his chair. He leaned across the desk, glaring. "I'll tell you what. I can make your life miserable. Think about that and then we'll talk again. Dismissed!"

Angrily, Desidra rose to her feet and stormed out of the office, slamming the door behind her.

Moments later she stood before the guard again. A phone rang, and he answered it. "Yes, sir," he said, then hung up and turned to Desidra. "Herkle says to admit you now. From your expression it looks like you had an argument with him."

"He's a pompous ass," she answered.

"Couldn't agree more." He waved her in.

When her shift was finished for the day, Desidra returned to her NCO apartment. The building quartered a number of army nurses, as well as civilian women who were phone operators and clerks on the post. A number of these women stood at the entrance of the complex, talking.

One of them, a nurse named Lou, called out to Desidra. "We're having a meeting. We need your opinion."

"About what?" asked Desidra.

"Some of us are missing china and clothing and pieces of jewelry. Have you had anything stolen?"

"Nothing important, just lightbulbs and a bucket of paint. I don't have much to take, only some clothing."

One of them laughed. "Don't say that too loud, or whoever it is will have you running around nude."

"I think it's a woman," Desidra said, recalling the scent she'd picked up previously: the odor of a human female.

Lou frowned. "We think it's the big gal who has the apartment next to yours: Marsha. She's strange and arrogant, thinks she owns this building and everything in it. We need to catch her in the act."

Desidra thought about this woman who crept into the living spaces of other people and took what she pleased. A vampire could catch her in the act.

And punish her.

"Marsha took your lightbulbs?" a woman asked. "How strange."

"Assuming Marsha is the thief," Lou said. "Nearly everything she took had value. That includes lightbulbs, since they're hard to come by in wartime. The thief must be stopped, but our rooms are unlocked. We have to trust one another."

"We were planning a dinner party last week," said another woman, "but the thief came in and removed all of our dishes. Later I saw plates and cups of the same pattern in Marsha's apartment."

"I saw her wearing a bracelet that looks like mine," Lou said. "I didn't accuse her because I thought she might have a similar one."

"Has anyone ever talked to her about her behavior?" Desidra asked. "She sounds psychopathic."

Laughter. "Marsha has a strange sort of logic, but go ahead and try!"

Moments later Desidra returned to her apartment. She

hesitated in the hallway by the door. Someone was inside again! She threw open the door, and a heavy human ran into her: a tall, brown-haired woman with wide shoulders and small breasts and tiny dark eyes planted in a round face. It was Marsha, looking like an oversized, petulant child,

"What are you doing in here?" Desidra asked.

"None of your business."

"This is *my* apartment."

The woman's mouth tightened into a thin line as she said, "I moved into this building *first*. No locks on the doors means I come and go as I please. This is army property, not private property."

"And that's why you took my lightbulbs?"

"I moved into this building before you and they were here when I came, so they're mine!"

"Actually they belong to the army," Desidra retorted. "Does the word privacy mean anything to you?"

The woman shook her head stubbornly.

Desidra advanced toward her. "That means I can come in your apartment anytime I wish."

"Don't try it."

"Is that a threat?"

"If you want it to be."

Desidra lowered her voice to an overly polite tone. "I'll tell you what. I have my little bit of space and you have yours. You stay out of mine and I'll stay out of yours."

"If I feel like it."

"Listen carefully, Marsha, for your own good. Don't come in my apartment ever again."

"I go where I please," came the response.

"If you come back, I'll do something about it."

"Go to hell," Marsha said, and she left.

So much for being neighborly, Desidra thought.

The vampire waited until midnight to take her revenge. Quietly, she glided through the hallway toward Marsha's door. Her feet didn't touch the floor. The loud sound of snoring came from the apartment.

A rush of excitement caught Desidra, and she tried to control her emotions. She passed through barriers into the bedroom and stared down at the sleeping woman. The mortal's mouth was open wide, like a huge baby bird waiting to be fed.

Instead of a worm, I'd drop a poisonous snake in that maw. Easily accomplished. I could bring one back and let it crawl down your throat.

Desidra lurked in the shadows for a long while, inhaling the odors of the room: burnt grease, cheap perfume, unwashed clothes, and stale cigarette butts. Intriguing. Humans had so many odors—they overwhelmed the sense of smell and left little space for taste or sight or touch. After a long while, Desidra bent over the sleeping human and bit sharply and quickly, then withdrew. This was a lesson for this foolish, selfish person.

The victim awoke immediately and rubbed the side of her neck. "What? What?" she cried out. She pulled the blankets up to her chin and tried to focus her vision in the low light. Her eyes widened.

Red eyes looked back at her. Glowing embers.

"Hello, neighbor," Desidra said. She stood over her prey, her mouth dripping blood. "You taste good. I'd like a bit more, so hold still."

Marsha leaped from her bed and ran screaming into the bathroom. Desidra could hear her pushing her heavy body against the door in a futile attempt to put a barrier between herself and Desidra.

Desidra grinned. *I'd love to slide through the walls and appear on the other side, beside you. But you've had enough for tonight.*

Desidra returned to her own room.

The following morning, when she left for work, Lou stopped her in the hallway.

"More problems?" asked Desidra.

"Not exactly. It's that crazy Marsha. She barricaded herself in her apartment, says a vampire attacked her last night."

"Poor woman," Desidra said. "She's lost her mind."

Desidra sought out Christopher and told him what had happened in the captain's office and in her apartment, and most of all about her trip to Japan. She attempted to describe her feelings for the human, Mitsuo.

Christopher spoke of happy times he'd been spending with Lance, then went on to complain about Captain Herkle. "The men hate and fear him," Christopher said. "He plays mind games with us, cares more about his personal power base than about the war. He makes money on the side on supply deals, and eats steak while the rest of us are thrown pig slop. He pockets the difference."

"We should drain his blood and suck the marrow out of his bones," she said.

"Not around here," Christopher said. "It could generate an inquiry and we'd have to leave. I don't know about you, but I'm enjoying myself here. I don't want to mess things up."

While he was not boastful, Desidra knew that Christopher's abilities as a soldier were receiving attention. There had been talk of promotion and more responsibility.

"Let's think it over," Christopher said. "We'll come up with a way to deal with him."

"All right, but we can't wait too long. One way or another we need to put him where he can't do any harm."

"We will," Christopher said.

"What do you think of mortals?" Desidra asked. "After all this contact with them, I mean."

"What do you think of them?"

She looked at the sky, then back at him. "Some I like, but some are evil beyond understanding. That probably sounds strange coming from a mind-reading vampire, but that's how I feel. Now it's your turn."

"I haven't made up my mind about them," he answered.

26

After the confrontations with Captain Herkle and her light-fingered neighbor, Desidra welcomed the trip back to Japan. Through the mists of early morning, she soared over Japan's mountainous beauty and descended to a town.

This was not far from her ultimate destination, Toyokuni's estate, and here she would reconnoiter for a while, letting her senses absorb the ways of the Japanese people so that she might better know this enemy. The gray misty weather would help her; there was no harsh sunlight to slow her down.

She found herself in the midst of a group of young Japanese girls dressed in neat black-and-white outfits. They reminded her of little penguins chirping and giggling their way along the street. Following them came several older women, bent and gnarled like aged trees but dressed in kimonos with youthful rainbow colors. The diminutive women sat in one of the abundant rock gardens, chattering softly to one another.

It was difficult to see any of these gentle females as enemies, in Desidra's estimation.

In the shops she passed, young women sold platters of fresh fruit arranged like jewels and sticks of incense. One place specialized in Chinese silk robes, and in the guise of a geisha, Desidra purchased a new garment to wear during the remainder of her visit. In the shop she donned the simple blue robe and told the shopkeeper to discard her old one.

This was a town of females, which made her wonder if the war had taken all the men, leaving only women and children behind to run things. It seemed to be the Japanese female's duty to stay behind, and this was in some ways similar to every other nation and tribe of people.

Wars were fought by young men.

Japanese history lessons had taught Desidra that in feudal times young girls were trained to repress their feelings, to be modest, unassuming, and indifferent to pain. Although they were supposed to retain all these attributes when they reached womanhood, these females were presented with *kai-ken*, pocket knives that could be used to defend themselves against attackers, or thrust into their own breasts, if loss of chastity was imminent. Some samurai females even tied their legs together before committing suicide, so that in their death throes they would not end up in an immodest position.

This was a country where self-immolation by disembowelment, the ritual suicide known as *seppuku*, had been until recently an honorable way to exit life under certain circumstances. Loyalty to the warlords was penultimate, and in matters involving dishonor it was preferable to commit suicide. It was this stern warrior code that set the standards affecting the character and manners of the Japanese people. In Asian philosophy, the soul was located in the stomach, and therefore, to set it free, one cut it loose from the body.

In Desidra's estimation, the swift death a vampire brought to its prey was far superior. It was as bloody a death as *seppuku*, but quicker and with less agony.

At a teahouse of pure architectural lines and spartan simplicity, she entered through sliding wood and paper screens and crossed to an outer deck. She selected a small table off to one side and ordered a cup of green tea. Below her, in a small pool lined with polished stones, white-and-gold koi swam in a graceful ballet.

The serenity around her was palpable. This teahouse and town seemed remote from the war, as if its people were unaffected by the ravages occurring in the Pacific and on the northern islands of their own country. Little bells tinkled inside the teahouse, and birds sang from a nearby tree. Desidra sipped her beverage and for the first time in a long while felt relaxed.

Memories of Midway shattered her tranquillity, and a deep sorrow set in for all the victims of war. She saw planes diving like fiery arrows into incinerated boats and young men screaming as death reached for them from the sea with long, cold fingers.

To be a vampire, to be undead, was better.

She left the teahouse and strolled on the hilly streets of the town. When people glanced at her, she occasionally let her disguise of Japanese features slide subtly to Caucasian and then back to Japanese, in no more than the blink of an eye. It amused her to watch people rub their eyes and do double-takes.

Finally she made herself invisible and flew to a garden path on the Toyokuni estate. The air was soft, an interesting change from the Arctic winds she'd encountered during her flight from Alaska. She assumed the form of Akiko once more and the guard greeted her as before, informing her she would be escorted to Mitsuo's room by the housekeeper.

Desidra waited, and when no one came she was about to find her way upstairs without assistance. Almost without warning the housekeeper appeared, her wide, flat face filled with an expression of irritation and distrust. "You're back?" she said in an unpleasant tone.

"It would seem so."

"Is it your wish to dine?"

"If your courtesy extends that privilege to me."

The woman frowned and twisted her hands. "I don't think we have time. Arrangements are being made for a meeting that will be held here tonight."

Desidra probed deep into the woman's thoughts, but

found only a glimmer of what the meeting was about. There would be military officers in attendance.

"You understand I can't feed you?" the housekeeper said.

"I'm a light eater," answered Desidra. "You needn't concern yourself with my belly."

"I won't! And you know the way to Mitsuo's room."

"Of course."

Abruptly, the housekeeper walked away.

Mitsuo welcomed Desidra warmly. "Akiko! I am pleased. I thought I might have driven you away during your last visit."

It was a much better greeting than her first meeting with him, she thought. Apparently he'd had an opportunity to think about her and recognize the benefits of her companionship.

She bowed politely.

"Please sit down," Mitsuo said.

There was a slight flush of pink on his cheeks, perhaps from excitement. She sensed he was physically aroused by her presence now, and she appreciated it. She seated herself on a chair by his bed. He was too pale and had not recovered from his wounds. She didn't penetrate his thoughts, but resolved that she would make an effort to avoid intruding on them.

I *trust him*, she thought.

"I want to know more about you," he said. "Tell me where you come from, what you've done in your life."

"I'm not very interesting." *What can I tell say that wouldn't terrify him?*

"Forgive me, but I must contradict you," he answered. "I find you intriguing . . . and something of a mystery, I think. Tell me about yourself."

She spoke slowly and with care. "I studied for a while in America. Linguistics and history. I speak English, Japanese, half a dozen other languages."

His eyes brightened. "So we have something in common. I studied in America, as well. What is your opinion of American culture?"

"Interesting." A safe enough statement, it seemed to

her. "It's very different from Japan's. A saying goes, 'Americans fly by the seat of their pants.' The behavior of many Americans reflect this."

Mitsuo looked puzzled. "I don't understand."

"It means they learn as they go and make their individual decisions accordingly. An independence of spirit."

"I liked the openness of its people," Mitsuo said, "the freedom from rituals." His voice faded slightly as he spoke.

Desidra cast a worried glance at him. "Are you tired? Do you want me to leave?"

"No, no, I enjoy hearing you speak. Your voice is musical. You are geisha, so you must have learned various musical instruments."

"Yes, I began to learn as a child." This was true, for she remembered the human child she'd been, singing in church and playing piano at home. Sharp, sweet memories burst out of dormancy into her mind, and she felt the long-ago melodies lift her spirits. "I love music," she said.

"Originally I studied economics," he said. "I wanted to be a businessman. But my father pointed out that I was samurai in spirit, as he is, and as my grandfather was. That's my destiny, to be a samurai courageous in the cause of virtue. So, I went to war."

"And war is a virtue?"

"The sword is the power that thwarts evil."

"The sword is power, and power is addictive," Desidra said.

"Power isn't what I seek."

With each passing moment she felt increasingly attracted to him. But she held back. There was time.

"I've been a poor soldier. Look at me. I should be somewhere else, fighting to hang on to the territory we took. Instead I lie in bed, helpless as a suckling baby. I have killed my wife and disappointed my father."

"Your wife made the decision to end her life. It wasn't your fault."

"By honor I have assumed responsibility for her death."

Desidra made a quick analysis. He was castigating himself because he hadn't revealed the full extent of his love to his wife before leaving for war. Now it was too late to tell her anything.

What sad creatures mortal were!

"At first I liked the idea of Western individualism," Mitsuo said, "but now I realize that too much individualism leads to chaos."

"By Japanese standards, perhaps," Desidra said. "But the world is larger than this island nation."

Mitsuo leaned back against his headboard and stared at the ceiling. "I'm very tired," he said, "but please remain. I would enjoy hearing another of your songs. The last one was stimulating."

She sang another vampire song for him, and shortly he fell asleep. She took his hand in hers. Though the room was warm, his hand was cold, too cold. She pressed fingers over his wrist. His blood pressure was dropping. A meaningless symptom in vampire physiology, but in a mortal it could signify imminent death.

She listened to his heartbeat. It fluttered, sped up, and fluttered again.

He's slipping away. I won't let him go!

Conflicting feelings assailed her. She wanted to nurture this man, but at the same time the ancient Hunger seized her, clawing at the cage to which she'd consigned it, raging for release. Her predatory instincts rose to the surface of her being like monsters rising from the depths of the ocean.

She strained for control, attempting to quiet the beast that wanted to leap and tear at the human's flesh.

Not this time! she told it.

Slowly and carefully she lay beside Mitsuo and held him in her arms and willed him to live.

Minutes passed, and an hour, then another.

Her efforts seemed useless. His vital signs were growing weaker.

Do it! screamed the beast in her head. *He's going to die anyway. Don't waste his fluids!*

I care what happens to this human, she answered. *I do this for my reasons, not yours!* She bit into the dying man's carotid artery and drank deeply for a few moments, then stopped suddenly.

"I want to give you my blood, to make you vampire," she whispered in his unheeding ear. "You are dying, and I don't want to lose you! But I can't make the choice for you."

She slipped off his bed and returned to the chair, where she waited.

For hours, Mitsuo lay as still as stone. Periodically she checked his pulse. It was unchanged, still weak.

She said a prayer she'd learned in her childhood, realizing as she did so that prayer was an unlikely tool for a vampire to use. "Hear me!" she said aloud to the God she believed had deserted her. "This prayer is for Mitsuo, the mortal. Keep him alive."

After a long while Mitsuo opened his eyes and stared into hers. "I fell asleep while you were entertaining me," he said. "I apologize for my lack of courtesy." He stretched his arms. "I had a strange dream. I was on a field of war, dying, but without pain. Then a wonderful release from all of my worries came over me."

"And how do you feel now?" she asked.

"Much better."

She checked his pulse at the wrist. It was stronger, which surprised her. Had the prayer worked? *If there is a God, he's answering Mitsuo's needs, not mine.*

"I must go for a while," she told him. "But I'll return in a few days, if you wish."

"I wish," he said with a smile.

Outside his door, Desidra became invisible again and flew down the stairs to the great banquet room below. The softly lit room was filled with men in uniforms and some in business suits. Long low tables were arranged in a pleasing pattern and covered with freshly cut flowers. Pretty young Japanese girls in pink-and-white kimonos served dishes of baked fish and exotic dark mushrooms, rice, and sweet desserts shaped like birds and chrysanthemums.

Desidra stood in a shadowy corner of the room, watching the festivities. Toasts were made with cups filled with warm sake, the first toast to their divine emperor, the second one to their host, Toyokuni. As the sake flowed, conversation became more animated and the men toasted their host ten times for the ten great victories and conquests he'd helped them achieve. It was he who had the power to contact the gods who guided them.

Desidra wanted to learn more about this, for she believed in other-worldly creatures. Not that she'd seen any, with the exception of vampires and ghouls, but she sensed something out there beyond what was easily explained.

It was why she'd prayed for Mitsuo.

But Japanese gods? What manner of gods could they be?

The banquet conversation became intense. "Our offensive strategy," said Kanji Toyokuni, "was designed to gain permanent control of the Pacific by establishment of bases on its key islands and some of the less important ones."

"True," said a naval officer. "Through our naval and air superiority, closing the Pacific to the American fleet, the war will be won."

"But a problem has emerged," Toyokuni said. "Allied attacks have us on the defensive."

Desidra laughed to herself. The vampire factor had turned the tide of war! First Midway, then the ambush-assassination of Yamamoto. More would follow!

"What do your gods suggest we do?" the officer inquired.

Toyokuni stood up with his cup of rice wine, and his resonant voice spun magic that captivated them for a time but revealed little information. Restlessness moved through the assemblage . . . whispered conversations.

"What do you have for us?" a man in a business suit finally demanded.

"Tell us what the gods say!" shouted an officer in a white uniform.

Toyokuni passed out pieces of rice paper, each bearing the same message printed in fine Japanese calligraphy. Desidra moved close and read one.

The message was cryptic, but she was able to interpret it. These fragile bits of paper held a defensive strategy for the Japanese that the Allies needed to know. When she had it memorized, Desidra flew from the house and back to the message center in Pearl Harbor. It was time for another coded message to be routed through channels.

Soon the Japanese would have their backs to the wall.

Several nights later Desidra returned to the young Japanese lieutenant's side. The rain raged as she approached, a violent spring storm that beat a drum song on the land and whipped her body with its frenzy. She descended rapidly, gliding in ethereal form through the tile roof and reappearing beside Mitsuo.

His room was shuttered, no light penetrated. She heard the rain's staccato rhythm. With her vampire eyes she saw Mitsuo slept, but not like a rock this time. More like a baby, with a peaceful smile on his face. She slipped from her wet kimono and lay naked beside him beneath the covers. The geisha likeness she had assumed for him was becoming more difficult to maintain, so she relaxed her powers and let go of the image she'd contrived. Her red hair fanned out across the bed and her long legs entwined around Mitsuo's.

He woke, leaned across her, and switched on a lamp. "Let me see your lovely body while we make love," he said. Immediately he let go of her, his eyes wide with shock. "Your hair is red, you are Caucasian! Who are you?"

"It's the fever you have," she answered. "It has given your eyes false vision. I am the same as always."

"But I thought you were geisha . . . Japanese." He clung to her. "Something strange is happening. I thought I was getting better, but this! You are Akiko, but you are not? Am I dreaming?"

"Does it matter?" she said, and kissed him.

"It doesn't matter," he whispered.

He pulled her tightly against him and made love to her in such a desperate fashion that she feared for his physical safety.

27

October.

It was well past midnight, and the house servants had gone to bed. From his study Kanji Toyokuni could see the guard in the gatehouse and pale lamps that lit the perimeter of the property. Not enough illumination to attract enemy aircraft, but enough to deter those who might wish to assassinate him. Two other guards, unseen from the master's vantage, were supposed to be patrolling the grounds.

One could not be too careful about security, Toyokuni thought. After all he was a man of importance, and a war was on.

He paced the floor, thinking about his son and the geisha, Akiko. Perhaps it had been a mistake to send for her in the first place, but Mitsuo had been severely damaged. Aside from his serious war injuries, he had been made apathetic and depressed by his wife's suicide. He was in desperate need of resuscitation. Hence the geisha Akiko, an expensive flower for the garden of Mitsuo's spirit.

A plaything to make his son more worthy of the Toyokuni name. For the sake of family pride.

Geisha meant "one with pleasing accomplishments," and she certainly had brought the listless young man back to life. But had she gone too far? Copulation for the release of tension was one thing, and of little importance. It was a bodily function performed by all animals. The most Kanji had expected of Akiko was that she would play a few songs, recite poetry, and then, if his son was still capable and she was receptive, they would sleep with one another. A physical function, no more.

Emotional involvement should never exist between a man of his son's station and a lowly entertainer, no matter how charming or talented she might be. It was dangerous. A geisha did not become the beloved of a samurai!

Perhaps he should have hired a *daruma* from the pleasure quarters, a professional woman to satisfy the sexual urges of his son. *Daruma* women bounced back like the dolls they were named for, legless toys that could be pushed and pulled yet returned to their original position each time. A *daruma* would never allow a client to fall in love with her.

Though Mitsuo had admitted nothing, Kanji knew that a bond was forming between his son and the geisha.How could this happen? How could a Toyokuni, meticulously schooled in the ways of his ancestors and the Japanese class system, fall in love with a woman so far beneath his social position? Always in the past Mitsuo had become enamored only of women from the finest families in the nation. Mitsuo's dear departed wife had been of that ilk, the daughter of Inazo Watanabe of the Japanese Diet.

Could it be that Mitsuo's education in America had weakened and contaminated him? For centuries Japan had disdained the undisciplined barbarian Westerners who first visited their nation as traders. The *Eliza*, an American vessel, had landed here in 1797 and made an unsuccessful attempt to open trade. Further attempts had been made, culminating in the visit of Commodore Perry, who sailed into Tokyo Bay with a fleet of American warships in 1853. Ultimately, trade had been established.

Kanji, and many of the military men with whom he associated, believed that Japan had a greater goal: territorial expansion. The Americans posed a threat to that and to everything Japanese. The war with America should have been initiated years ago, to keep the Western disease from spreading, as it had to his son. Mitsuo was no longer the warrior he had been trained to be.

Or was it the geisha's fault? Had she cast a spell on Mitsuo? The old man allowed this thought to sink in. Toyokuni believed in following his instincts, in listening to what the submerged powers of his mind were telling him. Yes, perhaps witchery and incantations were involved, and the geisha was not what she appeared to be.

With great dread Toyokuni plopped into a large leather chair at his desk and stared across the room at a few of his possessions: a blue-and-white Ming vase on a table, an expensive woodcut print on the wall by the door. The woodcut depicted the way his land had looked in centuries past, with Mount Fujiyama looming in the background.

Toyokuni, more than any of his ancestors, had called upon the Fuji-san demons that dwelled secretly in Mount Fujiyama. Always they had been of great service to him. Important military decisions were made with their advice: counsel that Toyokuni had passed on to General Tojo's war cabinet. Vast oil fields in Asia and the offshore islands of the continent had been taken over by Japanese forces based upon secret, strategically important information provided by the Fuji-san.

But each time Toyokuni employed the services of the volcano demons there was a price to pay, obligations that in the past had been paid by the war cabinet and the Japanese nation. Agreements had been inscribed in duplicate on thin sheets of stone, ostensibly so that the Fuji-san could keep their copies in the hellishly hot regions they inhabited.

Kanji Toyokuni knew some but not all the details of their mystical lives. It seemed that the Fuji-san had a taste for human eyeballs, because of their aphrodisiac effect on the nervous systems of the demons. Curiously, the eyeballs only tasted acceptable to the discriminating palates of the demons when extracted from humans who'd died from natural causes. Death by other means caused various chemicals in the bloodstream to taint the flavor and power of the organs.

Because of this need for naturally discarded eyes, the Fuji-san had no incentive to kill humans at will. As a result, a more convoluted approach was required to obtain the organs, and this involved the cooperation of human medical personnel to salvage and refrigerate these special body parts. Eyes chilled to temperatures between thirty-six and thirty-eight degrees Fahrenheit were preferred, for in this range they retained a firmness that enabled them to be swallowed whole with great delight, like grapes. Or so said the demons.

One member of Tojo's cabinet had resigned to protest the connection the Japanese military seemed to have established with creatures of the underworld. "Monsters without human values or concerns," the man had called them during a meeting with Toyokuni.

But the public announcement concerning this cabinet member's resignation put forth other reasons for his withdrawal, false ones that Kanji didn't need to recall in detail.

He rested his elbows on the gleaming surface of the inlaid wood desk and buried his face in his hands. Under the present circumstance, payment for demonic favors was a personal issue. His request involved the welfare of his son and not of the nation as a whole. The possible consequences worried him.

After a long pause he said in a trembling voice that betrayed fear and despair, "Fuji-san, come forth!"

And then he uttered the most ancient and secret of words, a word that had never been committed to paper in any language.

With his hands still covering his face, Kanji Toyokuni spread the fingers a little and peered out. He saw the Ming vase shake, as if from a slight earth tremor, and the container took on a soft red glow, highlighting the ancient cracks in its glaze. The vase tipped over on the table, but gently and in slow motion, as if it were a precious rare egg in the grasp of an unseen person. It did not roll from the table, but rocked softly instead, its mouth facing the man at the desk.

The interior of the vase glowed with a soft redness, and as on previous occasions grew steadily brighter until it bore within it a miniature and primitive violence: a tiny image of the Fujiyama volcano turned on end and about to spew its boiling contents toward the foolish, fragile human.

Fighting fear, Kanji peered deep into the redness, and it became the lava of the sacred mountain, but with a translucence like glass that permitted him to see minute shapes moving within it—millions of life forms. An odor of sulfur filled his nostrils.

The vase was full of lava now, and its red-hot, viscous mass began to spill out over the table and onto the carpet. Miraculously, no flames erupted. Suddenly the glow faded and with it went all light in the room, as if some giant creature had inhaled it.

Then slowly, the red light returned to fill the room.

Perspiration ran freely down Toyokuni's brow.

"We knew you would call us," said a voice from the red glow. A shadow-shape revealed itself in the red light of the room, a face in a shroud of burned and blackened skin, with arms like those of an animal, long and hair-covered. Where hands and feet should have been, claws protruded instead. The head of the creature was hawklike, with a long nose and eerie red eyes with bright blue pupils.

The visitor gave off an animal warren stench that was suffused with the odor of sulfur. Toyokuni tried to keep from gagging.

"I am Ichifura," the demon said, in a forceful, raspy voice. "What do you propose?"

Toyokuni had not previously dealt with this particular demon, but had found that each of them brought similar approaches and desires to the negotiating process. With his heart thumping hard, the Japanese gentleman walked across the room and opened the door of a small icebox. Behind him he heard the creature's breathing accelerate. The foul odor intensified.

Toyokuni pulled forth a sealed glass jar from the cold interior of the refrigerator. The jar contained two white-and-brown orbs. He turned and saw the demon trembling in anticipation.

With steady hands, not moving too quickly, Toyokuni

unscrewed the lid and placed the jar on the floor before the demon.

Warily, Ichifura moved close and inserted his long snout into the wide opening of the jar, as if to inhale the scent of a fine red wine. "Aah!" he exclaimed. "Most fresh!"

"One of my gardeners died yesterday," came the matter-of-fact response. "He was many years old. It was time for him to go."

"I see," the Fuji-san said, and with a smile added, "but the gardener does not."

Toyokuni forced a laugh, for it was considered impolite not to show appreciation for a Fuji-san's joke. Impolite and dangerous.

Ichifura inserted his tongue deep in the jar and curled it around one eyeball and then the other. The prizes were snapped back into his mouth and held there while the demon, in obvious ecstasy, rolled his blue-and-red eyes upward. The trembling ceased.

When he'd finished swallowing his obscene hors d'oeuvres, he asked, "What is it you wish from me, Kanji Toyokuni?"

"My son has become enamored of a geisha," Toyokuni replied. "I suspect that she is not what she appears to be."

The bright blue pupils of the demon stared intently. "And who is? Are you?"

Toyokuni ignored the sarcastic philosophizing. "Can you help save my son from her?"

"For the little treat you just gave me?"

"No, of course not. I can obtain more."

The demon shook its head. "No, we are already obtaining a good supply from our own sources."

"What is it I can offer you, then?"

The demon came close to the man and peered intensely into his eyes.

"You want my eyes?" Toyokuni asked anxiously. "After I die naturally?"

"What if I want them now? Would you blind yourself for your son?"

"But I thought . . . "

"You think we only take eyes from the dead?"

"Yes, for the taste and potency."

"What if I were to inform you that there are exceptions?"

For a moment Toyokuni hesitated. Then his loyalty to his only son took over. "In that case you may have my eyes. I'm ready." Another hesitation and a slight trembling. "How will you remove them?"

"I won't. That was only a test, to better understand your motivations. I see that you are willing to sacrifice much. The gift you have given me is enough for the small task you require." The demon paused. "You gaze upon me suspiciously. Do you think I have hidden motives?"

"You are a demon, after all, not a companion of the gods."

The Fuji-san uttered a sound that to Kanji sounded only a little like laughter. "My motive is only to understand and evaluate the person with whom I am bargaining. I am not greedy. And I truly savored the old gardener's eyes!"

"I am pleased," Toyokuni said. "And I trust you."

"Then you are a fool, Mr. Toyokuni. I will confide in you that we also sense something about the geisha. She is a most unusual creature, a type we have not previously encountered. We are curious to discover more about her and will help you." He took on a bemused expression. "Does this address your concerns?"

"Yes, but one question, please. What did you mean by your comment that she is unusual? In what respect?"

"That is what we intend to find out," said the Fuji-san, and he bowed slightly.

Toyokuni returned the courtesy.

28

"I must leave soon," Desidra whispered in Mitsuo's ear. "I'll return in a few days."

He murmured something in response, and she realized he was not fully awake.

They lay on a large, soft futon covered with blankets woven into patterns of flowers and beasts. Desidra's naked body pressed against her lover's, and she held him in a tight embrace, as if he were a child who needed to be shielded from the world.

She wondered if this was the bed Mitsuo had shared with his wife, but didn't ask him and didn't pry into his thoughts. He was almost hers now, and it wouldn't be wise to revive his painful memories and cause him to slip into the oblivion he'd just escaped.

Through a nearby window she saw the golden light of dawn tinting distant foothills and Mount Fujiyama. She reviewed her knowledge of the perfectly shaped snow-covered peak. Crustal movements of the earth had formed volcanic chains throughout Japan, and Mount Fujiyama was the most magnificent, it was said, a volcano more than twelve thousand feet high with a deep crater over two miles across. She'd learned from her studies that pilgrims from all over Japan's empire made annual visits to the shrines and temples that dotted the sides of this sacred mountain.

There was so much beauty in this country, not only in the landscape, but in the sense of harmony in the architecture and in the daily living habits of the people. So much of Japanese life evolved around nature—a reverence for it that was enmeshed in their religion, literature, art, and music.

It seemed odd to Desidra that the warlike samurai tradition had evolved in such a serene environment, until she realized that there was perfection and symmetry in the military training of the warrior class, as well as in nature. Samurai tradition had evolved in order to protect an extraordinarily beautiful and serene homeland.

The countryside almost made her forget the war, but not completely.

She disengaged herself from Mitsuo.

His breathing changed. "What did you say?" he asked, finally roused from sleep though his eyes were still closed. "I heard your words. Something about leaving?"

"I've work to do." She kissed his lips softly, only a feather touch. Their lovemaking had been intense, but of the human variety, and Desidra had been sorely tempted to throw caution to the winds and offer him something more: the Dark Kiss.

Should she give him her blood now?

No, she decided. He was improving. His lovemaking had been strong, and now his eyes were bright and filled with life, although he still could not walk.

"You don't need to work," he said, nibbling on her ear. His eyelids fluttered but did not open.

"My work is important."

He forced himself fully awake and struggled to sit up.

She helped him get comfortable with his back against the bed pillows.

"Japanese women do not speak in this manner," he said rubbing his eyes. "They do as the man commands."

"I've had enough commands to last me forever," she said, careless in her expression and putting her geisha behavior to one side. He hadn't looked at her since she had told him he was feverish. Should she remain Caucasian or become Japanese again? It was difficult to maintain the geisha image for too many hours.

She was comfortable in her defiance, because she sensed Mitsuo belonged to her more and more with each passing moment.

"You are difficult to control," Mitsuo murmured.

Control! The word brought to her mind the image of Romano. What was he up to at this moment? When would he come for her, as she knew he would?

Sooner or later, he'd arrive full of fiery anger. It would be sooner, she thought, because he knew she was growing stronger. Earlier, during a private walk in the woods near the Toyokuni estate, Desidra had tested her magic. She could spin and vault and hurl storms of wind with much more ferocity than she'd been able to accomplish under Romano's tutelage. In retrospect it seemed to her that he had restrained something in her, undoubtedly for his own protection, and now it was unleashed. It was progressing stage by stage, and one day her powers would equal or exceed his. She was certain of this.

But did she have enough time to prepare for him?

She nuzzled her lover. "I have responsibilities."

Mitsuo opened his eyes but didn't look at her. "The accomplishments of a woman are meant for home and family."

"And most of all for her man?" Desidra asked.

"Maybe."

"You think you are my man because we made love?"

"Yes, I think so."

He slipped back down in the bed and rolled over on his stomach. She saw the great scars of war emblazoned on his legs and back like unwanted medals, and she touched them lightly. He winced.

"I've been paid by your father," she said. "He purchased me for a price. Therefore, I am yours for a set time and an amount of money. Doesn't that change your mind?"

"No, Akiko. You're unlike any geisha I've ever met." He turned over until he faced her, and at that moment a bright finger of sunlight streaked its way across her hair. Mitsuo squinted to look at her.

"I think I still have a fever," he said. He ran his fingers through her red hair and studied the features of her face, the upturned nose, the large dark eyes. "You don't look Japanese."

"It's a woman's prerogative to change," she answered, and pressed her mouth against his. "One day we can be closer, with greater understanding. But not yet."

He frowned. "You're not Japanese, are you?"

"You must trust me, Mitsuo. There is more to me than you suppose. Would you like to be with me forever?"

"I'm confused."

"I know," she answered.

"One thing I know for certain. I can afford to keep you here with me, if you wish. I'm a very rich man."

He pulled the silken covers off his body. He was muscular and hairless. She found herself drawn by instincts long forgotten, by his smooth skin and quiet ways. This was different from the Hunger, the need for blood. This feeling was almost human.

"Forever?" he said. "Don't tease me."

"I'm not."

She'd used the word "forever" as mortal lovers sometimes did, and he had not taken her literally. If he only knew the truth, that she and Mitsuo could be united for the normal vampire life span of two or three thousand years! But not yet. He wasn't ready for such information.

Forever . . . eternity. Her mind whirled. Did so-called good mortals really live longer than vampires, in a heavenly life ever after? Were vampires condemned to burn in hell's fires? Intriguing thoughts, she decided, but could not be proved one way or another.

Mortals and their religious beliefs were so often linked to a fear of dying. If not for the inevitability of death in mortals, there might be no organized religion, since there would be no clergymen to encourage mortal terrors.

And if religious beliefs were true? If there was indeed a God? If so, she was damned forever!

Still, a couple of thousand years on earth with Mitsuo would be long enough to get to know one another. Without Mitsuo, her feelings would be entirely different. Without him the duration of a vampire's existence was a curse of loneliness.

She climbed out of bed and dressed slowly and seductively before him, letting him admire the movements of her body. When she finished dressing, she leaned over the bed and kissed him again.

"I'll miss you," he said, and ran his fingers through her long red hair. "I want to be wrapped in this again."

"And you shall be."

"Forever," he said.

She smiled, and with that she turned her back and walked toward the door, altering her image as she entered the hallway and hurried down the stairs. Once more she was the Japanese geisha, Akiko.

Desidra located a side door she'd noticed earlier and slipped through it into a mist that partially obscured her view of the gardens and outbuildings.

The temperature outside seemed uncommonly warm this early evening. As she walked through the light fog that covered the ground, she sniffed the air, trying to establish a sense of direction. An unsettled feeling came over her and then, inexplicably, fear bordering on terror. She wanted to bolt and fly away. Why?

Just ahead of her a patch of mist lifted, and Desidra found herself in a clearing. Two figures stepped forward from the mist, hideous hair-covered creatures with long noses and claws on the ends of their arms and feet. Bright blue pupils blazed in the midst of red eyes.

Desidra became a whirling cyclone and struck the creatures with quick strokes. They cried out and fell back, but four replacements emerged. Again Desidra became a cyclone, this time with fangs extended.

Once more she attacked, and this time three fell back, but the fourth remained and rose into the sky over Desidra. Before she could react, the creature descended and struck the top of her head with a tremendous blow, knocking her to the ground.

Surprised at the quickness and strength of her assailant, Desidra somersaulted away. When she looked back, she couldn't see the beast, and the mist closed in around her again.

She ascended, and as she drew even with the upper

branches of a tall pine tree, the mist began to thin.
Suddenly the tree trembled and hundreds of creatures
appeared within its foliage, shadowy shapes matching
those of her attackers, all with bright blue-red eyes.

This is not an illusion, she thought, *but a new kind of magic. I
must learn what it is, quickly. No time to waste.*

The tree broke apart, and the creatures swarmed about
her like obscene insects. At a frenzied pace they constructed
a cocoon that enveloped her. Absolute darkness closed
in, and her vision dimmed. She was buffeted about and
spun end over end. Assuming a survival mode, Desidra
whirled faster until she was a blur of speed, and out of
that spinning mass she suddenly burst out and up. But
instead of finding herself in clear sky and freedom, her
body rebounded against something pliant and strong.
The barrier held her and she sprung back, only to
encounter another malleable, impenetrable surface
beneath her. Back and forth she was buffeted from top to
bottom and side to side, as if she were in a rubber room.

I need to think!

With great effort she became motionless.

Stygian blackness enveloped her, and she felt as if she
was enclosed in the darkest, most distant place in the uni-
verse, far from any sun. But it was not cold here. She was
warm and getting more so, unabated by her internal
metabolic cooling mechanisms.

She touched one of her fangs with a fingertip, let it
draw blood. The dark redness ran freely. The heat seemed
to be weakening her. A faint, irritating buzzing filled her
ears and grew steadily louder.

She became conscious of a faint red glow all around
her, and the buzzing changed to a disconcerting, crackling
noise, as from a fire. She fought panic.

It was becoming too warm for this season.

In the blackness before her an oval shape began to
appear, and then beside it appeared a second of like size
and form. The ovals floated and shifted position and grew
brighter, taking in all of the redness and concentrating it
within, so that they were glowing orbs set in total darkness.

Two red vampire eyes staring at her from the pit of space.

Her own eyes, with flames burning inside them.

Hot, too hot.

No matter which direction she turned the flaming red eyes stared back at her.

Glancing around she realized that wherever her reflection had been it remained—imprinted there. Now there were red eyes everywhere, filling every square inch of available space. They examined her, gazed deep into her naked soul, cognizant of everything. She hissed and was about to hurl herself into the nearest surface when the eyes metamorphosed. Within their vampire redness appeared bright blue pupils, and she realized the eyes did not belong to her after all, nor to any of her kind.

These were alien life forms that appeared to function as a single organism, with shape-shifting powers. Unseen claws gripped her, and she felt herself rising in the midst of the organism, carried high into the sky. Despite every effort she could not free herself.

"Who are you?" she screamed, and her voice echoed through the darkness, repeating her own question.

No answer came.

The steely claws carried her for a distance laterally, and then whatever held her prisoner made a steep descent and deposited her in a dark, warm place. She could feel a hard, rocky surface, but even with her enhanced vampire sight could see nothing.

"You will remain here," a raspy voice commanded.

She heard a rapid fluttering of wings, which soon faded.

The surface beneath her rumbled continuously.

Her strength began to drain away, and something forced her backward onto a rough bed of rocks.

29

Christopher had always relied upon his parents to make decisions for him, and on the day that he became one of the Kindred, his sire had assumed that responsibility. Now for the first time in his life he felt as though he'd accomplished something of value: the creation of a private army of vampires. The force amounted to fifteen members, counting himself.

He wasn't used to being in a position of authority, with subordinates looking up to him, seeking his advice and instruction. Still, everything was going well, and he enjoyed this new role.

Whenever Romano came to punish him and Desidra, Christopher hoped his newly created army would effectively defend them against the sire's great powers. Sixteen soldiers actually, including Desidra. Romano wouldn't expect to face such resistance and would probably come alone. The old vampire's ego was as great as his strength, and he would assume that his two runaways would surrender immediately.

It was midday, early in November 1943, when the long, dark winter of the north was beginning its reign.

Christopher stopped at Desidra's apartment. She wasn't there, not in the steamer trunk, or anywhere else in the building. As he walked along the dark hallways, he heard a woman ranting inside her apartment. He stopped, placed his ear to the wall and listened. The sounds were clear now, but still gibberish. He picked up no scent other than that of a female mortal.

The human was shouting to herself, "Out, demon! Out, fanged woman!"

A religious fanatic, Christopher decided. In the past, he'd encountered others like her on the streets of Seattle, men and women dressed in sheets, pacing back and forth in the middle of the city, screaming sermons at no one in particular.

He began walking again.

Wait a moment, he thought. "Out, *demon*? Out, *fanged woman*?" He returned to the hallway outside the apartment and listened to the raving as it continued. A faint vampire trail was now discernible where he hadn't noticed it previously, a scent that may have been overcome by the more pungent odor of the mortal. Desidra had been here recently.

He knocked on the door.

After a few moments the door opened a crack, and he saw a frightened face peering out, a fat human face with a lipstick-smeared mouth and small eyes that blazed hidden fury. Behind the female lay darkness.

"Demons are loose in this complex!" the woman screamed. "Call the police!" She muttered nearly incomprehensible prayers, sobbed and wailed and clasped her hands together in supplication.

"Did someone harm you?" Christopher inquired in the most polite of tones.

"Are you the military police?" she asked.

"Not exactly."

"Then get the hell away from me."

Christopher let out a false breath, and as he did so it occurred to him that he was trying to behave like a human and the woman was not. "I'm offering to help you," he said.

She snuffled. "There was a demon in here, a red-haired woman with fangs. After she left, all the lights in my apartment went out, and I don't have any bulbs to replace them."

"Can you describe her?" He didn't bother to read her pathetic little mind. It must have been Desidra playing tricks.

"I just told you what she looked like, you idiot."

Christopher eased closer to the woman. On impulse he made his eyes blaze red and bared his long, razor-sharp canine teeth. "Did she look anything like me?"

The woman screamed again and slammed the door in his face.

"She's my sister!" Christopher called after her.

He left the building, filled with good cheer.

Desidra was not in the Signal Center, nor had she appeared at the small house Christopher shared with three other soldiers who worked for the Alaska Communication System, usually referred to as the ACS.

Privately he gave thanks to the army officials who had made the decision to move some ACS soldiers out of overcrowded barracks and into empty houses in Anchorage. The move was greatly to Christopher's advantage. His room in Anchorage was an ideal vampire hide-out, a center room with no windows, only a fan for ventilation, and an antique commode in a corner. Whoever had built the place had a strange sense of design, or perhaps it had been constructed by a person wanting privacy from the outside world, as he did.

Where was Desidra?

He flew to Mount McKinley, the magnificent pinnacle of which was poking through clouds in a steel gray sky. He remembered dancing with her here, and now, to refresh himself, he let the snow at the crown of the mountain sift over and around him like a blanket.

Then he dropped with fluid movement to a lower elevation. The mountainside was white with fresh snowfall. Some of the gray-black rocks still showed through, but before long they would be covered by the frosty blanket of winter. An icy breeze blew across his face, which he believed he would have enjoyed more had he found Desidra.

But she was not to be found.

He returned to his army post and located Lance, who was working alone in the mess hall, sweeping it with a push broom.

"I think Desidra's in trouble," Christopher said.

"She might have gone back to Washington," Lance suggested. "You told me she was impulsive." He stopped sweeping and put an arm around Christopher. "She knows what she's doing, wherever she is."

"I don't think she'd go to Seattle. Not since her banishment. Romano almost killed her for defying him. She couldn't risk another attack like that one."

Lance leaned on the broom handle. "You care about her too much."

"She's my friend, Lance. She would defend me the same as I'd do for her . . . or you. As a fledgling vampire you don't understand the depth of Kindred relationships. Desidra and I still care for Romano, too, despite loathing his behavior."

An extended silence came between them. At long last Christopher's countenance darkened, and he said, "I think she's gone back to her Japanese lover, and my senses tell me she's in trouble."

"If she's attracted to a mortal, why should we get involved?" Lance asked.

"You weren't listening," Christopher said. "I just told you I care about her."

Lance resumed his sweeping.

Christopher's thoughts held conflicting emotions. He wanted to leave immediately and follow Desidra's trail across the Pacific Ocean. "I'm a vampire," he said to Lance, "with all the power and responsibility that entails. I must be judicious, and this is what I intend to do. I'll do a little reconnoitering in Japan, looking for her."

"With your army?"

"Alone."

"You think she's in trouble, and you want to go there by yourself? That's crazy! We have a whole contingent of vampires to help you."

"They need more training."

"But they have some powers . . . far more than mortals . . . and this is an emergency."

"We don't know the situation yet. Maybe my senses are wrong, and I'd feel pretty damn silly barging in on her with a small army of vampires only to discover she's in bed with the mortal. An embarrassment like that could undermine my authority with everyone I've sired. Besides, neither you nor the others are prepared for the challenges of being a predator yet. You'll learn, but it takes time to develop the taste. Much pain and ecstasy is involved, which can only be learned through experience."

Lance swept under a table.

"While I'm gone I want you to take our 'recruits' on a Blood-hunt," Christopher said. "Let them discover what it's like to be the most intelligent predator in the world." He grinned.

Lance nodded. "All right. Take care of yourself."

"I shall."

Christopher became a mist that lifted through the ceiling and roof of the mess hall. He flew low over the Pacific Ocean to miss the storm clouds that had massed at higher altitudes. He didn't want to tarry, playing like a child in a mud puddle. But, oh, how he loved storms! Thunder rumbled above him like giants treading the skies.

He picked up Desidra's faint vampire scent and followed it to the Kuril Islands, then south toward Tokyo, the capital and largest city of Japan. Momentarily, he lost her scent and circled until he picked it up again.

Christopher approached one of the six large islands that constituted the middle part of three great arcs that formed the archipelago of Japan, then flew low over a volcanic mountain range that rose like a row of giant cones into the heavens. Near the province of Suruga he stopped and descended to the ground. The scent was weak, but it came from this general area.

Ahead of him, Mount Fujiyama rose majestically into the clouds. Desidra was somewhere in this vicinity. He was certain of it.

As he neared the sacred mountain, he was almost overwhelmed by a powerful odor . . . no, a loathsome stench. It wasn't human, which was usually bearable and sometimes quite delightful. So good, in fact, that he'd occasionally released his prey rather than bleeding it to death.

"I have standards," he murmured to himself.

Was Desidra with her lover? He sensed otherwise. She'd never associate voluntarily with anyone bearing that fetid odor.

At the base of Fujiyama he assumed the shape of an elderly Asian man, and in that guise hobbled along with pilgrims walking on a dirt road toward the mountain. They were mostly children and mothers and elderly men, all destined for the small Buddhist and Shinto temples built on the sides of the mountain. He listened to their reverent conversations and understood most of what they said, thanks to Desidra's help with the Japanese language during their idle hours.

A pool of silver water lay ahead, surrounded by bare cherry trees and dwarf pines. Stepping stones in the shapes of flowers protruded inches above the quiet waters. He followed the pilgrims over the water to the temple, as they moved from stone to stone with great care.

Just ahead a mother struggled to keep two young boys near her. The younger child, who appeared to be three or four years of age, held back, whimpering and protesting.

"Shhh," his mother said. "You will disturb the Fuji-san demons."

"What are Fuji-san?" the boy asked, wiping his eyes.

"Guardians of the mountain. If a child misbehaves, the demons come and carry him away. If a child lies, they come and rip his tongue out. If he refuses to go to the shrine, who knows what they will do?"

The child grew suddenly quiet, and without further complaint he followed his mother and brother.

Fuji-san demons? Christopher wondered what sort of creatures they were. He thought he'd seen a demon once, but it had turned out to be no more than an extremely old vampire, gnarled, sharp-toothed, and ugly. The beast within the Elder had corrupted his once beautiful features until he looked alien and monstrous.

I *don't believe in demons*, he thought.

But the thought didn't feel right. In fact, it felt terribly wrong. Something in his gut told him this. It told him something else, too.

There was no time to waste.

At the first opportunity he became invisible and leaped to the edge of the mountain's crater. He descended rapidly into its core. The heat was unbearable and the fetid stench overpowering—a curious combination of odors that included the smell of sulfur from the volcano, the faint odor of Desidra, and something else: a foul, stinking life form.

Fear bordering on terror rose within Christopher.

He flew close to the smoldering heart of the volcano, and the heat threatened to devour him. This was the most ancient of fears for human or vampire: fire.

He didn't see how Desidra could be alive here, and yet he still detected her faint but active scent. If she was dead, it had occurred recently—within moments, perhaps.

Am I next?

Hovering in the thick, uncomfortably hot air, he watched the fire below him, a hypnotic creature that begged him to leap into its center and do a death dance with it. It lulled him into a euphoric state, while every survival instinct screamed warnings.

Out of the flames a huge creature took shape and emerged. It rose toward him, its cavernous mouth screaming soundlessly. A long-nosed, clawed beast with spikes of fire spitting across its surface, it flew up at him rapidly, trailing blue and orange flames and molten teardrops of hot lava. Behind it Christopher saw three similar but much smaller beasts.

An odor from the bowels of this hell enveloped him in a thick, caustic cloud, and the hideous creatures were almost upon him.

He made a decision.

If there were more of these monsters hiding in the belly of the mountain, he could never rescue Desidra by himself. It was better to retreat this time and return with a contingent of vampire-soldiers. He must go and prepare for the battle he knew was inevitable.

He was certain Desidra was alive. All of his vampire senses told him so.

Just before the largest creature reached him, Christopher streaked upward and away. Behind him the keepers of the sacred mountain screeched a cacophony of alien sounds.

As Christopher lifted from the fiery mountain crater into the cool air, he suddenly felt a terrible pain in one leg and saw that one of the smaller demons had seized his ankle with fiery fingers.

Christopher kicked and whirled and tried to tear himself loose, but the creature had a death grip on him. The skin of his ankle was hot, and he saw the creature reaching out with his other clawed hand, trying to grab hold of Christopher's other leg.

Employing a maneuver that Christopher had never tried before, he spun and turned and whipped one way and another, so that the demon was unable to grab hold with the other claw, Christopher went into the most powerful spin he could muster, one that exceeded the speed of many great storms.

Suddenly, without warning, he came to a total stop, looked straight into the eyes of the startled demon, and with his free leg gave it a ferocious kick.

The fiend tumbled away, screaming furiously.

Before it could stabilize itself Christopher rose higher in the sky and climbed into the storm clouds for protection.

There, in the wind and rain, surrounded by the crackling sounds of thunder, he saw that he had suffered a severe burn and had lost some flesh on his left ankle. The foot of his right leg, the foot that had struck the demon, was also scorched and blistered.

30

Christopher crossed the Pacific in less time than he'd anticipated, looking behind all the while, until he reached the post near Anchorage. The sky was silver-gray, the overcast of late afternoon. A light coat of snow covered the earth, and there were significantly fewer birds around than there had been only a few weeks before.

Signs of the approaching hard winter.

He ducked inside his house. In the bathroom he tied a bandage around his leg. The wound would take a full day to heal, and he had to conceal it. He sat on his cot and thought about his duty as an American soldier and his more paramount obligations to fellow vampires, Desidra and Lance.

Well, I asked for it, he reminded himself. *I've cut myself off from Romano, thinking I could master my own fate. Time will tell if I'm right or wrong.*

Somewhere inside Mount Fujiyama, a safe distance from the lava, Desidra was trapped by fire monsters. He could only guess how many demons were residing in the catacombs of the mountain. A terrifying thought occurred to him: was Romano responsible?

No matter the number of demons, or who was behind them, Christopher was going after his friend. First he'd assemble his small contingent and explain the situation to them. Some training would be necessary to hone their newly acquired vampire skills. It shouldn't be too difficult. They were already soldiers, after all. His attack force would need shields, something to protect them from the fire and extreme heat, which could be fatal or debilitating. Invisibility or bird shapes would not work. What would Romano do in this situation?

Blast Romano, forget about him. You're on your own.

What Christopher had faced in the heart of the mountain was no ordinary blaze. He remembered the immense flame creature and its entourage of smaller clones. How could they exist? He suspected the work of magic and illusion, but the burns on his skin suggested otherwise. How could he overcome such power?

The fire at the heart of Fujiyama was reality, and he needed to take measures to protect his army from that. On further reflection he hadn't been able to come up with any sort of shield against the lava and flames, nothing that wouldn't drastically inhibit maneuverability.

We must keep the demons from dragging us in, he thought.

Abruptly, the beginnings of a solution came to him.

If demons could create illusions, so could he. The Fuji-san were attuned to fire, while he and his Kindred were the children of cold winds and snow and ice and darkness.

Why not fight fire with ice and snow and anything else that would defuse or destroy the demons? It sounded logical. Cold against hot. Natural enemies.

Christopher found Lance, who stood outside his barracks gazing up at the sky as it darkened. Lance was like a small child full of wonder, seeing things for the first time, through newborn vampire eyes.

"I thought you were gone forever," Lance said. He threw his arms around Christopher.

"I thought so, too." He showed Lance the burns on his ankle and foot.

"You've been injured!"

"Vampires heal rapidly, as you've yet to discover. My

leg is no problem; what I need are some ideas." He related what had happened at Mount Fujiyama, while Lance listened raptly.

"We need a diversionary tactic," Lance said presently, "one that will keep them away long enough for us to locate Desidra."

"Any ideas on how to do that? You have more experience as a soldier than I do."

"Give me a little time."

"My senses tell me she's still alive," Christopher said, "that she's holding out against their magic but weakening. I don't think we have much time to rescue her."

"This reminds me of the movies," Lance said uncertainly. "The kind of story where we're outnumbered fifty to one and still win."

"Forget that garbage. What do actors with fake medals and staged bravado know about real war?"

Lance looked up at the sky, then said, "I think I know what we could use as a diversion. You go down and coax the largest demon out, and he'll chase you like he did the first time. He sounds like an alpha dog, very territorial. While he's occupied with you, I'll lead the rest of our group against the smaller demons."

"Sounds good," Christopher said.

"I just thought of something else," Lance said, scuffling his feet on the hard, rocky ground. "What if the big one is only the leader of their guards? What if there's a bigger one inside the mountain, the holy-shit-get-me-out-of-here mother of all demons?"

"We can't let our fears work on us," Christopher said.

They polished up details of Lance's diversionary plan and envisioned an attack in which their small Kindred army swarmed into the volcano and drew the demons out, to do battle beyond the flames.

"It sounds dangerous, though," Lance said after a long while.

"Look at it this way," his companion responded. "According to modern science, we're already dead."

"A valid point."

"Get the men together," Christopher said.

* * *

He instructed them in the vampire manner of combat, making them perform maneuvers and exercises until he was satisfied that they understood. They learned quickly, and demonstrated impressive fighting skills. Their predator instincts served them well.

Within days they were ready for action. "We start out as birds," Christopher said at departure. Just before battle we change shape again. Watch for my signal."

The vampire army left Anchorage and took the same route Christopher had followed earlier. They looked like a flock of wild birds, off their usual track and buffeted by cold winds, but persevering. Below them, deep in the Pacific Ocean, Christopher could see Japanese submarines cruising like sharks searching for prey. They hadn't given up, despite the huge losses of the once invincible Imperial Japanese Navy.

Christopher sighed in the breathless way of a vampire and turned his attention to the task ahead. His odds seemed slim for a battle against a largely unknown and unquantified enemy, and he realized he'd be lucky to locate Desidra, much less rescue her.

Nevertheless, he intended to find a way.

During the battle at the mountain he'd glimpsed activity not far from the crater rim. The pace of combat with the demons had been so furious that he'd thought nothing of it at the time and hadn't considered it since. Until now. He recalled a number of the smaller demons gathered around what looked like a dark opening in the crater wall. In a protective formation? Yes, he thought so, and he thought he knew what they were guarding.

Desidra!

It all made sense, because if she was still alive she had to be kept away from the molten fires. The rush of blood increased in his veins.

When the mountain came into sight Christopher signaled to the others, and immediately their bird-shapes transmuted to grotesque, frightening forms. Christopher was silver ice and crystal snow with water gushing from his pores. He was an all-powerful water god with giant wings. The others who followed him were similarly disguised, but in different colors. Magenta ice and purple snow and bright blood ice . . . and the black snow of death.

Christopher led the way as they flew over the rim of the crater.

The large fire-beast who'd pursued him previously rose from the flames to meet him. No sign of the smaller clones.

Christopher spread his wings to increase his size and chanted a mantra, words without meaning to anyone but a vampire.

The demon hesitated for a moment, then burst upward toward Christopher. In surprisingly perfect English it shouted, "You shall not enter! I warn you, this is sacred territory!"

"Sorry, I can't hear you," Christopher answered.

And up the two of them went, screaming through the sky like dogfighting war planes, zigging and zagging, each seeking an advantage over the other. Finally, when Christopher was certain he had the demon out of its usual range, he led it in a loop that ended slightly below the rim of the crater. Making an unexpected move, Christopher hovered at the entrance to a small cave in the mountain's inner wall. It was the same place he'd seen before. There were no guards here now, and he detected Desidra's scent, but only weakly.

He was close enough to see that she was not inside.

The largest demon was closing in on Christopher, but cautiously, flying in a weaving pattern.

In the sky over Fujiyama, the Crimson Corps of vampires did battle with smaller demons, an activity that would keep the fire-monsters preoccupied. But what could he do about the granddaddy big one? And what if an even larger beast lay in waiting, hiding in the fiery lava of the mountain? He was forced to admit to himself that he had encouraged Lance and the others to follow him the way it was played out in the movies.

They were literally "flying by the seats of their pants."

He could feel the hot breath of the demon behind him,

curling around his neck and back, threatening to burn him into charcoal. But the creature kept its distance, not completely certain of the composition and powers of this strange water animal who had invaded its territory.

Christopher lunged at the demon, showering it with ice crystals that splattered and fizzled and popped against the demon's fiery body.

The creature retreated and watched from a distance.

Christopher agonized. Sooner or later it would make a move against him. Illusions could only be held for limited periods of time. Then something would flicker and change and the enemy would see through the deception.

Christopher continued his search, down the sides of the crater in concentric circles. The demon followed, still wary of this odd-looking being.

There was a darker shadow on the crater wall, a deeper blackness. *Another cave?* Christopher wondered. The scent of Desidra was strong here. He got close enough to see a narrow opening that led to darkness beyond. Suddenly a wall of fire burst up in the entrance, blocking it. Christopher shouted through the flames. "Desidra! Are you in there?"

"Christopher! Stay away or you'll be destroyed!" Her voice sounded weak.

He answered immediately in an ancient Kindred tongue, using words he hoped the demon would not understand: "I'm coming in!"

"No!" she implored him, in the same language.

"The fire that holds you is an illusion," Christopher said. "Its magic keeps you contained."

"That's not right. When I touch it, I'm burned."

"You've been weakened by magic," Christopher answered, unable to see her. "Let's try a little combined power . . . you and me on each side of the flames."

Hesitation. Then: "Okay. I'm ready."

Together they concentrated on the flames, attempting to will them away, calling reassuring messages to one another and remembering the lessons of magic that Romano had imparted to Christopher, and which he in turn had passed on to Desidra.

The would-be rescuer could almost feel the demon's

spittle upon him, splattering his backside with fire. He turned and saw the creature working its way closer, carefully and slowly.

At any moment it would attack.

Suddenly the flames blocking Desidra's escape began to recede until only a flickering rim of fire remained. Christopher stepped over it and entered the small cavern.

"Let's get out of here!" he shouted and they flew upward, the large demon directly behind them, clawing and spewing fire and shouting warnings in English.

"It doesn't understand our ancient language," said Christopher. "Stick with that and we'll outwit it."

Without warning, Desidra broke away from Christopher, turned, and flew straight into the face of the fire-monster. Before Christopher could react, she disappeared into the flames that composed its body.

He recoiled with shock. What had she done? Gone to her death?

The immense demon turned white-hot, and Christopher shielded his eyes against the light and the intense heat. When he opened them again, the demon looked different. Red flames surrounded its white-hot core, replacing the long-nosed face of the demon that now laughed at him, showing him his own fate.

And Desidra was gone forever.

As would be his own fate in about ten more seconds, thought Christopher.

Then the flames changed, and an icy wind struck Christopher, knocking him backward. He tumbled in the air. When he straightened himself he saw a familiar shape emerge from the demon.

Desidra!

Behind her the demon was no more than a skeleton of fire, dying and withering away. Turning, Desidra blew on it and it was extinguished.

Gone, entirely, except for wisps of smoke.

"How'd you do that?" Christopher cried.

"If you can wear an illusion, why not the demon? He was all show, a display to frighten off trespassers."

In midair Desidra hugged Christopher, and together

they surged upward. Above them the other vampires, Christopher's fledgling army, still circled, fighting the smaller demons. As the demons spewed fire, the vampires extinguished them with ice and water and snow bursts, striking them with their combined power.

Exactly as Christopher had instructed them.

But from below, out of the maw of the volcano, came more of the ugly small creatures, screaming toward them.

And something else, a shimmering, translucent shape encompassing the demons, forming them into one hideous creature.

"Up!" shouted Desidra through the smoke and fire. "As high as we can go!" She pointed to a great, black cloud hanging directly over the mountain.

Christopher motioned to Lance and the other vampires. They formed a triangle and flew in formation toward the refuge of the cloud. As they entered it, they welcomed its ice-breath with sighs of relief.

The remaining demons pursued them and made an attempt to enter the cloud, but it released a ferocious downpour of ice crystals. Sizzling and smoking, the Fujisan demons fell to earth, where their powers were further diminished by the snow that covered the ground.

Christopher watched them struggle and disappear, no more than evaporating wisps of smoke. An irregular shape of glimmering light rose from the snow into the air and, undulating, slithered over the rim of the volcano and disappeared down into it.

"Are you all right?" Christopher asked Desidra.

"Yes. Are you?"

"Do you think they're gone for good?"

"No, only for the moment. They're weakened but undoubtedly have restorative powers."

"What was that irregular shape?" Desidra asked. "The thing that looked like a triangle of light sliding into the mountain's crater?"

Her companion shrugged. "I don't know, but whatever it was, we didn't kill it."

"I worried it might be Romano."

"I don't think he'd come here," said Christopher. He

wondered whether it was a primitive life form that had existed for centuries and was disturbed by the battle. Or perhaps it was an ancestor of the demons.

"What did they say to you when you were held prisoner?" Christopher asked Desidra.

"That Kanji Toyokuni, Mitsuo's father, commanded them to entrap me, because he believes I pose a threat to his son. Kanji has a strong connection with the Fuji-san."

"Before we fly back to Anchorage, let's find a resting place," Christopher said.

She agreed and they flew to an area near the Toyokuni estate, a valley between two hills, where they curled up near each other within a crevice formed by two rocks.

The rest of the Crimson Corps, fatigued from the rigors of battle, tore foliage from the native plants and covered their bodies to protect themselves from the sun and any curious mortals that might pass this way.

Before nightfall Desidra and Christopher rose and sat on a small hillside. Below them a river rushed and gushed over rocks and gravel, making water music as it traveled. Sleeping flowers dripped dew, and feathered fans of golden bamboo hung in plumelike fronds over their heads. In the distance loomed Mount Fujiyama, with the purple of dusk beginning to close around it.

By appearance, all was tranquil.

"I find it difficult to believe what we've just been through," Desidra observed.

"You're here now and you're safe."

"Thanks to you and the others." She frowned. "We ought to go back and finish those freaks off, especially the mysterious triangular one that dived into the volcano."

"I'd rather go on a Blood-hunt," Christopher said with a yawn. "There's no nourishment in volcano-creatures. I'd rather sink my fangs into a human animal!"

Desidra laughed.

"Whatever the creatures are, they're no match for us," Christopher said.

"I wonder how they breed? Can they reproduce in great numbers? Or are they, like vampires, limited by tradition?"

"They may be more like us than you imagine,"

Christopher said. "After all, we got into the war with Japan to protect our territory, didn't we?"

"Yes."

"Well, I think that's what the light creature is doing. It's the watchdog of Mount Fujiyama, and the demons are its illusions."

31

Kanji Toyokuni paced the shiny floors of his house. Had the Fuji-san demons destroyed the geisha? His worries increased like bubbles in a boiling pot. Should he have called upon humans to perform the task—instead of supernatural creatures? No! With the geisha he was dealing with witchery, a treacherous female who had placed his son in a love-trance in order to manipulate him. Kanji Toyokuni had taken the most prudent course, the one most likely to stop her before she did serious harm to his family.

But he didn't trust the demons. They had their own agenda, and frequently it didn't jibe with his own. He wished they were under his command, unquestionably loyal and obedient to his wishes. In Japan, loyalty was a primary human duty. A fighting spirit went with a true and loyal heart. His own ancestors had engaged in continual warfare, dedicated to their lords even if it meant their own deaths. All Toyokunis preceding him had been adventuresome, aggressive males, perpetually prepared for war. The timid and the feeble were never part of the family.

He sometimes wondered if Mitsuo was fit to carry on the family name.

Kanji stopped and gently touched the porcelain figurine of a geisha. So beautiful and expensive. It was hundreds of years old, a family treasure. He smashed it to the floor and continued his incessant pacing.

Finally, tired of his restless thoughts, Kanji sighed and shuffled off to bed. It was late, and he was devoting too much attention to the matter he had left to the demons.

Let them handle it, he thought.

Within the mantle of the earth, a hundred trails of smoke passed through dirt and rock, streaking in the direction of Mount Fujiyama. From all sides, the dark vapors arrived simultaneously, surged up and over the rim of the volcano and down into the fiery molten core. They passed through the red-hot mass, moving without opposition against the direction and power of the lava flow. The smoke trails, each bearing a precious, sentient cargo, went deep into the flaming heart of the planet.

Far beneath the surface they merged into an incandescent, milky cloud, then compressed into a tiny burning point of light that penetrated an oxygen bubble and remained within it for a time, rejuvenating its collective self. Then it expanded, making the bubble larger, and larger still.

The bubble exploded.

Out of the earth, through the portal in the sacred mountain, a hundred Cimmerian stones burst into the sky, touched the clouds, and fell to earth. The rocks began to glow a soft orange. Within their depths something vibrated, Fuji-san remnants communicating with one another but only weakly. All except two flickered and fell into dormancy.

This pair shape-shifted into human forms, but with difficulty, and they walked on shaky legs like old men. At the boundary of the Toyokuni estate, they took on wings that barely carried them over the walls and back down. Moments later, wheezing and sizzling in a rain that had begun to fall, they stood in the bedchamber of a sleeping man, looking down on him.

The sleeper was Kanji Toyokuni, whose call for aid had led to the disastrous defeat of the Fuji-san.

One of the intruders placed his broad lips over the mouth of the sleeper and sucked the air from the lungs of the human.

Kanji Toyokuni awoke and tried to pull away. He made an effort to cry out but could not, for he was unable to free his mouth from the hot suction of the attacker. Another figure held his arms and legs down. In the last vision of his life, Toyokuni saw two ghoulish, glowing faces, and blue-red eyes.

A wheezing voice whispered in his ear, "You sent us on a suicide mission. We were unable to destroy the powerful geisha-creature and her allies. She and her kind are indestructible entities that have caused us much harm. Therefore, we extract payment from you for the damage we have suffered."

Toyokuni shook uncontrollably, and without air to sustain his life, went limp and died.

Unseen by the sleeping household, the Fuji-san quickly burned a chronicle of the events of recent days into the dark wooden stair treads of Toyokuni's house. The pictorial history of the family had a new tale to tell.

Badly weakened and in need of restoration, the Fuji-san demons returned to the womb of the volcano.

From the top of the hill where she and Christopher sat, Desidra looked toward Toyokuni's estate. Despite the heavy rain that beat against their bodies like a rushing river, Desidra could see lights around Mitsuo's home . . . more than usual. "Something's going on down there. I'm going to see what it is."

"You want me to go with you?" Christopher asked.

"No. You've done enough for me." She stood up and moved down the hill a few steps. "There are too many cars in front of the house," she said. "Maybe another military meeting. I'd better find out."

Christopher joined her. "I have worries, too. Sooner or later my army of vampires will be revealed for what they are, and all hell will break loose. Tricks and subterfuge can't fool our fellow soldiers forever. They'll begin to wonder why we never show up for meals, why we all work night shifts, and hate the sun." His face wore a pained expression. "I've been a good soldier, but in the long run it won't count for anything when the U.S. Army discovers the truth about me. I'll be banished from them, as you were by Romano."

Nearby bushes rustled as the Crimson Corps awoke and began to move about.

"I'm going to tell them to hide in rocky clefts along the upper sides of Mount Fujiyama," Christopher said. "If the Fuji-san still occupy the fires inside the mountain, as I suspect they do, why not vampires on the outside in the snow and ice?"

"As an occupation force?" she answered.

"Something like that. It has kind of a symbiotic sound, too."

"So, you'll be staying in Japan?"

"First I'm flying back to Alaska, he said. I have unfinished business there. A few more men to . . ." He paused and smiled, ". . . to recruit. It can't hurt to have more men here. What about you?"

Desidra didn't answer.

His stare was hard. "You're going back to Alaska, aren't you?"

"Stay out of my thoughts, Christopher!"

"Veil them from me, then, as I taught you."

"I shouldn't have to do that," she countered. But she did so anyway, and then said, "My cryptography contract is up this month, but the war isn't. I'm signing up for another year."

Christopher grinned. "What about the great love of your life? The enemy mortal you can't do without. Are you deserting him?"

"No, damn it!" she cried. "My task isn't finished yet! And a year is nothing. He'll wait for me."

"He's not a vampire. A year is a long time by mortal standards. Mitsuo might wander from your influence."

"I'll take that chance." She spread her arms. "Wait for me. I'll be back soon."

Invisible, she flew to the Toyokuni estate and found Mitsuo standing as rigid as a metal rod beside the body of his dead father. Desidra could see the anguish in his eyes and the physical discomfort he must be suffering. Several men, doctors or medical personnel from their appearance, leaned over Kanji Toyokuni's body.

One spoke to the grieving son: "I am deeply sorry for the death of your father. It appears he has suffered a heart attack."

I don't think so, Desidra thought. *The demons exacted their revenge for my escape.*

Desidra stepped closer to Mitsuo. She hoped this special mortal felt her presence, even though he couldn't see or hear her. She sent him her thought: *I'm here and I love you, Mitsuo. I feel your pain.*

Within minutes, Desidra had rejoined Christopher and they were far out over the North Pacific, bound for Alaska.

32

December.

The gray morning air was heavy, an oppressive force sitting on Christopher's head and shoulders, crawling up and down his spine. He stood with thirty-five other soldiers on an icy plateau, waiting. They wore full packs and carried rifles slung over their shoulders.

The vampire's senses were alert. Something strange was happening to the atmosphere. An earthquake about to shatter the ground beneath their feet? A storm blowing in from the sea?

He sniffed the brisk winter air but picked up only the spice-scent of fir trees.

He focused his attention on the men with him. They were restless, scuffing and scraping their feet against the ground, muttering to one another. Anger slid snakelike through the ranks.

Sergeant Miller, the noncommissioned officer in charge of the unit for this particular exercise, said to Christopher, "Where's Herkle? We're supposed to complete a ten-mile march and target practice today, and the men want to get it over with."

At that very moment a jeep came rumbling toward them.

"Captain's coming!" Miller bellowed. "Men, attention!"

The scraggly line of soldiers straightened their spines and sucked in their chests. Their facial expressions appeared as stiff as the rest of their bodies.

Captain Herkle stepped from the jeep and stomped forward over the permanently frozen earth. It crackled under his feet. He was the picture-perfect officer, Christopher thought. An outsider might conclude he was a noble example of the American soldier, but Christopher knew better. The captain reeked of arrogance and mean-spiritedness.

He walked up and down the line of men, scrutinizing them carefully. Pausing in front of a dark-skinned soldier, he punched the man's shoulders, first one and then the other. "What kind of posture you got, boy? Stand up straight!"

The man opened his mouth in protest. "I'm standing as straight as I can, sir."

Herkle snickered. "Then God help the U.S. Army."

The rest of the soldiers stared straight ahead, their gazes seemingly fixed on something in the distance.

Christopher perceived the men as one entity, operating like a piece of equipment, a well-tuned machine of violence. He resisted the urge to invade their thoughts. Sometimes it was more interesting when he didn't.

Herkle continued his examination. He stared at Christopher and snapped, "You some kinda pretty boy, Private Wilson? What kind of first name do you have? Christopher? I'd change it. Sounds feminine to me. Reports say you're a good soldier, but so far I haven't seen diddly from you."

Christopher stared straight ahead, eyes unblinking.

"What do you have to say, pretty boy?"

"Sir?" He looked into the hostile gaze of the captain.

"Aren't you going to argue with me, Private? Are you a fighting man or a wet rag?"

"A fighting man, sir!"

"Do you want to fight *me*, soldier?" Herkle thumped the vampire's chest. "Step out of ranks and take your best punch!"

"I can't do that, sir."

"Are you defying orders?"

"No, Captain. I can't hit an officer. It's against regulations."

"If it weren't against regulations, you'd blast me one?"

"I didn't say that, sir."

"Soldier, your eyes are a little red. Been drinking, pretty boy? Or are you tired?"

"None of that, sir. I'll be all right." Christopher concentrated on controlling his anger. With effort the redness in his eyes would diminish in a few minutes.

"I'm so glad to hear you'll be all right! I wouldn't want any of my men to be uncomfortable!"

I'd like to satisfy my Hunger on this SOB! Christopher thought.

Herkle's mouth curled up in a half smile that resembled a sneer. "Pretty boys make lousy Jap-killers. We'll test you out on this hike, see what you're made of. Sergeant! Load ten more pounds of rocks in this man's pack!"

Reluctantly, Sergeant Miller told a man to break several rocks free from the frozen earth. This was done, and they were crammed into Christopher's already full pack.

Go ahead and test me, Christopher thought. *I have fifty times the strength you'll ever have, you pigeon-chested, self-righteous fool. In less than a second I could bury my fangs in your neck, and a minute later you'd be dead.*

The Hunger was speaking to Christopher, telling him he needed blood. If not the captain, what alternative source of prey was there for him? Maybe he could sneak into the woods after target practice and find a rabbit or a fox.

Anything!

"Weaklings," growled the captain, scanning the unit. "Bunch of marshmallows." He signaled to the sergeant, and said, "We're doin' twelve miles today instead of ten."

A collective groan passed through the ranks.

"For that make it fifteen," Herkle snapped.

Silence followed, except one man coughed.

Sergeant Miller shouted, "Hup, one, two, three," and the men began to march double-file on a road that led into the forest. All of the men wore packs except Herkle, who followed at the wheel of his jeep.

At the midpoint of their trek, one of the newer recruits, a man walking in front of Christopher, stumbled over a tree root and tumbled down an incline into a small ravine. He lay unmoving on the snow.

Christopher removed his backpack and rifle and ran down the incline to assist.

"Get back up here, Wilson!" Herkle bellowed. "Let him get up under his own power. He's not hurt!"

The fallen soldier made an effort to rise, but fell back and groaned.

Ignoring Herkle's orders, Christopher examined the man's leg. A sharp edge of a bone protruded from the flesh.

"Looks like you broke it near the ankle," Christopher said to the fallen man. "I'll get you back up the hill." He slipped off the man's pack and weapon, and hoisting him over his shoulder clambered back up the incline, taking care not to give away his superior strength by moving too easily or too fast. He feigned a grunt, as though the man's weight was too much for him.

Captain Herkle stood by his jeep, his face red with anger. "I'll have you court-martialed for this, Wilson!" he shouted. "You disobeyed a direct order, and no one does that to me! Got that, pretty boy?"

"Yes, sir," Christopher answered in his most respectful tone, as he continued to huff his way up the trail. He laid the soldier on the ground, then went back down for the gear.

"Court martial, Wilson!" Herkle repeated.

"Do what you have to do, Captain!" Christopher shouted as he returned with the gear. "This soldier has a broken leg. He can't put his weight on it."

"You're just a two-bit private, not a medic. That soldier looks fit to me. I think he's gold-bricking." Herkle stepped forward and yanked the injured man to his feet. "Stand at attention!"

Painfully, the soldier rose and propped himself up on one leg, balancing himself against a tree, with the broken leg slightly off the ground.

The captain continued to shout. "Put that other leg

down on the ground where it belongs, soldier." He paused for breath. "Sergeant! Get these men moving."

"Hup one—two—three—," sang the sergeant, and the contingent of soldiers moved forward.

The injured man took a step, cried out, and crumpled to the ground.

The captain climbed back into his jeep and delivered a parting shot: "So maybe he has a little sprain. Okay, he stays here until we get back, whenever that is."

"You can't leave him out here alone," Christopher said, ignoring the sergeant's attempt to silence him. "There are wild animals in this forest, and it gets damn cold at night."

"He has a rifle," the captain answered. "If a bear wanders his way, he can shoot it!" He glared at Christopher and said, "At the rate you're irritating me, Private, you'll be in federal prison for the rest of your life." His jeep rolled forward.

Leaning over the injured soldier, Christopher whispered, "I'll be back to check on you. For now I've got to leave, or he'll have me shot. Keep your back up against that tree so nothing can get you from behind." The vampire rummaged through his own backpack, tossed his daily ration to the man. "If I'm delayed, this should give you some extra energy."

"Thanks, but what'll you eat?"

Christopher grinned. "Don't worry about me, I'll scavenge something." *Food that fits my particular appetite,* he thought.

He ran to catch up with his unit, while Herkle glared at him.

After several miles the road narrowed, becoming a rough trail. The marchers moved into single-file formation.

Herkle left his jeep behind and marched at the front of the unit. He carried no pack and walked rapidly, forcing the tired men to keep up. The trail traversed snow-covered roots and rocks and fallen trees, slowing the marchers.

Something rippled through the assemblage that Christopher's senses couldn't quite define. A mood that was gathering strength, coalescing into an atmosphere of ugliness.

Rage! Christopher realized. He had never encountered so much of it at one time in mortals. It exhilarated him, since human anger so often led to physical conflict and blood.

The trail led upward and the thick woods that had surrounded them grew barren and rocky. The men struggled over boulders until they reached a plateau overlooking the U.S. Army post.

Christopher looked down on the vast wilderness that surrounded the post. He had a sudden urge to descend into the wild forest and run naked with the other predators who lived there. He was nearly overwhelmed by his primitive desires, which were so intense that they threatened to expose him. It was difficult playing mortal.

He pulled himself loose from his instincts.

The captain was speaking to the sergeant. "We'll take another route to the target practice range. Down that side of the hill and around." He pointed.

"What about the man we left behind?" Christopher asked. "We can't leave him there!"

Herkle ignored him.

Christopher's anger began to match that of the men around him. *Stop behaving like a mortal*, he told himself. *Don't sink into the sticky morass of their emotions. Think straight.*

He accompanied the other soldiers down the side of the hill, conscious of ever-increasing tension the men were generating. One man communicated silently with hand signals to another, who in turn did the same to the soldier directly in front of him, and so forth.

Seconds later a man whispered the plan in Christopher's ear.

I *like that*! Christopher thought.

The targets of the shooting range loomed ahead, huge bull's-eyes. At the sergeant's command the soldiers lined up in their appropriate spots. Rifles were cocked and aimed at the targets.

Captain Herkle walked toward the assembled men. "All right you worthless crap-buckets, hit those targets or we hike another fifteen miles."

In unison the rifles came around and clicked as the

bolts brought shells into the chambers. Christopher, like his companions, put the hated countenance of the captain in his rifle sight.

"Fire!" shouted Sergeant Miller.

An explosion of sound ensued, thirty-six rifles firing simultaneously. In the midst of it there was a loud, short scream that the vampire found most satisfying.

And then there was silence.

Quickly the men slung their rifles over their shoulders. Four soldiers wrapped Herkle's body in a tarp. They carried it to the target range and dumped it on the ground, where it continued to bleed, discoloring the pristine snow. The area of the actual shooting was cleaned up.

"What a shame," Sergeant Miller said. "The damn fool wandered into the line of fire."

33

Hidden from view and the bite of a cold December snow-storm, a pair of vampires sat side by side inside a crumbling Buddhist temple.

"You are elusive as always," Christopher said. "I looked all over the army post for you and finally followed your trail here."

"Why have you come?"

"Herkle is dead."

"How?" Desidra asked. "You drained his blood?"

"No. The men were on a firing range and someone . . . no . . . *everyone* shot him. I was one of them. The army doctors found dozens of bullets in his body. The soldiers who were at the firing range told the investigating officers that the captain was daydreaming and wandered too close to the target area, where he was accidentally shot."

"By everyone?"

"That's the story they told the military police. There will be an investigation, but I think their version of what happened will hold up. There are no witnesses except the men who shot him."

Desidra shook her head. "I would have enjoyed giving him the coup de grâce myself. He deserved to die, but it was a terrible waste of good blood. We should have dipped our straws into the bastard when we first met him."

"Yes, a waste. All that fresh blood seeping out of the ragged holes in his body."

"How'd they clean it up?" she asked.

"Wrapped his body in a tarp quickly and moved it near the targets. Then the men scraped and dug with portable shovels at the killing site to clean it. Herkle was still bleeding, and he left a mess on the ground. They covered the area with snow and packed it down with fresh snow, so it looked like a number of soldiers had tromped across it."

"Didn't the Hunger drive you frantic, seeing all that blood?"

Christopher laughed. "Not likely I'd scavenge a drink while surrounded by the United States Army! Now, tell me why you came back here so soon."

She was quiet for a few moments and then took Christopher's hand. He followed her outside into the drifting snow.

"This is old Japan," she said. "The temple and its garden were probably designed and planted hundreds of years ago. The cherry trees have grown as crooked and twisted as some of our Elders and the wooden temple has lost its sheen. Still, harmony reigns here. The little bridge that crosses no water, the stunted pine trees, the carefully placed stones, all still exude something spiritual. The Japanese say that a garden should express the 'sweet solitude of a landscape clouded by moonlight.' This one does exactly that."

"You're turning poetic and Japanese," Christopher observed.

"I've lived with violence most of my vampire life," she said, "but I'm no different from any other animal. I need a quiet place to rest. When this war is over I want to be someplace other than a metropolitan area. There's no room for vampires in the cities any longer. The freedom of movement we once had is gone forever. I miss the Victorian days, when we dressed in grand clothes and lived in big, elegant homes. Until humans learned our secrets, and many of us were forced to live underground."

With a certain amount of sadness in his voice, Christopher said, "Yes, I was a young vampire in those days, too. I distinctly recall a particular mortal who invited me to his home one evening. We met in an English pub. One of the better ones. I was wearing a red velvet vest and black silk trousers and jacket, and my hair was more golden than it is today. I could see the man was impressed, and before the evening was over we had become dear friends. I adored him. He was a gentleman, well educated, well read, a man who respected my mind and wished to probe it further. I liked that. But I neglected to tell him of my appetites, and they overcame me. Unfortunately I destroyed him. Accidentally, of course, but I still feel the pain and guilt of my early carelessness. He was only thirty or thirty-five and should have lived out his mortal life span."

"It can never be the way it used to be," Desidra said softly. "Those days are gone, and for us so is the Seattle underground. Our future is Japan. Ironic, isn't it? Our future lies in a defeated nation. It's true nonetheless." She paused. "I love the harmony and beauty of this land!"

"You could never take up residence here because you wouldn't like Japanese discipline. I suspect your need has more to do with your lover, Mitsuo."

"Perhaps."

"No secrets, Desidra."

"What's the point of living for two or three thousand years, if you have no companion?" she said. "I don't want to grow old and beastlike, as many Elders do. I need someone who cares for me." She changed the subject. "What do you plan to do after the war?"

"My guess is that America will win in a few more months. Rumor has it that we're going to bomb the hell out of Japan to make them surrender."

Desidra expressed deep concern about Mitsuo's safety. "Bombs? If he were Kindred, he could escape from here easily. I may give him the Dark Kiss."

Christopher's eyebrows rose. "Is that a wise thing to do?"

"What about Lance? And all the others you've changed? You'd begrudge me *one*?"

He laughed. "From what I hear, your lover should be

safe in the countryside, It's the cities that will get the worst of it."

"So we bomb the cities and then what happens?" she asked.

"The Japanese surrender, and we occupy their country."

"How are you getting all of this information? I haven't told you anything, and you're not in the cryptography division."

"One of the vampires I sired got it from a former lover who talked too much. A cryptographer named Livingston."

"I know him."

"Anyway," Christopher said, "the U.S. Army will stay in Japan a while to make sure everyone knows what the rules are, and then they'll leave. That's the way war goes."

Desidra sighed. "And Innocent civilians get bombed and soldiers on both sides die and money that could be put to better use is spent on weapons of destruction."

"That's right."

"It's always the same, isn't it?" she observed. "It doesn't matter who starts or ends a war. No one actually wins. When I volunteered, my main purpose was to save vampire territory from the threat of fire bombs. But more and more I'm convinced our efforts should be directed toward shortening the war."

"Not much need for that. It'll be over soon anyhow, the way things are going. With my vampire army, I'm ahead of the game. We occupy Mount Fujiyama, and the U.S. Army will occupy the rest of Japan. By keeping the demons in check, we prevent them from releasing the mountain's killing power."

"And all the while the U.S. Army will think you're AWOL."

"Well, we can't tell them the truth: blood-sucking vampires helping the U.S. Army? Too bizarre. And if we do tell them, the government will cover up the story. John and Mary American Citizen will never learn the truth about us, and any vampire the government captures will end up being dissected in a forensic laboratory."

"How true. Vampires should fit in quite well here," Desidra said. "Unlike our own country, this land is mystical. Its people still believe in legends. They might even come to accept us, even though we're American vampires. They have their own vampire legends, you know."

Christopher nodded. "Let the Japanese people learn about us, so we can terrify the ones we want to target, the corrupt and depraved mortals who need to be drained of their blood."

They were interrupted by a resonant sound, familiar, deep, and accusatory. "Traitors!" howled a voice.

"Romano!" shouted Desidra. "He's found us!"

34

Prince Romano appeared before them, red eyes burning. He approached to within fifty feet, stopped suddenly, and stood silent and unmoving.

"It has taken me a long time," Romano growled, "but I've caught up with you. Did you think you could escape, Desidra? And you, Christopher-the-Deserter. I sent you to bring her back or kill her, not to form an alliance. She's mine, not yours!"

"I belong to myself!" Desidra called out.

A blue, sizzling surge of energy cut through the still air, shattering the peaceful solitude of the garden. It struck Desidra first, and like a giant hand slapped her backward against a stone pagoda.

"Leave us alone!" Christopher shouted. "We have no quarrel with you!" He released a high-pitched whistle.

"Who are you calling?" Romano asked. The typhoon of his anger invaded Christopher's brain, moving so quickly that Christopher had no chance to throw up a mental barrier.

Romano's expression darkened. "So you've been creating progeny without the authorization of your Elder? A little army of them, eh? Where is this invincible force? I don't see them answering your whistled command. Bring them forth and I'll destroy them." His sarcasm was palpable. "I know where they are. They're cowering somewhere, afraid to show themselves. Come out, come out, wherever you are!"

No one appeared.

Romano's blast of force struck again. This time Christopher reeled toward Desidra and fell across her. She pushed herself up against his weight, and they rose together to face their sire.

Without moving her lips, Desidra whispered to her companion, "When I nudge you, let your energy flow with mine."

"It won't work."

"Try it!" she said with ferocity.

Romano made no move to get closer to them. "Listen to what I say. I am your prince, your sire. You are under my absolute dominion, and you will return with me to Seattle at once! When we arrive I'll decide what your punishment shall be for breaking every tradition of the Kindred. Maybe I'll forgive you and maybe I won't."

Desidra thought she detected apprehension in his tone, but as usual she was unable to penetrate his thoughts.

He threw another powerful surge of energy in their direction. This time they were able to hold their position without flinching.

"I see," said Romano with a terse chuckle. "My wayward progeny have learned something during their wanderings, how to combine powers. It doesn't matter. You are suckling babes compared to me."

He tested them again, and a raging storm struck them head-on. Once more they stood silent and unbending.

"I have treated you gently," Romano said, "but I'll tear you apart cell by cell, if you continue to resist."

There was a change in Romano's demeanor. Very slight, but Desidra sensed it immediately, a stoop of the shoulders, a vague look in the eyes. A diminishment.

He's ancient, she thought. *He can't generate power for long periods, as he could when he was younger. He's resting for the moment. Is this an opportunity to disable him?*

She attempted to veil her mind as well as she knew

how, leaving false thoughts lying about to be picked up by an intruder. The trick Romano had taught Christopher. Could her sire penetrate it?

"Why not let us go?" Desidra shouted. "All we can bring you is anguish. Will killing us make your memory of us disappear? I think not. So, why do you pursue us?"

In a tired voice, Romano replied, "Because you're mine."

"If that's so, then we belong to you as a mortal child belongs to his parents. Mortal parents release their progeny when the children reach a certain age or state of maturity. Surely a vampire Elder is much smarter than a mortal. Wouldn't you agree?"

"What point are you trying to make?" Romano asked. He attempted to invade her thoughts.

Desidra sensed the invasion and thwarted it. "You are an intelligent being. I plead with your reason rather than your emotions." She climbed to the top of the temple's slightly curved roof, until she was able to look down on Romano. "Let us stay in Japan. Christopher and I will settle here."

"And I suppose Christopher's 'army' is to remain here as well? His unacceptable progeny must be destroyed, as our traditions dictate." Once again, Romano glanced around, showing more disdain than concern. "Where are the inferior ones?"

"Busy doing their jobs," Christopher answered. He described the mission to retain dominion over the Fuji-san demons.

Romano listened attentively. "You're either very brave or very stupid," he observed.

"The same could be said of you, sire," Desidra said with a stiff smile. "You came after us alone. That took courage."

She could smell the aging deterioration of the Elder, the steady ever-threatening, dry decay. He had used up most of his energy with the earlier bursts. She pushed a little harder. "Allowing us to remain here would be to your benefit, sire."

"Tell me how," Romano answered. "No! I will consider it."

He seated himself on a slab of stone beneath a giant

azalea bush. Desidra sensed his uncertainty. He was afraid of this land, of its people, and of these rebellious vampires.

"What's he doing?" Christopher inquired. "What does he mean 'consider'?"

She whispered in response, afraid Romano's ears might not be as worn as his eyes, "I just gave him a graceful way out, allowed him to save face. I don't know if he'll take it, though."

Presently, Romano stood up with renewed vigor. "I will grant you the right to remain here. With a provision. You can never return to Seattle! If you do, I'll kill you."

35

For a while after the departure of Christopher and Prince Romano, Desidra continued to sit in the temple garden. Snow sifted over her body. In her stillness, she appeared to be one of the garden's icons.

She disliked the warning from Romano, but out of discretion had not argued with him. Never to return to Seattle? Of course she'd return, but not until she was ready, not until she had the power to oppose anything the dark sire could throw at her. Romano alone in a distant land was not the same as Romano immersed in his power base, with his Kindred surrounding him.

She missed Seattle, with its fir- and cedar-covered hills. And she missed the immaculate white seagulls that soared above the bay, and the jagged, ice-blue mountains that towered to the east and west.

And Kweca! Most of all she missed Kweca, who had often met her in the city on one of the long piers that jutted out into the bay.

Did Romano's warning extend to the Makah Indian Reservation where Kweca lived, northwest of Seattle? She thought it did, and that the angry old vampire would not be pleased to discover her presence anywhere near him.

Patience, she thought. *That's what I need, and one day I'll go back.*

For now there were important decisions to be made, and they must be made carefully. There was information she'd picked up from Kanji Toyokuni's associates and servants, during meetings and whispered conversations. It formed an emerging picture that she must reveal to the cryptography unit in Alaska.

Japanese installations in the South Pacific were increasing. As the war turned against them, the Japanese military worked desperately, with feverish intensity, to build up supply bases near zones where they still planned to expand, even though they were obviously losing the war. It was the "never say die" philosophy of the samurai.

The need to blindly obey a leader was called by different names. Bushido by the Japanese and patriotism by the Americans. In such endeavors humans struggled for the ideals of duty, honor, and courage. Vampires had their code of ethics as well, Desidra *thought*, but there were vast differences between Kindred and mortals.

How can I make any sort of determination about my future? Desidra wondered. *In spirit I am neither vampire nor mortal but something in between. I have changed.*

For a few moments Desidra sat as silent as the statues in the garden. Even the breeze ceased all movement, as though it respected her silence. Then she rose to her feet, spread her arms against the crisp air, and flew. Back to Alaska. With her messages.

"I will return to you, Mitsuo," she whispered to the wind.

She was duty-bound to complete her work.

36

April.

Around the town of Anchorage, ice and snow began to melt beneath the spring sun, but a few inches below this soft outer covering the soil was permanently frozen, a sign that winter never completely left this part of the world.

Desidra worked long hours and stayed indoors as much as possible to escape the sun's rays.

"You never stop, do you?" Sergeant Miller remarked one day. "You work overtime when you don't have to. You take on other people's tasks. I never see you eating anything. Army psychiatrists might think you're running away from yourself. Are you trying to forget a bad love affair?"

"Far from it. There's a man I want to be with, but duty comes first."

The sergeant nodded and said, "War takes lives, including ours. Think about all the time and energy we've lost. This Signal Center *is* our life!"

"Not forever," she said. "I'll be leaving in the fall. I'll have put in two years by then."

The sergeant grimaced. "Guess you haven't heard the latest. They're asking civilian staff to sign up for work contract extensions."

"Which means?"

"You'll probably be here for another six months to a year."

Desidra bit her underlip. "Do you think this obscene war will ever end? Or will the killing go on forever?"

"You sound cynical."

"I'm being realistic."

"I hope you can hang on to your boyfriend, whoever he is."

But Desidra was optimistic. The war injuries Mitsuo had received would keep him out of military service, and she would visit him often enough to bond him more tightly.

She heard a soft curse, their lieutenant exhibiting displeasure.

"Uh, oh!" said the sergeant. "I'm getting out of here. He's looking our way."

The lieutenant rose from his desk and approached Desidra.

"Another one of those damned Washington G–2s has come to visit us," he grumbled. "I hate to see intelligence officers on the prowl. Take him to the officer's club, Desidra . . . anywhere. But keep him away from me. And remember, don't open your mouth around him. He'll try to pry information out of you. Something to hang us with."

She nodded reluctant approval, and a few minutes later a tall man strode into the Signal Center. Handsome with sandy hair, ruddy features and broad shoulders, he was a robust, healthy mortal. Desidra licked her lips.

Beneath his hearty exterior she detected a certain weakness, though she could not immediately define it. Later as she sat in the officers' club with the man, she discovered what it was. He drank excessively.

"Can I see your apartment?" he asked, his question slightly slurred. "You've shown me every blasted building on this post but where you live. We could go there and have a nice cup of coffee and get to know each other better."

"I don't think that would be a good idea," she answered.

"But I'm your guest."

"I think we should stay here."

He pulled his chair closer to her and threw an arm around her shoulders. "You know, you have great legs," he said. "Hey, how about another drink?"

"I think you ought to have coffee, instead. You can order it here."

"I'd rather go to your place."

It would be easy to disable him at this moment, she knew. But if she did, she'd expose her strength and what she was. Instead she'd have to teach him a lesson without hurting him or making him suspicious.

"All right," she said. "We'll go to my apartment for coffee."

On the way, he pulled her against him tightly. "Do you have a soft place where we can sit?" he asked. "A bed or something?"

"We can sit on chairs."

"I'm only going to be here a couple of days. Then I'll be on my way across the sea. Big battle coming up! I could get killed."

"What battle?"

"Operation Overlord," he whispered. "They're calling it D-Day. Massive military action with tons of bombs. We're going to throw everything we've got at those damned German batteries."

"It must be top secret. I haven't heard news of it in the Signal Center."

"We're gonna hit 'em between Cherbourg and Le Havre." He pressed his mouth against hers. "I think you should take me to bed, in case I get killed."

That could happen sooner than you realize, she thought. Still, she felt pity for him. He was so afraid of death that he was willing to reveal a top secret troop movement to a strange female, just so she'd "comfort" him.

"First show me where you're staying," she said.

He changed course and stumbled along the hard-packed dirt road that led to the officers' quarters.

"That building over there," he said, pointing. He stood on unsteady legs. "Hey, I thought we were going to your place."

She looked around, saw no one in the immediate vicinity. With a fluid motion she touched a nerve on his neck, causing him to collapse to the ground. In the shadows she slung him over her shoulder, stepped into the dark corridors of the building, and deposited him against the door of the commanding general's quarters.

The general would discover him in an hour or so and would be exceedingly displeased.

"Foolish mortal," she murmured. "You would have betrayed your country to bed a vampire!"

When she returned to her apartment, Desidra was startled to find Christopher sitting inside her steamer trunk. "What happened?" she asked. "Did the demons knock you off their mountain?"

"What an unfriendly greeting! I just came to visit you. We're doing fine on Mount Fujiyama, thank you. My Crimson Corps likes the weather and the solitude and we have a halfway truce with the Fuji-san."

"We haven't had much peace around here," she said. "After you left with your little vampire army all hell broke loose. The army still has an investigation going. They can't understand why more than a dozen men would go AWOL at the same time."

"How has it affected security?"

"It's pretty tight. For all of us."

"Yeah, well, my men were only regular army in support functions, not directly involved in cryptography or military intelligence. AWOL! If they only knew the truth, that we're actually doing more for the war effort than we ever could have done as grunts."

She nodded thoughtfully. "Do you remember that soldier who went AWOL and they didn't find him for weeks? Finally he turned up in a house of prostitution acting as official bookkeeper and drunk."

"I remember him. They threw the book at him. But they can't touch us."

"True. But to make things more pleasant here for the rest of us, would you like me to spread the rumor that you and the others have gone gold-mining in the Alaskan wilderness? That should lead the brass on a merry hunt."

"Don't confuse the army. I'd rather leave things as they

are." He scratched his chin. "Speaking of armies, I have seven Japanese in mine now, all selected carefully for their sympathy with the American cause. I even have one of the guards from Toyokuni's estate. You probably remember him—the big guy, Nukazawa. He had some old scores to settle with the demons, so I put him in charge of keeping them in check." He paused for a moment. "When are you coming back to Japan?"

"I've been told that I'll be staying here a while longer than I had anticipated." She paused. "As soon as I get out I'm going to marry Mitsuo."

"What? You're a vampire. You can have as many lovers as you want for centuries."

"Before I became undead," Desidra said, "I had dreams. A young man I loved was going to help me fulfill them. I think often of what I lost, and I want it back. I can't restore him, can't recover the past. It's dead and gone, so I'm taking other steps."

"Mitsuo asked you to marry him?"

"No, but he will."

"You amaze me." Christopher shook his head, revealing more than a modicum of displeasure. "Desidra, a dream is only a mirage. You see it, but when you reach out, it recedes. It's mortal and nevermore. You're not that young human girl any more and never will be."

"I think I can be happy with Mitsuo."

"When we were in Japan, Desidra, you told me you were considering making him a vampire and spending eternity with him. All those centuries are too long to spend with one person!"

"Are you saying familiarity breeds contempt? I don't agree. I hesitated to make the transformation, because I wanted to think about whether or not to give him the Dark Kiss. But now I'm sure. Our affection will grow deeper with time."

"You expect to make him forget his dead wife?" Christopher asked, struggling to comprehend what seemed unthinkable.

"I don't expect him to forget her. She'll always occupy a place in his thoughts, just as my young lover remains in mine. I can't understand why you're so opposed to what I'm doing. Don't you ever worry about loneliness?"

"Oh, no! I'll always have companions."

"My needs are different from yours."

"Shall I read your mind and learn details of your plans for that poor young man?" Christopher asked.

She bared her teeth. "My private life will remain exactly that. Don't forget you taught me Romano's method of concealing thoughts. Why are you so resistant to my happiness? Just because you like to change companions every few decades doesn't mean everyone has to be that way."

He arched an eyebrow. "There's nothing wrong with variety. In fact, it's more interesting, when you exist as long as we do."

"What about Lance? I thought you cared about him."

"I do. And I care about you."

She changed the subject. Christopher was her friend and entitled to his views. "Mitsuo wrote to me," she said. "He had an Eurasian friend mail it from Hawaii. Mitsuo can walk now. Isn't that good news?"

"He's the enemy! How can you work for the army and have an enemy husband at the same time?"

"My reasons are personal. For now I'd appreciate it if you'd watch over him. Make sure he gets what he needs. Promise?"

Christopher nodded. "I'll help, but I think you're throwing away the best centuries of your unlife."

37

December.

Desidra used her sleeping hours reconnoitering enemy installations, as she was doing now on a military base not far from the city of Hiroshima. Her shadow moved silently among the men she had under observation.

In the faces of these Japanese officers she saw resignation and anger, as if an immense tide was headed in their direction and they could do nothing to stop it. Though they spoke with bravado, their voices lacked conviction. They would follow the ancient code of the samurai: Never give up, fight to the death. Death was preferable to defeat.

They would be interesting prey, she thought, if she were inclined to dine. They would put up a good fight.

She left them and flew further east. A few miles beyond the Japanese army post, she assumed her geisha identity and stopped for a few minutes at a small park. The evening air was cool and smelled of wood smoke. She seated herself on a stone bench and listened to a pair of elderly men talking about the war. Both believed they were winning the war in the Pacific, and as far as they knew their Axis allies were doing the same.

They were sadly misinformed, thought Desidra.

According to American military predictions, the war in Europe was coming to a rapid conclusion. Once the

European theater fell quiet, America's military forces would turn their full attention toward the defeat of the Japanese in the Pacific arena. Based on her days in the Signal Center and personal observations about history, Desidra knew it was only a matter of time before America—the "sleeping giant" that had been of such concern to Admiral Yamamoto—would overwhelm the nation and culture of the Japanese isles.

One of the old men in the park coughed, a deep croupy sound that rang through the air like a defective gong. He pulled something from the sleeve of his black kimono and thoughtfully chewed what appeared to be leaves. She sniffed the air. Japanese herbal medicine.

Desidra watched him for a few minutes. He reminded her of an ancient woodcut she'd seen in Toyokuni's house. The old man's face was etched deeply with many lines, but he held his body as erect as a young samurai. An artifact of feudal Japan.

American culture, a homogenization of many nationalities and races, had a way of inundating foreign peoples. In her opinion, it "Americanized" them, took away what once had been unique to the citizens of a conquered land. Like the American Indian cultures, including that of her friend Kweca in Washington state, and native tribes in Hawaii and Samoa.

In Desidra's mind, the problem was linked to the Christian zeal of Americans, an innate and powerful desire to convert "heathen" ways and traditions to a more "God like" American path, despite the resistance of the native people.

It would be that way in Japan, as well, she predicted.

One of the old men in the park puffed on a long pipe, while the other talked about his family and his plans for his grandchildren. It was the sort of scene, thought Desidra, that could have been repeated, except for minor cultural differences, in any country in the world. Why couldn't mortals see how similar they were to one another, instead of fighting incessantly?

She remembered that Japan's desire to remain aloof from the rest of the world had caused America to sail a fleet of warships into Tokyo Bay under the command of

Commodore Perry in 1853. At that time a letter from the American President was delivered to the Japanese leaders, asking for "friendship, commerce, a supply of coal and provisions, and protection of shipwrecked persons."

The following year Japan reluctantly agreed to open certain ports to American trade.

And now they were at war.

She continued to sit in the quiet little park with its stone statues and lanterns and musical sounds of a stream running nearby.

How had this war evolved?

She'd visited Japan in the 1930s and remembered the complaints of Japanese leaders that Americans wanted to keep them from securing oil and other strategic resources. Under the circumstances it was inevitable that Japan would lash out.

The sneak attack on Pearl Harbor was not only premeditated, it was predestined. The military base was a bauble placed in the middle of the Pacific Ocean by the Americans, a jewel that was left inadequately guarded.

Intentionally? She wasn't sure.

Such thoughts were controversial, Desidra realized. Even with her vampire-insights and abilities her observations and suspicions would be difficult to prove. Still it seemed to her that the attack on Hawaii and the inevitable humiliating defeat of Japan were events inscribed on the slate of history in advance, with only small details left undetermined.

The two old Japanese men, unable to fight in the current war, discussed and analyzed Yamamoto's sortie from Hashirajima toward Midway some two and a half years earlier, on May 27, 1942.

"They pulled out of the harbor on Navy Day," said one old man. "You remember that date, the anniversary of Admiral Togo's 1905 victory over the Russian Fleet."

"Yes, in the Battle of Tsushima," the other man said. "Admiral Yamamoto was just a young officer then. He lost two fingers on his left hand during that battle."

"A brave soldier! It won't be long before we conquer the entire Pacific!" said his companion.

But they were doomed, Desidra thought.

Was her relationship with Mitsuo doomed as well?

He was still a human and prone to mortal weaknesses. She worried about an American bombing raid on his ancestral home. Rumors abounded about tactics that should be taken by the Americans to bring the war to a conclusion.

The curse of a vampire's longevity, she thought, was the ability to predict tragic happenings based upon a long view of history. It was a view that was not always pleasant.

She was afraid for Mitsuo.

38

June 1944.

Though the war in Europe ended in early May, the Japanese continued to build up their bases in the South Pacific. American military power descended upon them with increased ferocity. As a result, work hours in the Alaska crypto unit were lengthened to eleven hours daily, seven days a week.

This left little time for Desidra to visit Mitsuo.

Intermittently she skipped her sleeping hours and flew to visit her lover, as she had done this day at dawn.

Inside the Toyokuni house, she picked up Mitsuo's scent. Fresh. She knew exactly where he was. She compressed and slid through a closed door into the kitchen. She'd learned long ago to avoid the guards and servants and go directly to wherever Mitsuo was located.

A few feet away, he stood nibbling on something, near an open icebox.

She reassembled herself and became a black-haired geisha once more, this time as a Japanese woman instead of the Caucasian she'd been during her last visit. It amused her to do so.

"Akiko is here," she announced. "And I see you are feeling much better. Isn't this early for your breakfast?"

"Akiko? But how . . . ? I don't understand. Your hair is

supposed to be red." His face flushed with confusion, and he wiped his hands on a small towel. "I was taking a little food to help me regain my strength. So I could do this." He limped toward her and seized her in a tight embrace. "I've missed you."

She knew her appearance disturbed him. Based upon the white lie she'd told him before, that he suffered from a fever, he probably thought it was kicking up again, causing vision problems.

Sooner or later, if she proceeded with her plans for him, she would tell him the truth. When the transformation came, when he was Kindred, he would recover completely. His limp would disappear and he'd have superhuman strength. She would be giving him a gift, she rationalized, well aware that it was her own great need that had led her to this point. In a sense, he was more than a lover; he was her prey.

No! her thoughts screamed. *I came to save him! He will die if I don't transform him.*

"Come," he said, and pulled her up the stairs toward his bedroom.

She rode the undulating waves of his passion and drowned in its power. For a time they belonged to a larger creative force, one that overcame the differences between mortal and vampire. When the storm of their love subsided, they came to rest, side by side.

Mitsuo stared at the ceiling. "You are a remarkable woman," he said.

"Marry me," she whispered.

"It is customary for the man to propose matrimony."

She nuzzled his ear. "It's time you learned something about other cultures,"

He looked at her inquisitively. "Who are you?"

"I'm saving that answer for when we're married," she answered sweetly.

Seated at her workstation within the "vault" of the Signal Center, Desidra removed her shoes and placed her feet against the smooth surface of the lethal cylinder hanging in its metal hammock.

"Damn you, bomb," she whispered to herself. "You represent everything that's wrong with this world!"

She thought about a human bomb, Herkle. He was gone, dead for a year and a half now. She wondered if his ghost haunted Sergeant Miller's thoughts. The investigation had been swift. No one was accused of anything. This was war, and people were dying every day.

The men working beside her tapped away on their Sigaba keyboards, making little clicking sounds. Messages flew in and out of the center. Frank, the soldier who'd been sent to the psychiatric ward, had never returned to the unit. Since his departure, four other men had been unable to take the pressure and had also been dispatched to the psych ward. She missed them all, especially Frank.

She wanted to believe he was somewhere safe, buried in his own brain, hidden from harm. He was lucky in a way. No hope for the rest of the men here, however. Day by day, message by disturbing message, they would have to "sweat out" the remainder of the war and its terrible consequences.

As Mitsuo had said, the Japanese would never surrender. Did that mean a battle to the death for everyone? Even animals had better sense than that.

"Got a new guy here today," Sergeant Miller told her, breaking her concentration. "Hope you won't mind helping him a little, just to get him off the ground. He's already had some training."

A short while later Desidra looked up to see a stocky man seat himself beside her. She gave him a brief introduction. His was longer.

"Call me Brad," he said. "Actually it's Bradford Donovan Kurtis Smith the Third. But I prefer Brad. You can understand why."

She nodded.

He was restless in his chair. "I'm a recent graduate of Harvard. My grad gift was a white Packard with leather upholstery. I had my degree in hand and the world by the tail, and what's my reward? This hellhole."

"You'll get used to it," she said, and returned to her tasks. She'd been preoccupied with thoughts of Mitsuo and her own feelings for too long. It was time to concentrate on her job.

Naval movements in the Pacific were intensifying, and Desidra thought she ought to be doing something more active. The soldiers who surrounded her probably felt the same way.

Like them she was a physical person and needed a physical outlet. A good hunt, be it human or vampire! Maybe that's what was wrong with the spoiled, complaining puppy beside her.

Brad was fidgeting, staring at the message he was about to encipher. After a few seconds, he began to tap the keys of the Sigaba. "Maybe this won't be so bad, when I get the hang of it," he said.

"If you need any help," Desidra offered, "just tell me."

"You use null ciphers don't you?"

"Why do you ask?"

"My brother's an ensign in the navy, and he says they use null words or phrases at the beginning and end of each message they route out. Meaningless words or sentences. The beginning and ending is the most vulnerable part of a coded message."

"That's right," she said. "It makes decoding more difficult for the enemy. Do you have a question about that?"

"No. I didn't see anything in this message that indicated null ciphers, so I tossed in a few of my own." He held up two sheets of paper.

"What?" she said, alarmed. "Give me the original message!" Her voice was sharp.

He handed one of the sheets to her.

It was a routine transmittal to an American supply ship in the South Pacific. The communiqué was directed to the officer in charge. A simple message, the heart of which requested a simple action: "Divert one quarter of food supplies to Ilani."

She knew that "Ilani" was the U.S. Navy's code name for a small unnamed island near Fiji.

"Now let me see the message you sent out," she said.

He handed her the second sheet. She read it, and as she did so her anger rose. The null phrase at each end of Brad's version gave the message a different twist. "Strike the enemy on the head . . . divert one quarter of food supplies to Ilani . . . and have a good time at the picnic."

"The brass will kill you," she said to the new cryptographer. "If the enemy intercepts this, they'll think its an aggressive action. You've just made that supply ship a priority for them."

She tried to not to display too much anger, but this young man needed to learn something. "What kind of training did they give you?" she demanded. 'Strike the enemy in the head' has meaning. So does 'have a good time at the picnic.' Null ciphers should be gibberish, like 'Strike John jump fox go,' with the real message separated by double letters from the null ciphers."

"Oh," he said, looking somewhat bewildered. "God, how can I undo it?"

"You can't, you've already sent it out."

A few minutes later, Desidra told Sergeant Miller that she wasn't feeling well, and she left the Signal Center vault. In part this was true. She had an unsettled feeling in the pit of her stomach. All she could do now was damage control.

The message was probably still sitting in the radio room of the supply ship. If she moved fast, she could warn them and arrange for assistance.

Flying toward Ilani, she rode with the wind, following its scent and rhythm. "This way!" it whispered to her, urgently. "Hurry, hurry!"

And finally, after what seemed an eternity to her, there was the American supply ship below her.

To her dismay, deep in the turquoise sea, she saw several Japanese submarines cruising, sharklike, closing in on their target.

The Japanese have already intercepted the message! she thought. *They're getting in position for a kill.*

Quickly she dove toward the supply ship and entered its radio room. Messages were piled neatly and not so neatly on a small table bolted to the floor. No one was in there at the moment. She picked up the scent of the radio operator and followed it two decks down. In an outer cabin a man dressed in a captain's uniform stood near the radio operator. The captain held a sheet of paper.

The message!

Desidra had no opportunity to put a rescue plan into operation. There was a violent explosion, the ship shuddered, and fire erupted through the floor of the cabin. Flames rose in the air and a giant column of heat burst through the ceiling. The captain and the radio operator slid toward the fire hole and down into the inferno.

Torpedo!

Desidra pushed her shadow-self toward a wall, The ceiling was ablaze and what remained of the floor beneath her was dissolving rapidly, swallowing life jackets, medical gear, chart books. The heat was searing, and she envisioned the end of her existence. Finality. She could almost imagine a crackling sound, her own skin detaching itself from her body.

Every vampire's deepest fear: *fire!*

For a moment she was disoriented, overcome by the heat and the terror that reached for her with flaming fingers.

Resignation set in.

I'll die here. This boat will be my funeral pyre.

In a desperate last effort she lifted in the air, suspending herself between floor and ceiling. Like a living creature, the heat followed her. Disoriented by the fire, she was its prey.

Suddenly a second explosion rocked the ship. Beside her a ragged hole appeared in the outer wall, and seawater rushed through.

Cold, soothing water!

Using all of her strength she swam against the torrent and into the sanctuary of the sea.

A long distance from the ship the sea teemed with marine life.

Total awareness came to her of what war was all about.

Death.

Nothing but death.

40

July.

During the last few days of her work contract at the Signal Center, Desidra learned a secret that disturbed her deeply.

The Japanese had refused to surrender, and now America was about to test a revolutionary new weapon in New Mexico. An atomic bomb! The test would take place this month, and if successful, the new bomb would be dropped on one or more of four Japanese cities to be chosen according to weather conditions.

What were mortals doing to themselves? she raged. She had wanted the war to cease, had worked toward that end, but stubborn mortals were bringing it to a terrifying conclusion.

Mitsuo! The Dark Kiss must be given to him as soon as possible. As a vampire he had a chance to escape the consequences of this final battle.

Her marriage to Mitsuo must take place at once.

Alone, she flew to the foot of Mount Fujiyama, the place they'd selected for their wedding. Mitsuo had left the date to her, telling her he was ready, and she had said she would make the arrangements.

Now, she wanted to look around here and consider her decision.

The Shinto shrine was located in a quiet place off the regular pathway. It was ancient but well maintained and painted in bright colors of red and gold, expressing a passion not seen in the soft gray faces of other Japanese temples. Bronze-green vines climbed the columns of the shrine and surrounding trees were wreathed with wisteria, a flowering plant that gave the trees a misty appearance, as though they were bridesmaids draped with veils.

Near the shrine were two ponds connected by a wooden bridge that represented the "Bridge of Heaven" and contained a moon-gazing platform, a place for lovers or worshipers who wished to gaze heavenward.

Desidra's thoughts roiled along like a whitewater river, and she thought about the atomic bomb again. There was no heaven and no God for her. Maybe not for anyone. She had only the time she would spend with Mitsuo. If she lost him, there would be nothing.

As she walked around the shrine, Desidra found herself surrounded by pink and white azaleas, sweet box bushes, flowering plum trees, and a carpet of soft green moss.

If there is a God, she thought, *this place will bring me as close to heaven as I will ever get.*

For a moment she felt guilty about her desire to transform Mitsuo into a vampire, but she and her lover were similar, she reminded herself. Both were warriors without formal religious beliefs. Vampire and samurai. The merger seemed proper.

With help from Christopher, she found someone who would perform a Western ceremony, an elderly Eurasian monk living with a Japanese woman.

"You'll like him," Christopher said. "He asks no questions."

The two vampires strolled along the perimeter of a lake. Moonlight streamed across the calm water like a silver pathway. Desidra wished Mitsuo were here to share the scene with her.

Have you told Mitsuo he's getting married?" Christopher asked.

"Don't be sarcastic," she said with mock annoyance. "Of course I *told* him, and I *didn't* use my power of seduction."

"Not even a little of that? Did you put him in a trance?"

"No magic. None. Just the magic we find in each other."

"How romantic." His voice held a sardonic tone, but his eyes, red-tinged, revealed amusement.

"So I have your approval?" she asked.

"You do," Christopher answered. "For what it's worth."

"You're my family, Chris. The only real family I have."

"Then you won't be offended if I miss your wedding. I wouldn't care to shock the groom. He might not appreciate a man dressed in red-and-black velvet with a cape and high-heeled boots."

"I've always loved that outfit. You look grand in it. Go ahead and wear it."

"Actually, I can't make it. Have a date with a pack of demons."

They grinned at each other, fangs glistening in the moonlight.

Desidra and Mitsuo were married a few days later, surrounded by paper lanterns that flickered like fireflies in the semidarkness of early evening.

Her heavy silk kimono was red and indigo with silver plum blossoms embroidered across its surface. The colors of the night, white moon and deep blue sky and silver stars. She wore her red hair in traditional Japanese style, its color not much different from geishas she'd seen, who hennaed their hair, American style.

Western culture had already arrived on the Japanese isles, Desidra thought, even before the conclusion of the war.

The little Eurasian and his Japanese consort, the only other people present, bowed to show their respect for this strangely matched couple during this most extraordinary ceremony.

"You are beautiful," whispered Mitsuo in Desidra's ear.

And they said their vows in the silence of the shrine, as though all the bloodshed in the world had stopped for a moment.

Much later, spent from lovemaking, Mitsuo lay back on

the futon and said, "In spite of the suffering the war has imposed on this world, you and I found each other. You are my oasis. I am gradually regaining my physical strength, and the guilt that consumed me after the death of my wife has disappeared."

He leaned over Desidra and brushed his lips against her bare breasts. "I mourned my wife for many months, and then you came and brought me back to life." He pulled a small sheet of paper from under his pillow. "I wrote a haiku for you, to express what I feel."

She accepted it and read aloud:

> *"Cold moon wrapped in mist,*
> *and your eyes, midnight jewels*
> *whisper tales of love."*

"It's beautiful," she said, touched by his gift. She'd felt with certainty that she would make a vampire out of Mitsuo on their wedding night, fully bonding him to her. But suddenly it didn't seem so simple. As a banished member of a clan, she had no Elder from whom to obtain approval. What rules governed a renegade vampire? Rules prohibited what she'd already done.

Now, at the moment of decision, she could hear Prince Romano's voice, returning to her from long ago, instructing her in the ways of the Kindred. Telling her which actions were permissible and which were not. It had been a gentle, almost seductive voice, and she'd fallen into its trap.

But she was climbing out of it.

It had happened slowly, this separation from her sire and the awareness of herself.

Most of her life as a vampire had been a series of broad changes, of trends and general attitudes without specific sharp edges. She'd been growing as a woman and as a vampire concurrently, parallel awakenings that led inevitably to her ostracization from the clan.

She realized Mitsuo had been talking to her while her thoughts wandered. She trailed her fingers over his golden body. "I'm sorry, what were you saying?"

"I'm not a coward," he said. "I want you to understand that out of respect for my father and for you, I will return to the war soon."

"The war is lost for Japan," she said in a somber tone.

"Never!"

"Soon your emperor will speak to the people, Mitsuo. I can reveal no more. But it will be over before long."

"What makes you say such things? You're guessing."

She shook her head.

He smiled at her. "Then you must be a spy or have psychic abilities."

"Neither," she answered, and her thoughts wandered inward again.

It was as if her entire life, going back even to mortal times, had been a broad progression, a metamorphosis from stage to stage, an inevitable fate-driven course of events over which she had no real control. The small decisions she made had no influence on the big picture. Or so she believed.

She was somewhere on that continuum now, and a part of her personal metamorphosis involved the transformation of Mitsuo from mortal to vampire. His change would be an element of her progression and would intertwine with it.

The die was already cast.

Or was it?

All life and unlife involved the interaction of sentient and nonsentient beings, the effect of one upon another, give and take, action and reaction, push and pull. Great mistakes were made in the process, irreversible errors. Like this great war between mortals that would soon unleash a terrible bomb, a monster the world could never hope to contain, according to rumors that were rampant in the Signal Corps.

Whatever she did to her new husband would be irreversible for him, and also for her, the would-be creator of a new vampire. If she made a mistake she would have to abide with it for hundreds, perhaps thousands, of years.

"Do I make you happy?" she asked.

He laughed. "Is that a geisha question?"

"No! It's a wife question." She kissed him hard, her lips pressing against his, her body holding him down with her superior strength. The Hunger consumed her, and she moved from his lips to his neck, still holding him in place. He struggled against her, but could not cry out.

Fangs slid gently, sensually into his carotid artery and she drank deeply, gave him the Dark Kiss, draining the blood from his already weakened body. There was horror in the Kiss, but she clung to it, reveled in its passion, and submitted to its sensual call.

Mitsuo teetered on the edge of death,

"Now!" she cried aloud, and pulled away from him. From beneath the futon, where she'd hidden it, she removed a small knife. While he watched, dazed and losing consciousness rapidly, she drew the sharp edge of the knife across her left wrist. Blood spurted from the wound, and she held it against his mouth so that he could drink.

His expression was one of shock. He tried to resist, and her blood streamed over his closed mouth and down his chin; he moaned.

"Shhh, my darling," she said. "Drink! If you wish to live and love, drink my blood."

He stared into her red eyes and drank, as she commanded. When he was finished, she kissed his bloody lips. "Close your eyes, my dear Mitsuo," she said. "Sleep. And when you waken, I'll tell you my secrets."

Without words, he closed his eyes and slept. Quite peacefully, she thought.

She slipped from their bed and sat down at the small table which served as a desk in Mitsuo's room. She removed a fragile piece of rice paper from a box, located a pen, and began to write.

My dear Kweca,

It has been a long while since we last communicated, but I have never forgotten you. I'm married now to a Japanese lieutenant, and yes, I know what you are thinking. You believe this is a strange relationship for a vampire, especially an American vampire. But I need companionship, Kweca, to fill the centuries of my existence. It's too long a path to take alone.

I've learned a great deal from this war. Not so long ago, if you'd asked me to define the difference between vampire and human, I would have replied that the Kindred are carnivores—true carnivores—while humans are, by comparison, mere grass-eaters. But the war of mortals has changed my attitude, and I've reached another conclusion. There is a strong similarity between mortals and vampires. Both are predators hungering for territory and blood! There are subtleties of difference, of course, and we will discuss them at length when next we see one another.

She looked toward her sleeping husband, then resumed writing her letter:

There are exceptions to my conclusion. Mitsuo is one of them. I'd like you to meet him. I can't predict the future, but when this war ends I want you to come visit us. As always, I need your advice. Today I'm going to break the news to Mitsuo that I've transformed him into a vampire. I wish you were here to help me form the words, but I'll have to manage by myself. Somehow. . . .

DARE TO ENTER

The World of Darkness™ is a trademark of the White Wolf Game Studio.

BRIAN HERBERT is best known for his science fiction novels novels, including *Sidney's Comet*, *The Garbage Chronicles*, *Sudanna, Sudanna*, *Man of Two Worlds* (written with Frank Herbert), *Prisoners of Arionn*, and *The Race For God*. A recent novel, *Memorymakers*, was written in collaboration with his cousin, Marie Landis. He has received excellent reviews from such sources as *The New York Times*, *The Times of London*, *Publishers Weekly*, *People*, and *Kirkus Reviews*, and has appeared on a number of radio shows and panels to assist other writers.

His latest works include co-authored short stories written with his cousin, Marie Landis: *The Bone Woman*, *The Contract*, *Dropoff*, and *Blood Month*, as well as their co-authored dark fantasy novel, *Blood on the Sun*.

MARIE LANDIS has won numerous literary awards for her science fiction and fantasy stories, including the Amelia annual Horror Award. She is co-author of the science fiction novel, *Memorymakers*, a collaboration with her cousin, Brian Herbert. This past year she and Brian also co-authored the novel *Blood on the Sun*, as well as a number of short stories that have been published in *Dark Destiny I and II*, *Dante's Disciples*, and other anthologies.

The two cousins are actively involved in a number of new writing projects.